NEVER ON MONDAY

MAGGIE FITZROY

ISBN 978-1-7330262-4-6 (Print)

ISBN 978-1-7330262-5-3 (Ebook)

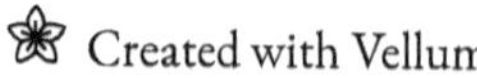 Created with Vellum

Dedicated to my sister Wendy, now in Heaven, who enthusiastically shared my love of books.

ONE

P hiladelphia, Pennsylvania
May 31, 1955

Dash it all.

I'd never seen a man as upset as the one sitting in my new, scantily furnished private investigator's office.

This was my first case—and yikes, he was my first client.

I hoped...

Wildly upset, Dr. Martin Paulson was weeping, wailing, gnashing his teeth.

"How could Nanette just vanish—where could she be?" He let the last word linger as a scream, then fixed his red, watery eyes on me, struggling to catch a breath between sobs.

"Doctor—"

"Where...where...where...? I don't understand. This doesn't seem possible."

Was it possible? Certainly.

"It's entirely possible," I said, struggling to keep my voice soothingly calm. "And I can think of several explanations for why your wife may have disappeared in the middle of the day from the boardwalk in Ocean City, New Jersey."

Maybe she'd been abducted. Maybe she'd had a mental breakdown. Maybe she'd run away.

I wanted to jump right in and solve his heart-wrenching mystery. If only he'd calm down long enough for me to ask him more questions, and to convince him I was the woman for the job.

I'd only received my private investigator license two days before. Framed and hanging on the bare wall behind my desk, my name, Story Smith, was written in big cursive letters for all the world to see.

Or at least, at that moment, for Dr. Paulson to see.

Except the middle-aged doctor wasn't seeing anything with his fists pressed to his eyes.

"Doctor..."

He bent forward and cradled his face in his hands. "Give me a moment...please." He moaned. "I just need a moment."

"Certainly."

I felt sorry for him, but also flattered that he'd come to me, a woman in a profession dominated by men. This was my chance. I wouldn't fail him. I'd find his wife.

One thing seemed clear so far: he had nothing to gain from her disappearance. He was either genuinely distraught or had the acting chops of Lawrence Olivier—Academy Award winning, for sure.

He'd rushed into my office with no appointment and just started blubbering, begging for help. So far, the only thing I'd learned in our few minutes together was that he was an obstetrician, that his wife's name was Nanette, and that she'd gone to the Jersey Shore for a day visit with her best friend, Carolyn, and never returned.

He had reported Nanette's disappearance to the police, but he didn't believe they were taking it seriously. And he preferred keeping her situation private for the sake of his practice and patients.

He had gotten my name at the police station from my brother Rob, who was there wrapping up his last case as a private investigator. Rob, newly married and looking for more stable employment, had just accepted a job with the FBI. When Rob overheard Dr. Paulson pleading with an officer, he'd urged him to come see me.

I took a deep breath and held the doctor's weepy gaze. "Please, sir, please steady yourself, so I can get more information. You say she disappeared the Saturday before Memorial Day?"

He dabbed his eyes with a soggy handkerchief. "Yes, that's right."

"Memorial Day was yesterday. So, four days ago?"

"Yes."

"What about Carolyn? Do you know what she has she told the police?"

He took a few deep, ragged breaths. "Carolyn said the boardwalk was crowded, which of course it always is on Memorial Day weekend. Nanette wanted to go into a candy shop for saltwater taffy."

"My favorite candy," I said. "Go on..."

He ran a hand down his grief-etched face. "Carolyn waited outside on a bench, but Nanette never came out of the shop. When Carolyn went in to look for her, nobody remembered seeing her. At all. It was like she was never there."

"How odd."

"Yes. Carolyn said the store was crowded. Lots of people waiting in line. Scads of kids. Loud, crazy, chaotic." He raked shaking fingers through his hair. "I suppose it's not all that surprising that nobody was paying attention to a lone woman. Even one as gorgeous as Nanette."

He reached into the pocket of his navy-blue blazer, pulled out a photograph, and handed it to me.

I studied it. She was indeed pretty. Early to mid-thirties. Sleek dark hair worn in a pageboy. Big, doe-like eyes. Coy, confident smile.

I looked back at him, wondering if Nanette might have left him on purpose. It was a possibility and probably what the police suspected. Maybe he cared for his wife too much. Maybe he was overly possessive. Maybe too controlling.

So many maybes. Including whether he would actually hire me. I needed this case. I'd quit my job, spent every cent of my savings to set myself up in business. And I needed to pay rent, put gas in my car, eat.

People told me I was crazy to quit a perfectly good job as a newspaper reporter, especially with the unique name of Story, perfect for a writer. That was my father's idea. He's also a journalist, and he had heard the name somewhere, and thought it pretty, and my mom agreed.

Anyway, here I was switching gears, at the age of twenty-six, to go into a dangerous field. Dominated by men. But I was used to being in a field dominated by men. In the newsroom, I'd been sadly relegated to write about fashion, society weddings, and country club soirees.

Boring. Since what I craved was adventure.

I'd pleaded for the opportunity to cover crimes, but that beat was off limits to me. Dubbed "a pretty young thing" by my editor, everyone in the newsroom joked that I'd soon be getting married and going off to have babies.

Little did they know. Because nobody knew. That I'd once been secretly engaged. And that it had ended tragically. And that it was my fault.

I'd probably never marry. I didn't deserve the love of a good man. My fiancé, Dean, had been a good man and look what happened to him.

No, I would need to make it on my own.

Fortunately, in addition to Rob, I had the support of my father, who helped me by opening a checking account in both of our names. It irked me that in 1955 women still couldn't open their own bank accounts, but that wasn't going to stop me.

Nothing was going to stop me from becoming a crackerjack private eye. A crackerjack female private eye.

I handed Dr. Paulson back the photo of his wife. "She's lovely... how long have you been married?"

"Fifteen years. She was nineteen and in nursing school. I was twenty-seven, just getting started in medicine when we eloped."

"Nanette is a nurse?"

"No." He lifted his chin, his expression etched with pride. "She dropped out of school to marry me, never needed to work. I have a very successful practice and I gave her the best life a woman could have...except for children." His voice breaking, he looked away. "We could never have them. But Nanette said she didn't care, that she loved me, that our family was complete with just the two of us."

"I see."

"Do you?"

"Yes, and I can help you. I will find her."

"How?"

"First, do you believe she could have been kidnapped? Or, is it possible she ran away?"

"Ran away?"

"I'm sorry, but I have to ask that."

"She did not run away." He spit the words out so forcefully it took everything I had not to show my surprise. "And if someone kidnapped her, they haven't contacted me for ransom."

I ran my fingers through my hair. I'd have to be more careful with my questions. Dr. Paulson obviously worshipped his wife, and I didn't want to add to his anguish.

I reached for a pad of paper and a pencil. "Okay, then, let's start with her friend Carolyn, since she was the last person to see her. What's her last name?"

"Lowell. Carolyn Lowell. L-O-W-E-L-L. She's also our neighbor and her husband, Alec, happens to be my best friend."

"Interesting." I jotted the names down. "My first step then, will be to go see Carolyn."

"Good...good." He'd reached into his shirt pocket and pulled out his checkbook.

Doggone! I was getting the case.

Holding my breath, I let myself relax. I told him my daily fee and he scribbled an amount on the check and handed it over.

"This is for a week." His tone was terse and final. "I'm hoping you won't even need that long, and if you find her sooner, which I hope you will, you can keep it all."

A week. I had one week. "What if it takes longer than that, Dr. Paulson?"

He shook his head, clearly not liking that question. "I am giving you a week. This is Tuesday, so until next Tuesday. My nerves can't take this. I have patients who need me. All my patients are women. I like women. I trust women. That's why I'm taking a chance on you. But if you can't find her, I'll have to hire someone else."

Like a man.

"Understood." I ripped a paper off my pad, handed it to him, and asked him to jot down Carolyn's address and phone number.

I watched him as he wrote. Now that he'd calmed down some, I sensed he was naturally serious, self-disciplined, and driven. And what some women would consider good-looking. Light brown hair going slightly gray, wide forehead, strong, square jaw.

But handsome is as handsome does my mother likes to say. Maybe his personality wasn't all that handsome. He was certainly capable of displaying strong emotions and maybe Nanette had grown tired of his storms. Another possibility.

He slid the paper with Carolyn's address and phone number back to me. "She lives on the Main Line, in Bryn Mawr. Let me know what she tells you."

"Of course." I kept my tone as optimistic as I dared. "I'll keep you updated, and hopefully will soon have some promising news."

But a woman gone missing is never good. I had to find her.

Quickly.

And—hopefully—alive.

Two

I'd known plenty of women like Carolyn Lowell and Nanette Paulson, which I told myself was an advantage as I motored down the leafy streets of Philadelphia's Main Line that afternoon, passing by grand mansions, some so grand they resembled small castles.

The Main Line, northwest of the city, was home to many of the area's wealthiest people.

Not that I was one of them.

But I had attended Bryn Mawr College as a day student, one of a very few middle-class students in a sea of girls from privilege and wealth. Since Bryn Mawr was in the heart of the Main Line, the Lowell mansion was easy to find.

I pulled up in front of it, parked, and looked it over.

It was grander than most of the other homes on the street, which was saying something. Three-story red-brick, white shutters adorning its many large windows. Massive Roman columns framing the front door, wide enough for a team of horses to pass through.

The home had an elegant historic ambiance, with cast iron horse head hitching posts on either side of the front gate. Magnificent white oaks shaded the yard, filled with red roses, purple iris, Black-eyed Susans, and at least thirty varieties of other colorful flowers.

I left the top down on my Thunderbird convertible, hopped out, unlatched the front gate, and headed up the walk.

I didn't have an appointment. I wanted to surprise Carolyn Lowell, and hoped she was home. I stepped up to the door, knocked, and held my breath.

I expected a maid in uniform to open the door. But this woman was no maid. She was a slim white-blonde with a head full of curls. She had delicate porcelain skin, blue-violet eyes, and a falsely-polite smile.

"Can I help you?" Her voice was high-toned haughty, as if she assumed I was there to sell her something.

"Carolyn Lowell?"

"Yes." Her tone sounded less assured as she looked me up and down.

I suddenly felt like I had at Bryn Mawr, inferior in social class and clothing. I was wearing one of my best dresses, black and white striped, cinched at the waist, and my black high heels.

But Mrs. Lowell, in a cream-colored blouse and silk skirt that clearly cost a fortune, did not look impressed. Only puzzled. "Can I help you?" She repeated the words with impatient annoyance.

"Yes, I hope so." I summoned my best confident smile. "In fact, I hope I can help you. My name is Story Smith and I'm a private investigator hired to find your friend, Nanette. I understand you were the last person to see her and—"

"Hired by who?"

"Her husband."

Eyes widening, her impatience vanished. "Come in, come in," she said eagerly, stepping aside and waving me into the cool interior of her palace. From the marble-floored foyer, she led me into her spacious living room carpeted with Oriental rugs, furnished with oversized sofas and armchairs, and decorated with paintings I could swear were Picassos.

She gestured for me to take a seat in a leather armchair in front of the largest fireplace I'd ever seen. She settled into a matching chair across from me. Her air of superiority gone, she met my gaze. "So, Martin hired you to find Nanette. I'm *so* glad. I'm *so* worried about her. I've been frantic, absolutely frantic."

She didn't look nearly as frantic as Martin had. I relayed what he'd told me about what had happened on the boardwalk, and she nodded.

"She went into Shriver's for taffy and never came out. I waited and waited and waited, then finally went in to get her. But she was gone. I was flabbergasted."

"No one in the shop had seen her, is that right?"

"That's correct. There were so many people in there, and I pushed my way through and around them and asked everyone I could, but nothing. No one remembered seeing her, not even the clerks."

"So, what did you do next?"

"I went outside and called her name, but nothing. Crowds streamed past me in both directions. I went into nearby stores, but nobody in them had seen her either. I felt so helpless."

"So, you called the police?"

"I had to. Couldn't think of what else to do. But they didn't seem too concerned. People lose each other on the boardwalk all the time. It's easy to get separated when it's so packed." She worried her pearls. "Now...it's been four days..."

"What do you think happened to her?"

She gave a deep sigh. "Abducted? Amnesia? Murdered? I don't know. I don't know."

Looking at her pained face, I believed every word she said, including that she didn't know.

"I have no idea. I wish I could be more help." Her voice was a ragged whisper.

"Was Nanette happy in her marriage?"

"Yes, I'm sure of it."

"How can you be sure?"

"She seemed happy. All the time. In the past year or so, she'd never been happier."

That could be important. "Do you have any idea why? Had anything changed in her life?"

"Not that I know of. I was just happy she was happy."

"Do you think she might have been pregnant when she disappeared?"

Carolyn raised an eyebrow at that question, as if she'd never considered the possibility and considered it utterly stupid. "No. She would have told me, and anyway, she didn't want children."

"Carolyn, there you are."

A tall man with wavy, dark brown hair came bounding down the wide staircase to our left. He wore a black shirt and black pants, and his deep, what-is-going-on-here frown only enhanced his good looks.

He came over to us.

"Story, meet Steve Evans."

So, this cool cookie wasn't her husband.

Carolyn touched one of her perfect curls and I saw something cross her face that I couldn't read but that struck me as curious. "Steve, meet Story Smith."

I stood. "Hello."

"Hello." Looking puzzled, he turned to Carolyn. "I've been searching all over for you. You had me worried."

"Steve, dear..." She gave him a sweet, don't-worry smile. "Someone was knocking on the door, so I answered it." She stood and nodded at me. "Miss Smith is a private investigator who Martin Paulson hired to find Nanette. Story, Steve is my bodyguard."

"Bodyguard?" The word came out of my mouth high and squeaky, betraying my surprise.

"Private investigator? You're a private eye?"

I resented the arrogant shock in his voice. "I am..." I stood taller, pushed my shoulders back, pulled myself up to my full five feet, five inches, or five feet, seven inches in heels. "Why do you look so surprised?"

"Uhm...It's just that..." His eyes moved from my feet to my cinched-waist dress, then to my shoulder-length locks. "I've never saw a pretty honey-blonde detective, in heels, no less. *And*, I've never heard of you."

"I'm newly licensed," I shot the words at him. "And I never heard of you." Although why I should have, I couldn't imagine. It just felt good to say that.

"Steve's a private investigator, too. A really, really good and successful one." Carolyn sat back down and gestured for me to do the same. "My husband, Alec, hired him to be my bodyguard for a while. Until Nanette is found. Which we all hope is soon."

Steve gave me a tight smile.

"Story is here to help find Nanette and she's been asking me some questions. So, if you don't mind, Steve…" Carolyn waved a hand toward the staircase. "Why don't you go ahead back upstairs. I'll be fine."

Steve shook his head. "No. Absolutely not. It's my job to keep you safe." He hitched his chin toward a sofa against the wall across the room. "I'll just go sit over there and listen, Carolyn. Don't worry, I won't interfere with Miss Smith's questioning."

Fantastic.

I was going to have an audience for my debut interview. An audience of one highly experienced private eye, whose confident presence jangled my nerves.

My mouth went dry.

I turned to Carolyn. Swallowed hard. Tried to ignore the sight of Mr. Handsome perched on the sofa just beyond her shoulder. Elbows on knees. Staring straight at me.

I felt like I was about to be graded. Which was ridiculous. I knew what I was doing. I focused all my attention on Carolyn. "Walk me through the day Nanette disappeared. Begin with that morning." My words came out smooth and confident. A good start.

Carolyn closed her eyes, like she was trying hard to picture it. "Let's see, I drove. We left that morning around seven-thirty. When we got to Ocean City, we headed straight for the boards."

"What time did you get there?"

"Around ten."

"She's already told all this to the police." Steve's voice was sharp and sarcastic. He stood and raised both arms in the air. "I really don't see how—"

"Please..." I shot him a frustrated glare. "If I could just continue..."

Irritation darkened dreamboat's face. He sat back down.

I turned back to Carolyn. "So, you strolled the boards for a while?"

"Yes."

"Did you go into any shops?"

"Yes, we meandered in and out of ones that struck our fancy. I bought a necklace. Nanette bought nothing, which come to think of it, wasn't like her. She loved buying things."

That could be a clue.

"What was her mood?"

"Cheerful, as usual."

"Tense at any point?"

"She's already told you—" Steve jumped back to his feet. Hands on hips, he looked at me like I was a child who just wasn't getting it.

"Steve, please, let me answer Miss Smith's questions," Carolyn said, giving him a sweet smile.

I wanted to strangle him.

He flashed me an I'm-sorry-but-not-really grin that made my chest go hot, then I really wanted to strangle him.

Carolyn turned back to me. "Nanette was her usual cheerful self. When she announced she was in the mood for some saltwater taffy, I told her I'd wait outside."

"What time was that?"

"Around eleven-thirty. It was probably close to twelve-thirty by the time I asked the manager of Shriver's to call the police."

"Manager of the candy shop?"

"Right. Shriver's Salt Water Taffy and Fudge."

"Then what happened?"

"Several officers came and walked up and down the boardwalk and a few went down onto the beach to look for Nanette. The more time that went by, the more upset I got."

"What was she wearing?" I asked. "Anything that would stand out? Make her easier to spot?"

Carolyn shook her head. "She wore a beige dress and white sandals, which looking back on it, was unusual for her."

"Why?"

"She usually wore bright colors."

I nodded. That could be significant, if she'd planned to disappear. Or not. Maybe she'd just been in a beige-mood that day.

"Carolyn, who's this?" Another man came into the room from a hallway to our right. He was beanpole thin, with a blond crewcut and a sharp chin. Dressed in a tailored suit, he exuded success.

"Alec," Carolyn said. "You're home early."

He glanced at me, threw Steve a questioning look, then walked over to me and frowned. "I don't think we've met."

He knew we hadn't met. And he wasn't being polite about it. His tone was suspicious and rude.

"She's a private investigator hired by Martin." Steve went over to Carolyn and put his hands on the back of her chair. He had large, strong hands. Serious, bodyguard hands. The kind that could land a hard punch if a situation called for it.

I stood. "My name's Story Smith," I said, reaching over to shake Alec Lowell's hand.

He squeezed my fingers, harder than necessary. I managed to keep a polite smile on my face, although it wasn't easy.

"She was just asking me some questions," Carolyn said. "Now if you gentlemen don't mind, I would like to get back to telling her what I know. I'm very glad that Martin—"

"Steve, how do we know this woman is who she says she is?" Alec glared at him. "Did you ask to see her license?"

Steve stiffened. "No, I did not." He came around from behind Carolyn's chair and looked me up and down, his gaze lingering again on my high-heeled shoes, then moving up to meet my eyes. "She looked harmless enough to me, didn't think it was necessary."

Harmless? Maybe it hadn't been such a good idea to wear heels. Maybe if I wanted to be taken seriously as a private eye, I should ditch the fashionable shoes. I made a note to myself to shop for some sensible flats, then snatched my handbag off the floor and pulled out my license.

Alec reached for it, then studied it. "Huh." He smirked. "Looks brand-spanking new. How much experience you got, honey?"

"Not much, I'd bet." Steve took the license out of Alec's hands, examined it, and handed it back to me. "Looks real."

"It is real, I can assure you." I turned back to Alec. "Martin Paulson is confident in my abilities, and that's what matters." I left out the fact that I had a week to prove myself and looked at Carolyn. "I will find Nanette. I promised her husband that, and I'm making that promise to you."

"*Gutsy.*" Steve applauded, giving me a heart-squeezing grin.

He let it fade. "But not exactly professional, Miss Smith. You'll learn. Not to make promises. That you might not be able to keep."

"See her out, Steve." Alec pointed to the door. "And going

forward, don't admit any more strangers into this house until we're sure it's safe. After all, that is your job."

"Why is it his job?" I asked. I wasn't intimidated by Alec Lowell. And it was one question I hadn't yet been able to ask. It had been burning in my mind even before Carolyn's rude husband had interrupted things. I turned back to her. "Why do you need a bodyguard?"

She let out a loud sigh. "Alec wants me to have one until Nanette is found. He thinks—"

"I believe she could be in danger from those who might have taken Nanette." Alec narrowed his eyes at me. "It's best to be safe so we don't need to be sorry."

"So...you believe Nanette was kidnapped?" I looked at Alec, then at Carolyn. Nothing she'd said had indicated she believed her friend had been kidnapped. And she certainly didn't look afraid of being kidnapped herself. Sitting demurely with her ankles crossed, she put her head back and closed her eyes, as if suddenly weary. "Alec thinks so," she said. "And I don't mind having Steve around." She popped her eyes open and looked at him with affection. A surprising degree of affection, for a bodyguard. "He's nice, and good company."

He was certainly nice-looking company.

But nothing was making sense.

I clearly needed to talk to Alec next, but the scowl on his face told me this wasn't a good time. And his dismissive attitude toward me made me think there might never be a good time. I'd just have to see what I could get from him now. "What makes you think Nanette was kidnapped, Mr. Lowell?"

He waited a beat, then scoffed. "Her husband is a wealthy man."

"Yes, but he hasn't received any ransom notes."

No one said anything. I waited for someone to say something.

"Maybe Nanette wasn't kidnaped for ransom," Alec finally said, his voice a low growl. "Maybe she was mixed up in something she shouldn't have been. Which means she might have put my dear Carolyn in danger."

He gave his wife a stern, say-no-more look, then turned back to me. "You have your work cut out for you, Miss Private Eye, and I wish you luck. I suggest you get to work because I have nothing more to say about the matter. Including what Nanette might have been mixed up in. I've no idea, just a feeling, so that's for you to figure out. Solving this mysterious tragedy is, I believe, why Martin hired you."

I gave a curt nod. "Yes, it is, and thank you for your time."

"See her out, Steve." Alec pointed to the front door. "And watch her leave. And in the future, don't let any more strangers in this house."

***

"What was *that* all about?" I whispered as I stepped out onto the front step with Steve, who reached behind me to close the door. "Your boss was unnecessarily rude to me, don't you think?"

"My *client*." He waved for me to go ahead of him down the steps. "And he's just scared. Which is why he hired me."

"Scared that his wife will be kidnapped? Even though there's no evidence so far that Nanette was snatched?" I waited for him to catch up to me as I walked toward my car. "Doesn't that strike you as strange?"

"Strikes me as lucrative." Steve gave me an aren't-I-lucky smile. "I'm being paid handsomely to do nothing more than guard the lovely Mrs. Lowell. While you, Miss Smith, have your job cut out for you.

And I wish you all the luck you will need." He halted when we came to the curb and I dug into my purse for my keys.

"Wait..." A tinge of respect slipped into his tone. "Is that T-Bird yours?"

"Sure is." I palmed my keys in my hand and looked over at my sleek white ragtop with its robin-egg-blue seats. "Like it?"

"It's a beauty."

"Thanks."

"Problem is, it's rather attention grabbing." He cocked his head and looked back and forth between me and my car. "As, I might add, are you, Miss Smith."

"Story..." My cheeks went hot. "You can call me Story. And what exactly are you getting at?"

He waited a few seconds, then slid me a smile that crinkled the corners of his eyes. "I think you know."

"Do I?"

"Do I have to spell it out for you? Your car is eye catching, which means it might not be the best vehicle for you. Private eyes need to blend into the scenery, not stand out. In this..." he waved a hand. "You will definitely stand out."

Of course, he was right. But the Thunderbird had been a gift. A hard-earned one. It was also my pride and joy, and I had no interest in trading it in for a boring car. Not that it was any of his business.

It was time to change the subject away from me. I backed up and leaned against the side of my pride and joy, folding my arms across my chest. "So, Steve," I said. "You're a professional private investigator, and I'm betting you're really good at it. So why hire yourself out as a bodyguard? Isn't that a bit below your talents?"

He stared at me, then shrugged. "I told you, it's lucrative. What's it to you?"

"I just find it curious."

He shrugged again. "No big mystery. I'm in business by myself. No partner. Just me. I go where the money is. Alec Lowell wants me to guard his wife? Sure. I'm happy to do it for a very nice fee. Probably a lot more than you're getting from the good Dr. Paulson."

I had no doubt about that.

"Plus, I get to live here, in this luxurious mansion, for the foreseeable future. Or, at least until you find Nanette Paulson and it's clear Carolyn is no longer in any danger. I hope you find her. Alive and well, God willing. But until you do, I'm getting paid by the day."

Something moved in his eyes, like a passing cloud that came and went so fast I might have imagined it. But I was good at reading people, I'd honed that skill as a reporter, and what I saw in Steve's wide-set deep brown eyes looked like envy.

It was envy. Despite his boasting, he envied me. Envied the meaningful challenge before me, while he was stuck in a fancy mansion playing guard dog.

"I'll find her." I lifted my chin, now even more determined.

"This is your first case, isn't it?" He stepped toward me. "That's why I never heard of you. We all know each other in this town."

I didn't answer. I yanked my car door open and slid in. "Nice to meet you, Steve Evans," I said. "I'm sure I'll be seeing you around." I turned the key and let the engine purr. "Until then..." I gave him a perky salute.

He returned my salute. "I'm sure I'll be seeing you around. Best of luck, Story. And by the way, I do love your car."

Carolyn Lowell hadn't told me anything useful. Not much that I didn't already know, in any case. But my visit to her hadn't been a complete waste of time. I'd discovered that she had a bodyguard because her husband believed her friend Nanette might have been mixed up in something nefarious.

Which was puzzling. And which may or not have been true.

But what now?

Back at my office, I considered calling Martin Paulson to ask him about Alec Lowell's assertions, then hesitated. Dr. Paulson hadn't even hinted to me that his wife could have been involved in anything shady or dangerous. And even mentioning that his good friend, Alec, believed she might could send him into a tizzy.

Which right now was the last thing I needed.

I picked up the phone and dialed my brother Rob. His receptionist put me straight through.

"Story," he said, sounding happy to hear from me. "I hope you're calling because you got the case. Did Doc Paulson hire you?"

"Sure did, and thanks for recommending me."

"Happy to. You deserve it. And I have confidence in you."

"You should, you trained me."

"That's true."

"He's giving me a week, Rob. One week."

"Okay." He paused. "That's fair."

"You think so? I'm nervous. Scared I'll fail."

"You? Scared? Doesn't sound like the Story I know. Anyway, who told you this would be easy?"

I smiled. I'd caught the P.I. bug while going undercover on a case with Rob last Christmas, and there had been nothing easy about it. "Yeah. You're right. Not easy. Just exciting and fun."

"I recommended you for this case because I know you'll succeed. And when you do, you'll be off to a great start. It'll do wonders for your reputation as the new gal in the biz."

"The only gal that I know of." I squared my shoulders. "Hey, Rob, have you ever heard the name Steve Evans? He's a—"

"Private investigator. In Philly. Why?"

"So, you do know him?"

"I've run into him from time to time." There was wariness in Rob's voice. "Why?"

I twisted the phone cord around my finger. "He's working as a bodyguard. Protecting Carolyn Lowell, the woman who Nanette Paulson was with when she disappeared. Apparently getting paid handsomely for it. But something seems off."

"How so?"

"Carolyn's husband is insinuating that Nanette could have been involved in something crooked but says he hasn't a clue as to what it might have been. Just a feeling, he says. It's all rather vague."

"Hmmm."

"What do you mean by hmmm?"

"I think it's odd that Steve Evans is working as a bodyguard," Rob said. "He's a very good PI. Why him?"

"The money, he says."

Rob laughed. "That makes it even stranger. Steve is wealthy, very... or so I've heard. Family owns a large estate out in Chester County. Birdsong, I think it's called. Went to private schools, probably has a trust fund, quite sure he doesn't even need to work."

I leaned my head back and stared at the ceiling. The Nanette

Paulson case was getting more mysterious. Or maybe I was just complicating things in my mind. Steve Evans probably had nothing to do with anything.

I needed to focus on the missing woman.

"Story? You still there?"

I sat forward and untwisted the phone cord. "Yeah."

"Watch out for Steve Evans. He's quite the lady's man."

I frowned. "So?"

"So, he's good-looking, right?"

"A hunk...so?"

"So, you noticed."

"I'm not blind."

"So don't fall in love with him. I've heard many women have. He's broken a lot of hearts. Don't let him break yours."

I couldn't believe what I was hearing. "What are you talking about, Rob? I don't expect to ever see the man again."

"Well, if you do, I'm just warning you. He goes after pretty woman who have a lot going for them, then just leaves them, with no warning, when he tires of them. Or so Piper told me. One of her best friends, Claudia, thought she was going to marry him. Kept expecting a ring, which never came. She's been a basket case ever since he left her in the dust."

Piper was Rob's wife. They were newlyweds. He'd met and fallen gaga in love with her during that case we'd worked undercover at Christmas. I liked Piper. She was sweet and had a lot of friends, and I had no doubt what she said was true.

Although I didn't know what it had to do with me.

"Thanks for the warning about Steve Evans, Rob," I said. "Good to know. But I don't think I'm in any danger on the romance front. I'm focused on my business. And excited about this case."

"That's my girl. What's your next move? You must have one."

"Of course."

"What is it?"

"I need to go to the Ocean City boardwalk. I'll head over there tomorrow. Look around. Ask questions. Check out the place where Nanette Paulson vanished."

"Sounds good," Rob said. "Maybe you can find out something the police missed."

"I sure hope so." I pushed aside the twinge of doubt tightening my chest. What if I didn't? What if I was wasting my time?

"Do you have a photo of Nanette Paulson?" Rob asked.

"Yes."

"Good. Make sure to take it with you."

"Of course, thanks for the reminder."

"You can do this, Story."

I summoned a smile. Dear Rob. He was right. And I was going to prove him right.

THREE

I crossed the Ninth Street Bridge into Ocean City the next morning. It was the first of June, and school wasn't out yet, but the town was gearing up for the summer season.

There was more traffic than I'd expected. Early vacationers, carting beach chairs, were heading to the beach. The streets were shiny clean, all the buildings freshly painted, everything pristine.

Such an unlikely place for a mystery.

Parking was hard to find, but after much searching, I finally located a spot about a block from the boardwalk and parallel parked.

I dabbed on lipstick, donned my favorite sun hat, put my top up, and got out of my car. I was happy to have a working excuse to spend time in one of my favorite places, where the very air has the scent of saltwater and suntan lotion.

Ocean City, with its long stretch of pearl-white sandy beaches, is one of South Jersey's most popular shore towns. Growing up, I visited often with my parents and brother Rob, who is four years older than me. Some summers we'd rent a cottage with some of my aunts, uncles, and cousins.

On an island between the Atlantic Ocean and wide bays separating it from the mainland, the place was designed for families like ours. Founded in 1879, it's modestly quaint and historic. Victorian mansions, beach homes, small cottages, with a downtown shopping area and the two-and-a half-mile-long boardwalk.

Lined with shops, eateries, and amusement arcades, the boardwalk is the town's centerpiece. A place designed for innocent fun.

But a woman had disappeared from there. And I wasn't there for fun.

I climbed the steps to the boards and headed to Shriver's.

How in the world could a woman just vanish from Shriver's?

I couldn't think of a more unlikely place. The popular candy shop, which opened in 1898, is centrally located, and the oldest business on the boards.

Opening the door, I was instantly captivated by the salty sweetness of vanilla and caramel wafting from the pastel taffy displayed in glass cases. My mouth watered.

"May I help you?" A young woman called to me from behind a counter filled with chocolate, vanilla, strawberry, and pistachio flavored bars of fudge. "You look like you're having trouble making up your mind. Would you like a free sample?"

I would have loved a free sample. I was practically drooling. But I needed to focus on my mission.

"No thank you. Actually...I'm not here to shop. Although everything sure looks yummy."

She drew her brows together, then brightened. "Oh, then are you looking for a job?"

"No..."

"Then...?"

I took a deep breath and smiled. "I'm actually here to look for a woman. She came in here the Saturday before Memorial Day and then disappeared. Were you by any chance working here that day?"

"I wish I was." She grinned, revealing a mouth full of braces. She had a freckled face, wore her red hair in a ponytail, and the nametag on her uniform dress said her name was Jane. "I heard all about it from my coworkers. They said cops were everywhere, looking for the lady. So, they never found her? That's sad."

"Yes. But why do you wish you'd been here?"

"Because maybe I would have noticed her. At least, I hope I would have."

I looked around the shop. "Are any of your coworkers here now who were working that day?"

Jane bit her lip and looked over at the other counters. She pointed to the saltwater taffy. "I think Peter was. He's the manager. You could go ask him." Then she turned and pointed toward the back of the shop. "And that's where they make the fudge—see the big machines through the glass window? People can stand there and watch. I bet some of the candy makers were here that day. It's worth checking."

I agreed. A man behind the floor-to-ceiling observation window was mixing brown goo in a huge metal vat with a giant wooden spoon. While focused on what he was doing, he had a clear view of customers watching him.

I couldn't talk to him behind glass, so I decided to see Peter first. I waited till he was done ringing up a sale, then told him who I was, and that I wanted to confirm that he was on duty the day Nanette went missing.

"Sure, I was here," he said, blinking at me from behind thick glasses. He looked to be in his mid-forties, with short, sandy hair, and a serious demeanor. "I didn't see the lady, though. Told the police that. We all did, all of us who were working, and customers, too. Strange, but not really, because it was so busy."

I pulled Nanette's photo out of my purse and showed it to him, hoping it might trigger something in his memory. "Are you sure you didn't see her?"

He shook his head. "No, sorry."

"I understand." I met his gaze with a hopeful smile. "Were any of the people in the back room, who were making candy, here that day? Maybe I could speak to them?"

He looked over and shrugged. "I suppose. Bruce, the big guy doing the stirring, he was here. But he already told the police he didn't see anything that could be helpful. Still, if you want, let's go talk to him, you've come all this way. From Philly, you said?"

I nodded, and he came out from behind his counter and waved for me to follow him. He weaved his way around a few more counters and then to a door I hadn't noticed, on the north wall of the shop.

A sign on it read, "Employees Only." He pushed it open. On the right a small hallway led to a closed door, which Peter said was his office, and a short hallway to the left led to another closed door. "Come on in," he said, opening it. "I'll introduce you to Bruce."

Bittersweet odors of sugar and cocoa hit me as soon as I stepped inside. Bruce looked up, looking happy to have an excuse for a break.

Unfortunately, he didn't know anything about Nanette Paulson. "I hardly ever look through the window to see who's watching me," he said. "So, no, I can't say that I saw her. Wish I could."

I nodded, then glanced over his shoulder. There was another door.

Partly ajar. It led to the outside, to the back of the boardwalk. If we hadn't turned into the candy room, we would have been able to walk out that door, instead.

"Peter..." I said, my heart beating faster. "Who uses that door?"

He shrugged. "It's for deliveries. Why?"

I looked at him, then at Bruce. "I know only employees are allowed back here. But if a customer snuck in, then slipped out of the building through that delivery door, they might not be noticed. Right?"

Bruce stared at me. "If they snuck in at the right time, when everyone back here was too busy to notice, I suppose..."

Peter nodded. "If they were subtle and quick, and if the store was busy and crowded, I guess they could get away with it. The question is, why would they want to?"

———

Before leaving Shriver's, I bought a bunch of saltwater taffy. I couldn't resist. When it comes to candy, it's my weakness. So yummy and so chewy. Some people like to smoke, some people like to drink, I like saltwater taffy. I'm goofy that way.

I popped a strawberry piece in my mouth, then headed up the boardwalk, going in and out of jewelry stores, women's clothing boutiques, souvenir shops, amusement ride arcades, pizza joints— flashing Nanette's photo, to no avail.

I was discouraged, though not surprised.

Heading back down the boards, I grabbed a slice of pizza and a Coke from one of the pizza places. I went over to a bench to eat my lunch, then stood and rested my arms on the boardwalk railing behind me, gazing down at the beach scene below.

A few sunburnt kids, who must have been playing hooky, were chasing each other, squealing loudly as they ran in and out of the cold ocean.

Seagulls circled colorful beach umbrellas, calling ha-ha-ha. Adults relaxed on lounge chairs or lay spread-eagled on towels.

Lifeguards perched on white wooden towers by the water's edge were keeping a close watch on swimmers in the waves.

Warmed by the mid-day sun, I scampered down the steps to the beach and showed Nanette's picture to lifeguards up and down the shore.

But I didn't get anywhere there, either. All the lifeguards said they probably wouldn't have noticed a woman fitting her description strolling along the sand. But they would have noticed, and rushed to rescue her, if she had gone into the water fully dressed.

I left the beach and drove to the town's police station.

There an officer confirmed that no sandals or clothing matching what Nanette had worn that day been left behind. I had to assume she had not gone into the ocean and drowned.

"It's possible the lady had a bathing suit on under her clothes and for some reason didn't tell her friend she was going swimming," the officer told me. "But we have no proof at all that she was even in Ocean City that day. Only that friend's word for it."

Which was true. I only had Carolyn Lowell's word for it, too.

But why would she lie about such a thing? I thought back to my meeting with her. While she had struck me as a bit uppity, she also struck me as truthful. If she and Nanette had not really gone to Ocean City, where would they have gone?

Walking back to my car, I popped another piece of saltwater taffy in my mouth and jawed on it to quell my frustration. Then I put my top down and cruised west across the bay back to Philadelphia.

Relishing the breeze on my face, I kept asking myself what could have happened to Nanette.

Where was she?

I ran the possibilities through my mind as I crossed the Garden State on the Black Horse Pike, letting the wind wrestle my hair as I drove past dairy farms, dive bars, diners, veggie stands, and patches of deep woods.

Could she have been abducted? Murdered? Left for dead in one of these woods?

Could she have experienced a sudden mental breakdown, forgot who she was? Was she being sheltered by someone unknown who'd taken a fancy to her?

Might aliens from another planet have snatched her? I laughed out loud. No. That did not happen.

But what if she had purposely snuck out the back door of Shriver's?

Maybe she'd felt threatened, thought someone was stalking her? And they were—and grabbed her.

Maybe she had suddenly felt sick, had to throw up, then, embarrassed, had crawled into a hole somewhere and passed out, permanently.

Or maybe she'd planned to disappear all along, and carefully plotted her escape?

She might not have gone out that door. But my trip to Ocean City hadn't been a complete waste of time.

Because now I knew that she could have.

It was getting late by the time I got back to Philly, but I decided to stop by my office on Walnut Street before heading home.

I live alone in a tiny one-bedroom apartment in Manayunk, a modest neighborhood in the city that hugs the Schuylkill River, not too far from my office downtown. But right now, there was nothing and no one waiting for me at home, and I wanted to type up a report about my day in Ocean City.

Rob had taught me the importance of writing daily reports while everything was still fresh in my mind, so I parked my car outside my office building, climbed the stairs to the second floor, and headed down the hall to my office.

An envelope with my name on it was taped to the door. I was ripping it open when I heard a noise behind me and turned.

"Hi." A middle-aged woman with light brown hair and soft, friendly eyes greeted me. "I see you got your note. I wasn't sure when you'd be back."

"Hello," I said, confused. "I'm new here, just moved in a couple of days ago. Haven't even had a chance to put my name on the door." I paused, then introduced myself. "And you are...?"

"Wendy Castillo." She gave a smile that lit up her face, which matched the good cheer in her voice. I suspected she might be one of those people who managed to stay perpetually perky because we were standing in the middle of a drab, narrow hallway, carpeted with a brown, threadbare runner, lit by dim ceiling lights, which barely illuminated dingy gray walls.

I couldn't afford the rent in anything finer.

She pointed to the only open door in a line of closed doors along the hallway, two doors down from mine. "That's where I work," she said proudly. "I'm Jonathan Miller's secretary and receptionist. He's a lawyer. Just getting started...so, so far, there's only him and me."

"Nice to meet you, Wendy." I reached over to shake her hand. "So far, there's only me. I mean, I just got my private investigator license, and since I'm just starting out, I can't afford a secretary or receptionist...not that there's any need...yet."

She widened her grin. "There might be, though." She pointed to the envelope in my hand. "A man came by a little while ago, and was knocking on your door, pretty loud. I came out and offered to help him. He seemed upset, so I suggested he leave a note on your door." She nodded her head at it and then looked at me, her eyes gleaming with curiosity, as if hoping I'd share the contents.

I slid out the single piece of paper tucked in the envelope. It was a short message from Martin Paulson, scrawled in big letters. I read it silently to myself: "Any news about Nanette??? What have you found out so far??? Why don't you answer your phone?!!!"

I hadn't answered my phone because I was out looking for Nanette.

Irked, I looked at Wendy, smiled, then folded the note and put it back in the envelope. I fished my office key out of my purse and unlocked the door.

Wendy still stood there, looking expectantly hopeful, but I wasn't about to reveal what the note said.

On the other hand, I didn't want to be rude. "Would you like to see my office?" I waved for her to come in with me. "As you can see, I'm just getting started."

I had two rooms. A small front area, with a wooden desk and chair, which would one day serve as my receptionist's office, when I could afford one, even part time. Beyond that was my office, which had a larger, metal desk, a phone, my typewriter, a window that overlooked the street outside, and a door that I could close for privacy.

"Very nice." Wendy's eyes gleamed. "I can't believe you're a private detective. How exciting."

"Thanks. "It is exciting."

"I admire you," she said. "And I'd like to help you."

"Really? How?"

"How about you get a sign for your door that says if you're not in, for clients to leave a message with me, down the hall, at office number 212? That way you'd kind of have a receptionist. Right?"

"Kind of..." I looked at her doubtfully. "But what about your boss? Jonathan Miller? Would he be okay with that?"

"He'll love it, I'm sure. Because maybe you guys could work out a deal. I could do some part time work for you, and you, in exchange, could maybe do an occasional investigation for him. What do you think?"

I grinned. "I love it."

"Fantastic." She handed me her boss's business card, which she pulled out of a pocket in her dress. "Have your clients call me at this number if they can't reach you. I'm sure Mr. Miller will agree to this. And now you and I can be friends."

Four

I didn't know Wendy Castillo. Yet. But I needed all the friends I could get in my business.

Things were looking up.

The next morning, back at my office, I called Dr. Paulson's practice, but he wasn't in. I gave a message to his receptionist that I had spoken to Carolyn Lowell, had gone to Ocean City, was actively working the case, and would be back in touch soon.

I had more questions for the doctor. I needed to know more about Nanette's life, and to interview more of her friends and family.

But first I needed to speak to Carolyn again, despite her husband's animosity toward me. Which was, itself, curious. Why *did* she need a bodyguard? And what crooked stuff *could* Nanette have been up to? Surely, Carolyn could give me a hint, or at least the names of some of their mutual friends, who might know more than she did.

I also wanted to size her up, to see if maybe she'd been lying about going to Ocean City.

I'd just have to risk going back to see her. Risk getting physically tossed off her property. By her hunk of a bodyguard. I smiled to myself. I'd like to see him try. But...he wouldn't do that to a woman? Would he?

I smiled all the way to the Carolyn's house, and realized I was still wearing a let-him-try grin on my face when Steve opened the door.

"Story." He stared at me. "Back so soon?"

"I know I'm not supposed to be here..." I raised my chin. "But I need to ask Carolyn a few more questions."

"Oh."

"May I come in?"

He stiffened and glanced behind him. "Carolyn is home...but..."

"Come on. I know what her bossy husband said, but it's not like I'm dangerous. You won't be putting your charge in any danger from me."

He flashed me a sideways smile and held my gaze. "How do I know you're not dangerous?"

My face grew warm at the sight of him standing there all dressed in black, his dark brown eyes taking me in as I took him in. Not moving. Keeping a firm hold on the door.

I slid him a-you-must-be-kidding look.

His eyes twinkled. "Well...you don't look dangerous." He lowered his gaze to my feet. "Although, those sneakers you're wearing today do look a bit more intimidating than the heels you had on before. I see you're learning."

Yes, I was. Today I was wearing white pedal pushers and a short-sleeve cotton blue top. Casual though professional, and easier to move around in, in case I needed to do any serious moving. Like running. Or, God forbid, fighting off bad guys. Or resisting efforts by one serious bodyguard to escort me from the premises of the Lowell estate.

"Then, I can come in?" I asked, peering hopefully over his shoulder. "It won't take long."

He shrugged. "Okay. I guess...sure." He waved me inside and called for Carolyn, then gave me a warning look. "Alec's at work, but you never know with him, so make it quick."

"Story..." Carolyn greeted me as she came down the stairs, dressed in tennis whites. "I didn't expect to see you so soon again. Does this mean you have news?" Her eyes lit up. "Good, I hope."

"Unfortunately, no."

She paled. "Not bad...?" she whispered.

"No, no. Not anything solid. Yet." I looked at her, then at Steve, then back at her. "Although I did go to Ocean City yesterday and discovered that Shriver's has a back door that Nanette could have slipped out of. Or, been forced out of, but that only generates more questions, which is why I'm back."

"I see." She hesitated, then waved for me to take the seat that I had sat in before, then settled herself down across from me.

Steve went back to his sofa.

"How can I help you?" she asked, a sliver of nervous impatience in her voice. "I'm getting ready to go play tennis at the club, so I don't have long, and I don't see what else I can tell you. And Alec will be furious if..." She waved a hand at me. "I'd rather not deal with his anger if I can help it."

"You can help me, and I'll be quick. I need a list of Nanette's other friends. Does she also belong to your club? Is it a country club?"

"Yes, The Whispering Pines Country Club. And yes, she has lots of friends there. Like me, she practically lived there. You know, golf, tennis, swimming, martinis. Happy hour."

What a lifestyle. Play all day. Play more at night.

I pulled a notebook out of my purse. "How many close friends would you say Nanette has? And could you give me some names? I'd like to get a more complete picture of her life. Maybe someone knows something you don't."

"You mean, like a secret?"

"Possibly. A secret that might explain why you need a bodyguard."

"Wait." Steve stood up and came over to us. "I don't think you should give Story any names of Nanette's friends without asking their permission first, Carolyn. It's only fair to them."

She glanced at Steve, then back at me. "I suppose he's right. Why don't I talk to some of the girls today at tennis, then get back to you? Anyway, I'm pretty sure Nanette didn't have any secrets."

"Your husband apparently thought she did. That's why Steve's here." I turned and gave him a what-are-you-trying-to-do look. Suggesting that Carolyn should get Nanette's friends' permission to talk to me only delayed things, making it harder for me to find her.

"Mom!"

Mom? I didn't know Carolyn had children. I turned. A teenage boy was making his way down the stairs, one insolent step at a time, his expression part confusion, part scowl. Gangly-thin, he had a face that might have been good-looking if not for his sullen expression, and the acne that dotted his cheeks, nose, and chin.

"Freddie," Carolyn said. "I didn't know you were home." She glanced at me. "Story, meet my son, who I thought was at swim practice. Freddie, this is Miss Smith, a private investigator looking for Mrs. Paulson."

Freddie hopped his way down the rest of the steps and came up to me. "Nice to meet you." He looked me straight in the eye. "A lady detective. How cool." He glanced over at Steve. "I never met a detective in my life, and now I got two of them in my living room. How lucky can a kid get?"

"Freddie, you're being rude," Carolyn said. "My best friend is missing and this a serious matter."

"Ain't it, though." He pursed his lips.

"Freddie. You *know* we don't say ain't. It's uncouth."

"Yeah, yeah. Just like I *know* what's really going on here, Mom. Like, why you have a fulltime bodyguard all of a sudden. Who's moved into the guest room next to my room." He slapped his forehead. "Oh, wait. No, I don't know why. Can somebody tell me?"

I was so glad he'd asked.

"Dad thinks I might be in danger. That's all I can tell you right now." Carolyn propped her hands on her hips. "And anyway, why aren't you at swim practice?"

"Coach cancelled. And don't change the subject. Why are you in danger? Were you and Mrs. Paulson involved in something bad?" Freddie stomped over to Steve. "Come on, somebody tell me something. I deserve to know."

"You'll need to ask your father," Steve said. "He hired me to keep your mom safe, and so that's what I'm doing, just doing my job."

"Following her around all day? Wherever she goes? Don't you think that looks kinda suspicious? Like what am I supposed to tell my friends?"

I saw an opening and dove for it. "Why are you worried about that, Freddie? What do you think your friends will say? Have you heard any rumors about Mrs. Paulson?"

His eyes gleamed. "No rumors, but the lady was a flirt. Flirted with every man at the club. Young, old, didn't matter."

"Freddie!" Carolyn's face went pink. "How dare you speak like that about my friend. She was just overly social."

"That's one way of putting it." Freddie snickered.

I looked over at Steve. Arms folded across his chest, his expression remained neutral, as if he was trying to distance himself from the conversation. But what was he was thinking behind his hired-help demeanor? He looked uncomfortable in it, and I bet he had a million questions he would've asked if he were in my shoes.

"What do you mean by flirtatious, Freddie?" I asked. "How exactly did Mrs. Paulson act?"

"Stop!" Carolyn stamped her foot. "This conversation stops right now. Nanette was just very outgoing, so what? Story, I do not give you permission to question my son. I'm afraid he doesn't know what he's talking about."

I bet he knew a lot more than he'd already said, but it wouldn't do to aggravate Carolyn by disrespecting her wishes. I needed her list of Nanette's friends. "I'm sorry, Carolyn," I said. "I didn't mean to upset you by questioning Freddie. It's just that I want to find Nanette as quickly as possible. I hope you understand."

She let out a deep sigh. "I do."

"Then can you please talk to Nanette's friends at tennis, and get me some names and phone numbers?"

"Alright."

Freddie slid me a sarcastic grin. "If they're honest, they'll just tell you what I did," he said. "That Dr. Paulson's wife is a sex pot."

———

After taking leave of Carolyn Lowell, it was time to go see Dr. Paulson. After calling his office to confirm he was in, I drove there, hoping to at least get a few minutes of his time between appointments with patients.

His office was in a high rise next to the University of Pennsylvania Hospital. It was also as busy as I'd expected, or more so. Pregnant women filled every seat in the waiting room, and I almost felt guilty asking the gray-haired receptionist for a few minutes of the doctor's time.

She gave me a frosty look. "I'm afraid that's impossible. If you're with child, and are having an emergency, you'll need to go to the emergency room."

Did I look pregnant? My fiancé, Dean, had always told me that I needed to gain weight. That I was too skinny. I leaned toward her. "I'm not pregnant," I whispered. "I'm here about Mrs. Paulson."

She widened her eyes. "Oh...I see. Then, just a minute, I'll go ask."

Thirty seconds later she returned and led me into an inner suite of rooms, all with closed doors, then into a conference room at the end of the hall. "He'll be with you momentarily," she said, then left.

I took a seat at a long table in the center of the room, where the walls were dotted with images of adorable babies. Boy babies. Girl babies. Twin babies.

Fortunately, I didn't have long to wait. My client came in minutes later, dressed in white pants and a white lab coat, looking anxious and hopeful at the same time. Which was a huge improvement from the last time I'd see him.

"You have news?" he asked, sitting across from me. "Good, I hope."

"Nothing yet. But I do have more questions."

He frowned, not even trying to hide his annoyance. "I'm a busy man. couldn't your questions wait? When my receptionist said you were here, I thought—"

"I'm sorry, doctor, but when would be a good time?" I shot back. "I'm well aware that you're busy, and I wanted to catch you between delivering babies. No one is in labor now, correct? So, could you please give me a few minutes?"

His frown softened, and he shrugged. "Okay. What do you want to know?"

"First, I'm wondering about the total lack of publicity about Nanette's disappearance. Your receptionist seemed to know about Nanette, but your patients still don't?"

"No. I need to keep this low key. I don't want my practice interrupted, or my patients, many of whom are in a delicate condition, alarmed." He leaned forward and met my gaze. "I just want Nanette found, which is why I hired you."

"Of course." I studied his face. It was growing flushed. Although he wouldn't admit it, a part of him had to suspect she might have left on her own for some reason, as opposed to being abducted. Now was not a good time to press the matter, however.

"I need to talk to some of Nanette's other friends," I said. "I've asked Carolyn to get me a list, but in the meantime, can you suggest anyone in particular I can talk to? What about her parents? Siblings?"

He shook his head, then sighed. "Nanette grew up in an orphanage. I am her only family. As for friends, Carolyn will have to help you there. Nanette spent far more time with her than with me." Pain sparked in his eyes, then guilt. "I'm afraid that my practice kept me so busy I didn't have much time for my poor wife, although she knew it couldn't be helped. She knew what she was getting into when she married a doctor."

"Did she complain?"

"No, never."

"Carolyn said she was very outgoing, that she had many friends."

"Yes, that's true."

"Was she equally outgoing with men?"

He dropped his jaw at the question. "What do you mean?"

"I mean, is it possible that Nanette was so socially extroverted that she could have given someone the wrong idea?"

I didn't want to come out and ask if she was flirtatious, but hoped he got my drift.

"No," he snapped. "That's ridiculous." He narrowed his eyes. "Are you suggesting my wife might have been having an affair? Because if you are, you are way off track, and I should fire you now."

"I didn't say that," I said, keeping my tone calmer than I felt. "I just got the impression from Carolyn that Nanette was rather...cheerful, charming, vivacious?" I didn't dare bring Freddie into the conversation or use his description of sex pot.

He relaxed his shoulders, leaned back and smiled. "Yes, it's true Nanette was...is... an uncommonly charming woman. Who deserved more of my time."

"But surely doctor, you and she spent some time together. When you went out, or were there occasions when you could commit to being with her without being interrupted?"

His eyes lit up. "Actually, yes. Whenever possible, I always tried to make it home for dinner. Unless one of my patients was in labor, of course."

"That's something, good for you. I'm sure she appreciated that."

"She did." He allowed himself a half smile. "Nanette's a good cook. She took pride in serving me wonderful meals."

"So, the two of you did spend time together," I said. "Don't be so hard on yourself."

"Only, never on Monday."

I wasn't sure I'd heard him right. "What about Monday?"

"On Mondays, Nanette volunteered at a homeless shelter in center city. So, we never had dinner together on Mondays. That was her special night, a time she devoted to the poor."

I tried not to show my surprise at this side of Nanette. Carolyn hadn't mentioned anything about her doing charity work, but it was another lead. Significant, or not, it was another place I could go to find out more about her.

"Tell me more, doctor," I said. "What is the name of this shelter, and where is it located?"

"Do you think it could be important?"

"I don't know, but I need to find out."

"I'm not sure of the exact name, and she always took a cab to get there, so I'm not exactly sure of the address. Something like City Mission, I think on Vine Street. I'm sorry, I don't have more information."

"Don't be," I said. "This is a start." I stood up. "I believe there are several missions on Vine Street. I'll go there and ask around and then let you know what I find out. In the meantime, if you can't reach me by phone, a receptionist who works down the hall from my office, Wendy Castillo, is now taking messages for me—I believe you met her earlier today." I jotted down her office number and handed it to him. "Keep in touch."

He nodded, looking more hopeful, and confident in me. Which was heartening.

"Don't worry," he said. "I will."

———

I phoned Carolyn when I got back to my office to ask her what she knew about Nanette's charity work with Philadelphia's downtrodden.

She didn't know much. Not the name of the homeless mission, or the address, only that it was somewhere in the vicinity of Vine Street, in what was known as the Tenderloin District.

"She didn't really talk about it," Carolyn said. "Only that she found working with society's unfortunate souls very gratifying. As far as I know, she just cooked and served meals."

"Did she ever invite you to go with her?"

"No, and I didn't volunteer. That section of Philly gives me the willies."

"Why?"

"You know why. It's filled with bums, drunks, and crooks. It's dangerous."

"But Nanette wasn't afraid to go there?"

"Guess not. Maybe she should have been."

"Do you think it might have had something to do with her disappearance?"

"Oh..." Carolyn whispered conspiratorially. "I didn't think of that. Maybe..."

"I'm going to go over there tomorrow, ask around," I said. "I know there are several missions on Vine Street and I'll find out which one Nanette volunteered at. Maybe someone will know something."

"Be careful."

"I will."

"Take Steve with you."

Steve? "Steve? You want Steve to go with me? But he's your body-guard, not mine. And what would your husband say?"

"He won't have to know."

"But what if he finds out?"

"I'm not worried about Alec, I'm worried about you."

That was nice of her, but I preferred to work alone. If I was going to make it in this business, I would have to prove that I could. And that I was fearless, and that I could take care of myself.

"Thank you," I said. "But I don't need Steve to go with me."

"Oh, but I insist," Carolyn said. "Steve is going with you, and that is that."

FIVE

Steve was not going with me. I didn't work for Carolyn, and she couldn't tell me what to do.

The next morning, I drove to my parents' house for breakfast. They live in the heart of Germantown, a Philadelphia neighborhood on my way to Vine Street, where I planned to head after breakfast, alone.

My mom, June, wasn't as enthusiastic about my new career as my father, Ralph. But both greeted me warmly with hugs, and kisses on the cheek.

I'd called to let them know where I was headed that morning, so I wasn't surprised when my dad peppered me with questions and my mom showered me with warnings.

"Have you ever been there?" my father asked. "Are you taking a gun?"

"You better take a gun," my mother said. "And a big, strong man like your brother, too."

"I've never been there." I walked over to the kitchen table, where coffee and orange juice waited for me. "But I know how to get there."

I unfolded my napkin and put it in my lap, then looked over to the stove where my father had started scrambling eggs. "And I don't own a gun."

"You better get one," my mother said, plopping a bowl of oatmeal in front of me. She pushed the sugar bowl in my direction, then sat across the table. A look of distress darkened her normally tranquil face. "I'm worried about you, Story. Don't know why you're doing this."

"Doing what?" I dumped a spoonful of sugar in my cereal, keeping my voice casual, as if I didn't know what she was referring to.

"Being a detective. It's no job for a woman."

There it was. Again. I shrugged. "It is for me."

My father handed me my eggs. "Story has her mind made up, June, so there's no use trying to talk her out of it. Best just to be supportive." He patted my shoulder. "I'll go with you."

He was dressed in his old plaid flannel robe and scruffy slippers.

"Thanks, Dad, but you're not dressed, and I can't wait." I salted my eggs. "Anyway, I need to do this on my own. Don't need my father to go with me. Don't need my brother. Don't need Steve Evans."

My mom leaned toward me, eyes wide. "Who's Steve Evans?"

I sighed. "He's another private eye, who's working as a bodyguard right now for a witness in my case."

"Bodyguard?" My mother's eyes went even bigger. "Why does this witness need a bodyguard?"

"That's one thing I'm trying to find out." I dug into my eggs with casual nonconcern. "Anyway, I'm hoping to learn more today. About a lot of things." I was beginning to wish I'd not stopped by for breakfast.

"By all means take this bodyguard with you." My father went back to the stove. "Why not?"

"Why?" I glared at him. "You wouldn't be having this conversation with Rob."

"Story..." My father sounded as exasperated as I felt. "You are not Rob. You are a young woman, very attractive, and quite frankly, very naïve. I've been supportive of you up to this point, but now I wish you would listen to me, and respect my advice. Take some precautions. Buy yourself a gun. Learn how to use it. And take a man with you today. Take this Steve Evans fellow. He could be useful."

I didn't say anything. I studied my father's extremely concerned face and sighed. He was right. I did need a gun. I was in the kind of business where I needed a gun. But I didn't need a man.

Especially Steve Evans.

Problem was that it would take time to buy a gun and learn how to use it and time was something I didn't have right now.

Plus, taking Steve along was better than my dad. I suspected Steve would be happy to go with me, which, for some reason, didn't gladden my heart.

Still...

"Okay, okay, I'll take Steve." I said. "I'm pretty sure he has a gun."

***

"Religious missions, cheap hotels, seediness, decay—and bars, bars, and more bars, each grungier than the next." Steve clicked his tongue as we motored past Franklin Square, also known as Bum's Park. "This place reeks of alcoholism and failure, quite a cautionary tale on the wages of sin."

I could only nod in agreement as I gripped the wheel, appalled, and more frightened than I wanted to let on. We had my top up, but in my pretty car we stood out like a gleaming diamond in a garbage dump.

I cut my gaze to Steve beside me in the passenger seat, then back to the scene at Sixth Street and Vine. As I'd suspected, he'd been eager to come along. Thank God he'd come with me, too, although I had too much pride to show my gratitude.

We had the windows open for air and I nervously glanced out mine. A stiff breeze knocked a beer can and food wrappers down the street, but the sad scene was no competition for the bitter stench of urine.

Researching the area, I'd learned there were three large missions on Vine Street: The Sunday Breakfast Mission, the Galilee Mission, and the Salvation Army Harbor Light Center. None matched the name Dr. Paulson had given me, so I'd suggested to Steve that we start with The Sunday Breakfast Mission, which contrary to its name, served meals every day of the week, and not just breakfast.

I edged myself closer to Steve after we parked and walked toward the large, plain, solid brick building. Its grimness reflected the gravity of its mission: saving souls while providing food and shelter.

Knowing what I knew about Nanette Paulson so far, she struck me as the type of woman who would stand out here even shinier and flashier than Steve and I did in my T-Bird. And, if she came by herself, it would have made her more vulnerable. How good of her, how noble.

How risky.

We stepped inside, and I immediately felt safer. Long tables took up most of a vast room, clearly the dining hall. Which, unlike the street outside, was clean and neat. At the back of the room a swinging door led to what I assumed was the kitchen.

"May I help you?" A nearly bald man dressed in gray, and wearing a clerical collar, hurried toward us, a confused, tentative smile on his face. "We don't serve lunch for another forty-five minutes, I'm afraid."

"Oh, we aren't looking for a meal," Steve said. "Just—"

"Let me." I put a hand on Steve's arm to remind him this was my case. "We're here looking for a woman." I handed him my picture of Nanette. "We are told she volunteers at a mission in this area, but we're not sure which one. Does she look familiar?"

"Volunteers how?" He studied the photo.

"Serving meals, cooking in the kitchen...maybe? Her name's Nanette Paulson."

He handed the picture back to me and shook his head. "I'm sorry, no. I've never seen this woman before."

"We must have the wrong mission, then," Steve said. "Thank you for your time, pastor."

"Father Gregory, and you're welcome."

"Wait," I said, not finished. Something was bothering me. "Do you have many volunteers here, Father Gregory? Women like the one we're looking for? Nanette is a doctor's wife, from the Main Line. Forgive me, but it seems to me she would stand out in a place like this. Am I wrong?"

His kind eyes crinkled as he smiled. "You're not wrong. Most of our volunteers are not wealthy women, although we do have a few who come with a church. Do you think that's the case with your doctor's wife? Maybe she volunteers at another mission as part of a church group."

"I don't know, that's a good question," I said.

"We offer shelter and meals to save souls for Jesus." Father Gregory pressed his hands together as if in prayer. "In exchange, mandatory attendance at religious services is required, which means most of our volunteers are affiliated with a church in some way."

If Nanette was a religious churchgoer, her husband hadn't mentioned it, nor had Carolyn. I made a mental note to find out.

"Thank you for your time, Father." I signaled to Steve with my eyes that now I was ready to go. "You've given us good information, and hopefully we'll have better luck at one of the other missions."

Back out on the street, I braced myself against the dirt and squalor, trying not to stare at the men openly taking swigs of cheap malt liquor. Or at the ones curled up on the sidewalk. They were sleeping off a hangover, I supposed. What a sad, desperate life for those poor souls.

We hadn't gone more than half a block before a man dressed in dirty rags stumbled up and begged me for money.

Steve grabbed my arm and steered me away, then into the Galilee Mission a few doors down.

"I can take care of myself." I pulled free.

He took my arm again and tightened his grip. "Don't be stupid," he whispered. "Remember why you're here, to find Nanette. Not to prove how brave and tough you are. Although I don't doubt for a moment that you're one tough gal." He gave me a wink.

Was I? I was beginning to have my doubts. Fortunately, the mission's dim interior hid my suddenly very warm cheeks. How tough could I be if I couldn't even control my reaction to a good-looking man's sexy wink?

Unfortunately, no one in the Galilee Mission had ever seen or heard of Nanette.

And we had no better luck at the Salvation Army Harbor Light Center, or any of the several smaller missions off Vine Street.

Something wasn't right. By the last mission, it hit me. "What if Nanette didn't really volunteer to help the poor?" I mused aloud to Steve. "What if that was a lie? What if she'd been lying to her husband about that?"

"I've been wondering that, too." He gave me a hopeful look. "So, are you ready to give up here and go home?"

No, I was not. Not nearly ready.

"Give up is not in my vocabulary," I said as we stepped back outside. I looked up and down the street, at all the other places we hadn't checked out yet. The cheap hotels, grimy pawnshops, sleazy bars.

"Story, what are you thinking?" Steve's tone was ominous.

"That so far, we've only talked to the folks who run the missions. What about the people they serve? Maybe one of them has seen Nanette."

"I don't think that's a good idea..." He took hold of my arm and yanked me away from a drunk making a grab for my ass.

This time I didn't pull away from Steve. I kept walking as if nothing had just happened. My legs were shaking so bad I was sure he could feel my jitters. Which I would *not* let deter me. "We need to go into some of these bars and ask around," I insisted.

Steve pulled me to a stop. "You do know that a lot of these people around here are not sane. Not in their right minds. Right? What do you hope to gain by talking to them?"

"There might be a mission we missed. I need to exhaust all possibilities, and then, and only then, will I be willing to go home. One way or another, I need to find out whether Nanette really did volunteer around here, or whether she was lying. In which case, what was she really doing on Monday nights?"

Steve let out a long, exasperated sigh. "Okay, you have a point." He pointed to the bar we were standing in front of, a grimy hole-in-the-wall called Joe's...something. The small, nondescript sign hanging over the door was faded and missing a bunch of letters.

"Let's start here," Steve said. "And whatever you do, Story, stick close to my side."

SIX

It was so dark and smoky inside Joe's that at first, I didn't think the joint had any customers.

Then, once my eyes adjusted to the gloom, I saw that the bar running from front to back was lined with sad-looking men on stools. They were hunched over, as if using the edge of the bar to prop themselves up. Most held a drink in one hand and a cigarette in the other.

The place reeked of stale tobacco, body odor, and despair.

I steeled myself, pulled out Nanette's photograph, and walked up to the first customer who made eye contact with me. He was a young man with dark scraggly hair, hollowed out cheekbones, and empty eyes, which brightened when he saw that I wanted to talk to him.

"Can I help you, doll?" he drawled, almost slipping off his seat.

I showed him Nanette's picture. "I'm looking for this woman. Have you ever seen her around? I think she might volunteer in one of the soup kitchens around here."

He leaned forward, squinted at it, shook his head. "Nope. Never saw no woman around here pretty as her." He grinned. He was missing most of his front teeth. "Except maybe you, doll-baby. I'd offer to buy you a drink if I wasn't so broke."

"Hey," Steve growled behind me. "Watch yourself, Story."

I ignored him.

"I kin buy you a drink, hon," the much older man next to the young guy announced. "How about a glass a wine, little lady?" He pulled change out of his pocket and slapped the coins on the bar. A dime and a nickel. "Barkeep, one Sneaky Pete for my friend here. And make it quick. She looks real thirsty."

I wasn't, but I didn't see any point in being rude. The bartender handed me my wine and I politely took a sip. It tasted like rotten grapes, although I managed to swallow it without grimacing. Ignoring the burning in my throat, I put the glass down. Everyone at the bar was staring at me.

Good. Might as well take advantage of that. Holding up Nanette's picture with both hands, I asked in a loud voice: "Has anyone seen this woman around here? Maybe volunteering at one of the missions? Serving food? Cooking in a kitchen?"

They shrugged and shook their heads.

"Told you this would be a waste of time." Steve muttered. "What are you going to do now? Drink up? Or should we just get out of here?"

"I seen her!"

I glanced back at Steve, then peered down toward the end of the bar to see who'd shouted that.

A man with a long, gray, matted beard slid off his stool and ambled toward me. Rocking back and forth, smelling like a brewery mixed with vomit, he nodded at the picture in my hands. "Yep, that's her. I seen her down at the Purple Lantern."

"When?" Steve asked sharply.

"I dunno. Seen her more in once." Gray Beard sniffed. "Wouldn't forgit that face."

I turned and gave Steve a let-me-ask-the-questions-look.

"Where's the Purple Lantern?" I asked.

"Just down the street, about three doors," another patron shouted. "Big purple sign, purple door. Can't miss it."

I looked back at Steve. "Okay, then, let's head there next."

"What about your Sneaky Pete?" the guy who bought it for me asked.

I pulled a dollar bill out of my purse and handed it to him. "I appreciate your generosity, but I need to go. Buy yourself and your friends a round, on me."

With a wave, I headed for the door and Steve followed.

"Wait." Steve put a hand on my arm when we got back on the street. "Do you believe him? What in the world would Nanette Paulson be doing in a bar around here? Volunteering to feed the poor is one thing but hanging out in a bar with down-and-out drunks is another."

"I don't know what to believe." I broke away from him and made a beeline toward the Purple Lantern. "But I need to check it out."

The Purple Lantern sat wedged between a pawnshop and Sam's Hotel, a seedy looking firetrap with a sign in the window advertising cheap rooms for the night.

Its faded plum-colored front door was propped open, and the interior loomed dimmer, dirtier, and more dangerous than Joe's.

I glanced back at Steve, coming up behind me. Part of me wanted to wait for him, take his arm, waltz in like we were a couple. And part of me wanted to go in alone. Because if I was to make it in this business, I'd need to face my fears and get used to going solo.

I didn't have to wrestle with my ambivalence for long. As I hovered by the door, a drunk ran up and grabbed Steve's jacket. "Can you spare a quarter, sir?" He shook Steve as he begged. "Anything...anything..."

Hoping to avoid the bum, I let Steve fend for himself and slipped into The Purple Lantern alone.

Once my eyes adjusted to the gloom, everything looked gray. Gray floor, gray walls, gray lumpy men on barstools slumped over drinks. Much like at Joe's, but somehow sadder. The brightest object in the joint was a framed liquor license hanging over the long mirror behind the bar.

I took a deep breath and tried to push away the queasy feeling that suddenly made it hard to breathe. Something was very wrong. A society woman married to a doctor would not frequent a place like this. Nanette wouldn't even step foot in it. Joe's was sleazy...but this place was pure hell.

A man slipped off his stool and came over to me. The hairs on the back of my neck prickled. Tall and muscular, he had a crazed look in his eye.

I wanted to turn and run out the door. But I also wanted to find Nanette. So, why not talk to this nut? Snatching her photo out of my purse, I held it up for him. "By any chance, sir, have you—"

He batted the picture out of my hand and snaked his fingers

around my wrist. "I know what you want, sugar." His leer and sloppy-slurry words gave me the creeps. "Come with daddy."

Daddy?

I pulled away. My heart raced. My chest squeezed. My legs wouldn't move. And damn it, they needed to move.

He grabbed me again. I tried to pull away, but his grip was too strong. "No! What are you doing? I only wanted to ask you a question."

"And sugar, I only want you." He squeezed my wrist so hard that pain shot up my arm. "Let's go." He shoved me toward the rear of the bar.

"Stop! Help! Someone! Help me!"

No one reacted. He pushed me past a line of men slumped over on stools. A few turned to look at me with confused, unfocused eyes, then looked away.

God help me, they were all in a drunken stupor.

I turned, tried to kick my attacker but missed.

He laughed.

I grabbed for an empty barstool. He shoved me away from it. I fell to my knees. He yanked me to my feet. "Keep moving!"

"Help!" I shouted at the bartender.

But he was working a beer tap at the other end of the bar and didn't even turn around.

I glimpsed myself in the grimy mirror behind the bar. Hair askew. Eyes wild. Mouth wide open in a scream. Like some poor woman in a horror movie, helpless to escape some awful fate.

No! Not me. I turned and launched myself at my monster's face. Clawed for his eyes. Missed. My nails dug into his cheeks, drawing blood.

He growled, then grabbed my shoulders and shoved, shoved, shoved me toward what looked like a rear door.

I screamed. "Help! Somebody...help!"

Where was Steve? Why hadn't I waited for him?

"Shut up." My attacker gave me another hard push, reached over me, thrust the door open, and shoved me through.

I landed on my knees, stumbled to my feet. Blinking against the harsh sunlight, I looked around.

I was trapped in a grungy courtyard. Enclosed by tall buildings. Piles of trash. No way out. Nowhere to run.

He grabbed my blouse, ripping it as he yanked me around to face him. His nasty, black-toothed grin made my stomach lurch.

He pulled me toward him, then dragged me backward toward the door and kicked it closed.

"Don't..." My plea came out as a whimper.

He put his hands around my neck and chuckled. "Nobody can hear you now, baby. You're mine." He pinned me against the door, holding me in place with one hand while his other hand fiddled with his belt.

Oh, God. No. He was going to rape me.

I kicked his legs but that only made him laugh.

I tried to knee him in the groin, but he stepped in too close and tightened his grip on my neck.

"Please, no..."

Grinning with anticipation, he pushed his pants down.

Cold terror shot through my veins. I started shaking.

He leaned in to kiss me.

I turned my head, felt his gross wet lips graze my cheek. His breath smelled like rotting garbage.

I gagged, but he was squeezing my neck so hard it sounded like a gurgle.

With brute force, he grabbed my skirt and tugged. I heard the waistband rip.

Black dots swirled before my eyes. I couldn't breathe...couldn't breathe...

The door behind me bucked. Someone was trying to force it open. Someone who was shouting my name.

Steve? With all my strength, I jerked hard to my right to unblock the door.

I landed on the ground with my attacker on top of me. He grabbed my skirt and tried to rip it off.

The door flew open. Steve ran out and yanked the beast to his feet.

He slammed him against the building so hard that his head flew back and hit the bricks with a thunderous thud. He slid to the ground, ending up flat on his back. Pants down to his ankles. His privates in full view.

Steve helped me up. "Are you okay?"

"Oh, my Lord...he could have...but he didn't..." My teeth rattled so much I could hardly get the words out.

"Thank God. You shouldn't have—"

"I know. I know." I collapsed against Steve, and he held me tight. "I might throw up. If you hadn't come when you did..."

"You're okay, you're okay. You're safe now."

I squeezed my eyes closed. "Is he alive or dead?"

"He's still breathing. And bleeding, the bastard. Looks like you got a good swipe at his face."

Police sirens wailed in the distance.

My neck hurt. My head hurt. My knees stung. I opened my eyes and looked down. They were bloody.

My legs wobbled, I suddenly felt dizzy.

Steve tightened his grip around my waist, then lowered me to the ground. I leaned back against the wall and closed my eyes again.

"We need to get you to a hospital." Steve's voice was tight. "But first we have to wait for the police."

"I'm fine. I'll be okay."

"I hope you're right. But we need to get you checked out. And it looks like your left hand is bleeding."

I opened my eyes and stared at it.

Steve took my bloody hand in both of his. He ran his fingers along the side. "There's a deep gash. Don't you feel it?"

I hadn't. Until he mentioned it. Too much of me hurt worse. Especially my pride.

Steve kept my hand in his as he settled down next to me, but he didn't say anything else. He wanted to, I was sure. He wanted to tell me that I should have listened to him. Should have waited for him. Should have known what I was getting into as a P.I.

I was grateful for his silence. Because I didn't need him telling me what I already knew.

I was still silently berating myself when police officers arrived, hauled my would-be-rapist to his feet, arrested him, and dragged him away.

———

I was stuck lying on a gurney in the E.R. It was mid-afternoon and I was waiting to see a doctor, aching all over, but at least I'd stopped shaking. I rolled my head toward Steve, sitting beside me. "I don't need to be here. All I need is a few Band-Aids for my hand."

"That's a deep cut. I'm sure you'll need stitches."

"Whatever. More importantly, why had I ever thought Nanette would step foot in a sleazy place like The Purple Lantern? Now I'm convinced she never volunteered to help the poor, either."

"The question is, what was Nanette really doing on Monday nights?" Steve met my gaze, looking as perplexed as I felt. "And did it have anything to do with her disappearance?"

"That's what I need to find out." I didn't sound nearly as confident as I would have liked. I needed to buck up, get my beginner's confidence back.

But I was a mess. Mentally. Emotionally. Questioning my life choices. What had made me think I could make it as a P.I. in a tough, gritty city like Philadelphia? As a woman, in a man's world? Was I nuts?

I didn't dare voice my doubts out loud. I didn't know Steve well enough. Plus, he was my competition, and it wouldn't do to have the competition know how weak I felt.

I sighed. "Maybe Alec Lowell is on to something. Maybe Nanette was involved in something shifty." I pulled the flimsy hospital blanket up to my neck.

Steve touched my uninjured hand. "You feel like ice. Should I get you another blanket?"

"Okay, thanks. I'm so cold. I can't get warm."

He was back in a flash and draped the blanket over me. Why did they make hospital blankets so thin? I wanted Steve to warm my hand with his. Hold my hand and not let go.

His skin on my skin. That's what I really wanted.

No, no, no. I didn't want to feel what I was feeling for Steve. I also didn't want him to know how I felt.

"I'm beginning to think it's a good idea Alec hired you," I blurted out after a long, awkward silence between us. "For Carolyn's safety."

"You're *beginning* to think that?"

"Yes, at first it seemed odd. Weird. Suspicious. But now, I don't know."

"Lots of things about this case are weird." Steve narrowed his eyes as he met my gaze. "Remember what the police told us? They couldn't find anyone in The Purple Lantern who'd ever seen Nanette."

"Yes. I'm so glad they found her photo on the floor, where that freak knocked it out of my hand. And that her disappearance is still an open investigation."

"Except, they made it pretty clear that they believe she left of her own accord."

"Right." I sighed. "It doesn't help that Martin Paulson doesn't want missing woman posters tacked up around town. I understand that he doesn't want to upset his patients or harm his practice. Still, does that mean his patients are more important than his wife? Maybe that could be a reason she left him, if she did."

Steve and I looked at each other for another long moment. Too long. Where was the doctor? I wanted to go home. Take a long, hot shower. Put my nightgown on. Go to sleep and wake up tomorrow ready to solve this case. I only had a week, and I was getting nowhere. Fast.

"It seems a sure bet that the drunk that attacked me had nothing to do with Nanette," I said, not liking the hopeless, poor-me tone in my voice.

Steve pressed his lips together. "At least he won't hurt you again. If there's any justice in this world, he'll spend the rest of his sorry life in the pokey. If not the mental hospital, which is where he really belongs."

"Which leaves me nowhere as far as my case is concerned. So far all I have is an injured hand along with a bruised neck and a bruised ego."

The curtain around me flung open. Finally, a doctor. He yanked my blankets off. What a jerk. At least I was dressed. He asked Steve to step outside the curtain, so he and a nurse could examine and treat me privately.

It took a hell-of-a-long hour for them to bandage my knees and assess my hand. Three stitches later and I was a free woman.

Steve and I threaded our way through the parking lot to my car. Steve held up my keys. "I'm driving."

"You just like driving my T-Bird."

"I knew you were a smart cookie."

"Tell you what, you can drive to the Lowell mansion. We'll drop you off, then I'll drive myself home." My voice didn't leave any room for argument.

Steve opened the passenger side door for me. "Agreed."

"You've been gone a long time. I hope Alec Lowell doesn't bust a gasket."

"Oh, he had no idea I was going with you." Steve started the car and slid me a sideways grin. "And for Carolyn's sake, I hope he never finds out."

"I hope he doesn't for both your sakes."

"What?" Steve turned toward me. "You think he'll fire me? I doubt that, but even if he does, I'm not worried. I'm damned good at what I do."

He pulled onto the street. He looked so right behind the wheel. Like he drove my car all the time.

"You are good, Steve," I agreed. "Darned good. And thanks again for your help today."

He turned back to me and held my gaze. Too long. The car drifted onto the shoulder.

He jerked the wheel and put the T-Bird, and his attention, back on the road where they belonged.

I was finally feeling warm again. All over. Outside. And inside.

Not good, not good, not good.

Rob's warning about Steve came back to me. Don't fall in love with him. Lots of women had fallen for him. Was I proving to be the exception? I needed to be the exception.

I glanced at Steve again. Darn, why did he have to be so good looking? I didn't need that. I didn't need my heart doing flips whenever I looked at him.

I could not let this man distract me from my mission.

Which was to make it on my own. I made a promise to myself there and then that I would.

SEVEN

Alec was seething when Steve pulled up to the Lowell mansion. Clearly waiting for us, Carolyn's short-fused hubby came running out the front door the minute Steve parked my car.

Steve hopped out, and Alec slowed his pace, stomping across his lawn with a thunderous expression that boded trouble.

We'd been gone too long. The sun was beginning to set on what had been a long, long day. Steve and I had been gone hours longer than originally planned, and I felt a twinge of guilt.

The top of my car was up, and I didn't want Alec to see me. I was also in no mood for a confrontation if he did—so I slid over into the driver's seat, ready to take off.

Only I didn't. My curiosity got the best of me. I wanted to see what would happen next. I rolled my window down all the way and watched Steve stroll toward Alec with a cool swagger.

"Where were you?" Alec yelled. "I hired you to protect my wife. And you've been gone—what— all day?"

Steve shrugged nonchalantly. "I'm sure Carolyn's fine. Where is she?"

"In the house, you fool." Alec waved a hand at the wide-open front door.

"Alec!" Carolyn ran out toward him. "Calm down, will you? What will the neighbors—"

"The neighbors be damned!" Alec waved a fist at Steve. "When Carolyn told me you'd gone off with that girl detective, I couldn't believe it. What the hell did I hire you for? Not to be the assistant to some crazy dame who thinks she's Sherlock Holmes."

Steve's eyes flicked over to me then back to Alec. "Carolyn assured me she'd stay inside with the doors locked, so I knew she'd be safe. What—do I have to stay by her side every single minute of every single day?"

"*Yeah.* That's what I'm paying you for."

"Doesn't make me your slave, Lowell." Steve stepped back and folded his arms across his chest. "I don't need your money. Maybe I should just quit."

Alec's angry glare evaporated. He shook his head. "No, no, don't do that. No need for that." He glanced over at me and then turned back to Steve with a pasted-on-phony smile. "It's just that..." he cleared his throat. "Never mind...never mind. Where did you and Miss Smith go that was so important?"

"We wanted to check out a lead about Nanette Paulson!" I shouted. I didn't like being called girl detective, and I didn't care if the neighbors heard me. "It was in a dangerous part of Philly, so Steve was nice enough to go with me."

Alec narrowed his eyes to a squint, walked over, and peered in my window.

I immediately regretted opening my big mouth, wished I had just driven away when I'd had the chance.

"What in hell happened to you?" he asked, eyeing my swollen neck. "Your neck's turning purple. Somebody try to strangle you?"

"What?" Carolyn ran over and saw my torn blouse and my bandaged hand. "My God, what happened, Story?"

"It was a good thing you insisted Steve come with me." I held her shocked gaze. "It turns out Skid Row has some mean drunks, and I had a run-in with one of them."

Carolyn clapped a hand to her mouth.

Steve nodded. "Nanette must have been lying to her husband about volunteering there, Carolyn. Because we couldn't find anyone who recognized her picture."

Carolyn turned and looked at him. "But Nanette wouldn't lie. Why would she lie about such a thing? About volunteering to help the poor? I don't believe it."

"Well, I think you better believe it, dear." Alec's tone was triumphantly sarcastic. "I told you that your so-called best friend was probably wrapped up in something dangerous. With dangerous people."

"But she wasn't..." Carolyn shook her head.

"No? Look what happened to our girl detective here. That's why I hired you a bodyguard, Carolyn. Because I care about you so much."

I pressed my lips together to keep from saying something I shouldn't. Alec's concern for his wife felt overblown. Fake. And he wasn't making sense.

"I'm going to keep looking for Nanette." I reached for Carolyn's hand and gave it a squeeze. "I aim to find out the truth about what happened to her, but in the meantime, it won't hurt to have Steve as your bodyguard. Just in case."

I wanted Steve to keep his lucrative gig. I would have felt guilty if he'd lost it because of me. Not that he needed the money, if Rob was right about him. But what did I know at this point? Damned little. Maybe Carolyn was in danger.

"Thanks again for your help, Steve," I called over to him. "But I can take this case from here."

"Good!" Alec declared. "My wife has told you everything she knows—so good-bye and good luck and please don't come back." He turned and stomped up the walk.

Steve came back over to me. "I'm sure you'll find Nanette," he said with an everything-will-be-okay smile. "You have a lot to learn, but you have the makings of a great private eye, and I'm sure I'll be seeing you around."

"Gee, thanks. I hope so." I beamed. His words of encouragement were just what I needed.

"That is if you don't get yourself killed..."

"Gee...*thanks.*"

I couldn't believe him. After what we'd just been through, how dare he tease me.

But he was only telling the truth. Warning me. That I had a lot to learn, and I needed to learn it—fast.

I started the car and gave Steve a stiff wave. "See you around. I guess."

———

Wendy motioned to me from behind her desk as I passed the open door to her office.

I could not believe she was working so late.

After leaving the Lowell residence, I'd gone home, showered, and changed clothes, and was ready to type up a report of what had transpired that day. I was too keyed up to do anything else—like sleep.

"Hi, Wendy," I said, glad to see her. "Working the midnight oil? You sure are dedicated to your job."

She grinned and shrugged. "I love it. And I have a lot of work to catch up on since I took some time off earlier today."

"Any news for me?"

"Nope. Quiet as can be around here. No visitors for you, that I know of, and no messages."

I nodded. "I'm not surprised. I haven't started advertising yet."

"Maybe you should." She flashed me a cheerful grin, then squinted at me with a sudden look of shocked concern. "Hey, are you okay? What happened to your hand? And your neck looks kind of red. And your eyes...too."

I winced. They were bloodshot. From almost being strangled to death. After I got home and examined my face in the mirror, I'd realized how awful I looked.

But then I'd forgotten how bad I looked. Maybe I needed to wear sunglasses and scarves for a while. I gave Wendy a wry smile. "I'm okay. I've just had a super long, rough day so far, that's all."

"You want to talk about it?"

"Not really..."

"You sure?"

I kind of did want to talk about it. I didn't know Wendy yet, and maybe it would be foolish to trust her, but she had volunteered to be my part-time receptionist, and she sure seemed nice. God knows, I did need a pal.

"Well..." I held her compassionate gaze. "I've been hired to find a missing woman and she is proving to be quite a mystery. Her husband thinks she's a saint. Her best friend's teenage son thinks she's a slut. And her best friend's husband thinks she was involved in something shady and dangerous."

Wendy's eyes went big, and she waved me into her office. She pointed to a chair next to her desk, and after I sat down, she leaned toward me and whispered, "Is that why you got beat up?"

"No...yes...maybe? I got caught up in a lie my mystery woman was apparently spreading before she vanished. I shouldn't say any more than that."

Wendy stared at me, like a million questions were running through her head.

I stood up. "I have work to do. I need to get going. I'll talk to you later, okay?"

"Sure." She cheerfully put her fingers back on her typewriter keys. "See you later."

———

I unlocked my door, sat down behind my desk, inserted a piece of paper into my typewriter, and started typing.

One-handed, because my bandaged hand ached.

My neck throbbed. My head started to pound. My heart began beating so fast I couldn't concentrate.

I started to shake. Then I began to sob. Silently. I let my tears run down my cheeks.

Who was I kidding? I'd come close to getting raped. I'd almost died.

I was hurting and in shock. I wasn't Super Woman. I needed to go home.

Tomorrow was another day, and my report could wait until then. It wasn't as if I was going to forget anything that had happened between now and tomorrow.

Or ever.

EIGHT

A good night's sleep did me a world of good.

The next morning, feeling much better physically and emotionally, I bathed, dressed, ate breakfast, and was back at my office by nine o'clock.

My left hand still hurt but I considered myself lucky I was right-handed.

Still, after a few sentences, I stopped typing. This report would be going to Dr. Paulson.

So... how much should I reveal about what I suspected at this point? That Nanette had been lying to him about her Monday nights?

No. At this point, that might only get me fired. I had to stick to the facts about my activities. List the places where Steve and I had gone. Who we'd talked to. What they'd said. Leaving out what had happened to me. No need for him to know about that...

I stared at a piece of chipped paint on the wall. Maybe I shouldn't even say that Steve had come with me. Was that necessary?

I heard footsteps coming down the hall.

Like Wendy, I'd left my door open for air.

I looked up, expecting to see Wendy.

But it was Carolyn.

"Knock, knock," she said breezily, then walked in, ignoring the surprised look on my face.

She was dressed to play tennis. Again. White pleated skirt, white blouse, white sneakers. Hair up in a ponytail, tied with a white ribbon.

"Hi...?" I stood up.

"Hi." She looked around. "Nice office. I'm impressed."

"Thank you. You're being kind." I stared at her, puzzled. "But I'm surprised to see you here. And to see you again so soon. Does this mean you have news about Nanette?"

She sat in the client chair next to my desk and crossed one tanned leg over the other. "Not really."

Now I was truly confused. "Where's Steve?"

She waved a hand. "He's waiting for me out in the car."

I blinked. "Okay..."

She stood up, pulled her chair around to face me directly, sat back down, and leaned forward. "You must think I'm a bit of a flake."

I just stared at her. "I don't think anything of the sort. Why would I?"

She bit down on her lower lip. "I apologize for the way my husband has been acting. I don't know what has gotten into him. He's not been himself. I think Nanette's disappearance really has him rattled."

"Of course, that's understandable."

"Only he doesn't have to be so rude."

"Well, he has been rather rude to me. But that's not your fault."

"It's not, but it makes me want to help you."

I nodded. "Thank you, but you already have. You've told me everything you know, and even loaned me your bodyguard, incurring your husband's wrath. Which, by the way, I'm sorry about. But you must have known how he'd react if he got wind of it."

"I knew, and I didn't care."

"I see." I studied her face. It was growing flushed. "But why didn't you care?"

"Because he's being ridiculous and I'm tired of it. Insisting that I need a fulltime bodyguard. Insisting that Nanette was involved in something bad. Insisting that she was mixed up with bad people, even criminals. Doesn't he realize I would have known if that were true? That I would have seen something, heard something? He's treating me like I'm a child."

"I admit, I have been wondering about that," I said.

"I want to help you find my best friend. And I can, thanks to Alec."

"Okay...?"

"I want Steve to keep assisting you."

I widened my eyes. "Steve?"

"Yes. Why not?"

I could think of a few reasons.

"Not just Steve, but me, too," she said.

My jaw dropped.

"Look, Alec wants Steve to guard me day and night. So...might as well put him to work doing something useful. He's a very talented detective."

"And, let me guess. He's bored being a bodyguard. And he envies me."

The corner of her mouth lifted in a half grin. "He hasn't actually come out and said so, but yes, I can tell he does."

Oh boy.

"No thank you, Carolyn." I shook my head. "I need to solve this case on my own. Dr. Paulson hired me, after all."

"No one has to know."

"What do you mean?"

"You can keep all the money Martin is paying you. And you'll have two secret assistants. Steve, and me, since he's guarding me, and he and I need to stick together. Don't you want to find Nanette? I do!"

Of course, I wanted to find Nanette. More than anything, I wanted to find Nanette.

Who was I to turn down help that I could really use?

This wasn't about me. Steve could teach me a lot. If I didn't let him take over the case, which I most definitely would not. Even though I knew he'd try. "I don't think Steve will like the idea of being an assistant," I said, meeting her anxious gaze. "Have you run this idea by him?"

"Sure. He's all for it."

"But how would the two of you pull this off? I mean, how will you be able to keep Alec in the dark? As you've noticed, he doesn't like me. Doesn't want me around."

Carolyn gave a sly smile. "As long as you don't come to our house, I don't think we'll have a problem. He wants Steve to follow me around like a puppy and he doesn't seem to care where we go or what we do. When I go to the club, Steve goes to the club. When I go shopping, Steve goes shopping. When I play golf..."

"Steve plays golf?"

"Really well. Tennis, too. The perfect bodyguard."

"I bet all your friends are jealous."

"Why? Because he's so good looking? Yep." Her smile faded. "Only Alec doesn't seem to care about that, either. He doesn't seem jealous of Steve at all. Which I don't get. He could have hired somebody ugly."

That was true. And what I'd been thinking, too. Another odd puzzle piece to this challenging case.

I needed to set my pride aside. I could use all the free and secret help I could get.

"Okay. Let's bring Steve in here and we can talk," I said. "And together we will find your friend."

———

Posh.

That word kept coming to my mind as Carolyn gave me a tour of her ritzy country club later that morning, Steve dutifully trailing a few feet behind us.

Posh tennis courts, a dozen or more.

Posh 18-hole golf course, perfectly manicured grass glistening in the sun.

Posh low-slung white-brick club house, which overlooked an outdoor patio filled with tables and umbrellas, and beyond that an Olympic-size pool. Where beautiful adults sunned themselves on lounge chairs beside sparkling blue water while teenage lifeguards watched squealing kids splash and play.

Perfect place, perfect people, perfect life.

Thankfully, Carolyn was willing to personally escort me around Nanette's world. The club was private, and I would have had a hell of a time even getting past the guard. Let alone fitting in.

Strolling onto the pool deck, with all those pretty people, I was glad I'd worn dark glasses and a summer scarf to hide my not-so-pretty eyes and neck.

"Hello, Carolyn." A deeply tanned bleach-blonde waved to us. Stretched out on a lounge chair, she sported huge cat-eye-shaped sunglasses and a bikini so teeny half her breasts were on display.

She lowered her shades, eyeing Steve and flashing him a flirty smile. "And hello handsome, so good to see you again."

"Hi, Tina." Carolyn gave her a flutter-finger wave. "And yes, Steve's still with me. If Alec has his way, he will be for a while, too. At least until Nanette is found."

Tina giggled and grinned. "Oh, goody."

I was dying to see Steve's expression, but he was behind me. Carolyn put a hand on my arm. "Tina, meet Story Smith. She's a private eye who Martin hired to find Nanette. She's here to meet some of her friends, learn more about her life, which hopefully will lead to some clues."

"Goodness, yes." Tina flicked a glance at me then moved her gaze back to Steve. "What a dreadful thing, Nanette just up and vanishing like that. Scares me to death. What if her kidnapper comes for one of us next?"

"Kidnapper?" I couldn't keep the surprise out of my voice. "What makes you think she was kidnapped?"

She sat up straighter and reluctantly pulled her eyes away from Steve to look at me. "Because she would never have left on her own accord. I would think it would be obvious. Nanette had everything a woman could possibly want. Somebody kidnapped her. And I'm scared."

Scared? Really? No, this woman looked relaxed and well-oiled in shiny suntan lotion, maybe even slightly tipsy. The drink beside her chair was bright orange with a striped paper umbrella sticking out of it. She picked it up and took a sip.

I needed to press her for more. I glanced behind me to see Steve's reaction to the kidnapping theory, but he was playing the role of aloof, observant bodyguard. Dressed in khaki pants, a white cotton shirt, and boat shoes, he didn't look at me. His eyes, behind dark sunglasses, were scanning the area, looking for potential danger in paradise.

This was great. He was sending me the message that he was not going to interfere with my interview. I was on my own.

Yay.

I sat down on the unoccupied lounge chair next to Tina and leaned toward her. "Please, tell me more. Do a lot of people here at the club think she was kidnapped?"

Tina pursed her bright red lips. "Probably. Anyway, Alec does. Why else would he hire Carolyn a bodyguard?" She cut her eyes back to Steve. "I wish my hubby would hire a gorgeous guy like Carolyn's got to squire *me* around."

Was she serious about being scared? Or just playing some kind of flirtatious game?

"Who do you think would want to kidnap Nanette?" I asked. "Any ideas?"

"Unfortunately, no."

"Do you think she could have gotten herself in some kind of trouble? Maybe got involved with the wrong people?"

"Goodness, no. Not Nanette."

"Do you think she could have given some man the wrong idea? I heard she could be quite the flirt."

Tina gave a tinkling laugh. "Oh, she could flirt. But she flirted with everybody. You know, in an innocent way."

"Everybody?"

"Yeah, all the guys." She pointed a shell-pink fingernail at Steve. "She would have flirted with you, for sure."

Steve acted as if he had not heard her.

I was kind of enjoying this, except that I was getting nowhere.

"Tina," Carolyn said. "You're just being naughty. You don't know anything at all."

Tina stuck her tongue out. "So?" She slid her sunglasses back over her eyes and melted back down into her chair. "Just trying to help."

"Not much help." Carolyn put a hand on my arm. "Come on, Story, let's go talk to some of the tennis players."

Steve and I followed her over to the courts, which were packed.

We walked up to a match where men and women were playing mixed doubles. We stood to the side until they finished, then Carolyn motioned for one of the men to come over. He was tall and slim and looked to be around forty. I wondered why he had the freedom to play tennis in the middle of a workday.

"Looking for me, Caro?" He gave me a welcoming smile. "Hello."

"This is Gary Abel," Carolyn said. "He was one of Nanette's favorite tennis partners. Gary, meet Story Smith. She's a private eye looking for Nanette and she's casting around for any information that might help. Since you played tennis with her most every day, she'd like to ask you some questions."

"Wow, I don't know what I can tell you." Gary wiped sweat off his forehead with a small towel. "It's a mystery. I miss her. I love her. I want her back. But don't we all?"

His use of the word love caught my attention. I pointed to a bench. "Could you and I go have a seat over there, so we can talk some more?"

He shrugged. "I suppose so."

We sat down next to each other, and I turned to face him. "You said you loved Nanette. By any chance, are you talking romantically?"

He laughed. "No, no, no. She was just fun to be around. And a hell of a tennis player."

"I see."

He pointed to Carolyn and Steve, who were waiting for me on the other side of the court. Standing side-by-side, they appeared to be in deep conversation. "You know, Carolyn's husband, Alec?" Gary asked.

I nodded.

"Alec also played a lot of tennis with Nanette. Did Carolyn tell you that?"

"No..."

"He did. They were quite a two-some. Martin Paulson's a busy baby doc, but when he and Nanette did come to the club together, they often played mixed doubles with Carolyn and Alec. A lot of the time, they switched up partners, and I have to say, Alec and Nanette made quite a team."

I made a mental note to ask Carolyn about that, then brought my gaze back to Gary Abel. "What did you think when you heard Nanette disappeared?"

"I was devastated. Mystified."

"What do you think might have happened to her?"

His face darkened. "Somebody took her. But I understand Martin hasn't received any ransom notes."

"Do you think someone could have become obsessed with Nanette, kidnapped her, not for ransom, but to keep her as a…" I hesitated. Should I say it?

"Sex slave?" He shrugged. "I would hate to think that, but a woman that pretty and charming…it's possible."

I glanced back over at Carolyn and Steve, still deep in conversation. If someone didn't know better, they could be mistaken for a married or dating couple, they had that kind of easy comradery.

"Why do you think Alec hired a bodyguard for Carolyn?" I asked.

He sighed. "I think Alec is just being overprotective."

"Alec suspects Nanette was involved in something shady."

He shook his head. "No idea why he would think that." He pressed his lips together. "I'm sorry I can't be more help. Wish I could."

I stood up. "I wish you could, too. But thank you for your time, Mr. Abel. I hope to have some good news for you soon, to have Nanette back here playing with you before you know it."

"I pray that is so."

So did I. Another day was winding down and I still wasn't making much progress. I didn't have many more days before Martin Paulson would replace me.

I was getting nowhere at the club.

Steve and Carolyn were still talking when I walked back over to them. A tiny tinge of jealousy crept into my chest when he started laughing and then she started laughing and neither looked over at me.

Nope. I would not allow myself to feel any such feelings. Like Rob said, women liked Steve.

Carolyn clearly did. Good for her, that was her business. I needed to stay professional.

I gave myself a mental shake and took a deep breath. Steve was giving me space to do my job. So, what was my problem?

Neither he nor Carolyn needed to help me. They could have easily just gone about their days playing tennis and golf together, bodyguard and damsel-in-potential-distress, having fun in the under the sun while I worked my case by my lonesome.

I needed to cultivate more gratitude. And a better attitude.

"How did it go, Story?" Carolyn gave me a tentative smile when I came up to them.

"Alright. I didn't learn anything new." I looked at her, then at Steve. "Only that Alec used to play a lot of tennis with Nanette. Is that true?"

Steve lifted an eyebrow.

Carolyn shrugged. "Yes. So?"

"It's probably nothing. I'm just wondering why you didn't tell me that Nanette and Alec often teamed up against you and Martin Paulson."

Carolyn sighed. "I didn't think it was important."

"Maybe it's not," I said. "It's probably not." I had to be careful not to make her angry, but at the same time something bothered me about it.

"Hey, want to go over to the golf course?" Carolyn asked.

"Okay," I said, meeting Steve's gaze for the first time that day when he lowered his sunglasses and gave me a look that said, "good job."

Or maybe I'd just imagined it.

We strolled onto the course at the eighteenth hole.

Four women were getting ready to tee off. Carolyn introduced me, and I asked if any of them had any ideas, crazy or not, as to what might have happened to Nanette.

They all offered ideas. None of much help.

"I can't imagine..."

"She was such a happy person..."

"Such a sweet woman..."

"And a great golfer..."

So, there I was. Left with what I already knew. Nanette had spent much of her life playing tennis and golf, with nothing to suggest she'd been involved with drug smuggling, prostitution, bank robbing, or anything remotely illegal.

"Did she ever talk about her volunteer work with the poor?" I asked the foursome.

They looked at each other and shrugged.

"Not really," one of them said. "We all knew she volunteered, but she was very humble about it. She didn't like to talk about it, although we all thought she was a saint for doing it."

I smiled.

Right.

I turned to Carolyn. "I think I have a pretty good picture of Nanette now. Or at least her life here at the club." An idea came to me. "When Nanette wasn't here, what else did she do with her time?"

Carolyn looked back and forth between me and Steve and shrugged. "Mostly shopped."

"Shopped where?"

"She had some favorite stores. Why?"

"Could we go visit some tomorrow?" It sounded lame, but I was desperate.

"Sure." Carolyn smiled. "I could take you around. Steve and I can take you around. Glad to."

Steve looked like he'd swallowed a toad. "Shopping is one of my all-time favorite things to do, ladies." He coughed. "Can't wait."

———

Nanette had extremely expensive taste in clothes. No surprise.

It also came as no surprise to me that Theo's, a famous Main Line boutique, was one of her favorite stores.

I'd heard all about the place from my Bryn Mawr College friends, but I'd never had the nerve to shop there. From what they said, it was the kind of place where you didn't dare ask the price of something. If you did, you clearly didn't belong. And you certainly wouldn't be able to afford it.

Carolyn ushered me and Steve in when the place opened at noon. It was a Sunday, so I considered myself lucky they were open at all.

The clock was ticking, ticking, ticking on my investigation. I wasn't sure what I could possibly learn here that would get me any closer to finding Nanette, but I had to try.

I had to keep digging into her life.

We were the day's first customers. I scooted ahead of Carolyn and Steve, then stopped, looking around in amazement.

The display racks were so organized, they looked as if they'd been arranged by a genie waving a magic wand. Untouched by human hands. Everything perfectly draped on hangers, nary a wrinkle.

Dresses arranged by color lined one wall. Blouses and skirts and slacks adorned racks in the center of the room. Shoes, flats and heels, casual and dressy, sat grandly on display next to a wide floor-to-ceiling mirror.

The carpet was so squishy it was like walking on a cloud. Frank Sinatra crooned softly in the background, his voice coming from a record player...somewhere.

I caught a glimpse of myself in the mirror. My maroon skirt and striped blouse looked like they'd come from Sears. Because they had. I gave myself a little smile and shrugged. At least the redness in my eyes was fading, as were the bruises on my neck.

"May I help you?" A clerk greeted us from behind a long counter near the back, next to a row of curtained dressing rooms, each curtain a different color. Pink, purple, blue, red, yellow. How pretty. How perky.

The young dark-haired clerk matched the curtains in perkiness. With a grin that twinkled her eyes, she looked from me to Steve, then to Carolyn. "Hi, Mrs. Lowell." Her eyes slid back to Steve. "Hello." Then to me. "Hello."

Carolyn introduced me but not Steve. I assumed it was because she didn't want the entire town to know she had a bodyguard, although it was probably already common knowledge.

"Story," Carolyn said, "this is Minnie. Ask her anything you want because she knows Nanette well."

Minnie's happy smile faded. "I'm so, so sorry about poor Nanette. And so worried about her. How can I help?"

"First, how often did she shop here?" I asked.

"Oh...every week at least. Maybe a couple of times a week."

"What did she buy?"

"Lots of things. Pretty much whatever caught her eye. She has an account here, in her husband's name of course."

Nanette sure was spoiled, but I kept that opinion to myself. "Did she talk about where she planned to wear these things that caught her eye?"

"Not really. She just always said she wanted to look pretty. That she needed to look pretty. She seemed to crave compliments, or at least reassurance, if you know what I mean."

I didn't know what she meant. Everything I had learned about Nanette so far painted a picture of a woman supremely self-assured.

I turned to Carolyn to ask her what Minnie meant.

But she and Steve had wandered over to the dresses. Carolyn held up a frilly flowered number and grinned as Steve nodded his approval. She had him hold it while she went back to flipping through hangers, looking for more.

I pressed my lips together. Good for Carolyn, she might as well get some shopping in while we were here.

I turned back to Minnie. "I'm afraid I don't know what you mean. From what I've heard about Nanette, she exuded confidence, and she certainly had her husband's unconditional adoration."

Minnie shrugged. "Nanette liked to hear that she looked pretty. If you told her she looked smashing in something, she'd buy it. But it was never a lie. She looked good in everything."

I bet Minnie was on commission. She must have loved seeing Nanette walk in the door. "Did Nanette ever come in here with her husband, Dr. Paulson?"

Minnie shook her head. "Not that I know of. I never met him."

"Did she ever talk about him? Say anything about wanting to look pretty for him?"

Minnie shook her head again, then began fiddling with bracelets on a display rack on the counter. "Although, come to think of it, she did act like a woman in love."

In love? "Why do you think that? What about her—?" I turned, distracted by Carolyn's giggles. Over at the dresses Carolyn and Steve were busy. His arms were full of items she'd picked out, and by the amused smile on his face, he clearly enjoyed being her pack mule.

And she was enjoying his undivided attention.

"Nanette just had that look of being in love," Minnie said. "She'd be all dreamy-like when she was admiring herself in the mirror, pinching her cheeks, fluffing her hair. Especially when she was buying fancy outfits, like for a special date."

Special date? I was under the impression Dr. Paulson's busy practice didn't allow for many special dates. I looked over at Carolyn for clarification, but she must have slipped behind one of the curtains because Steve was standing there alone. His now-empty arms folded across his chest, he met my gaze and gave me an I'm-just-doing-my-job grin.

Yes, he was doing his job, guarding Carolyn, and quite well. No one was going to dash into Theo's and snatch her away. Not if Steve Evans could help it.

"Can you describe some of the recent dresses she bought?" I asked Minnie. "Anything you can remember might be helpful."

Minnie brightened. "The week before she disappeared, she bought a candy-red satin dress and matching heels. And...let's see...a pearl necklace and a pearl bracelet...and Whispers of Roses—a new perfume we just got in...heavenly." Minnie gave me a funny look. "But don't ask me where she planned to wear that outfit, Miss Smith, because I have no idea. She didn't say, and I didn't ask. It's not my job to pry. Although she did look darling."

No doubt. But now I really needed to talk to Carolyn, who had come out from behind the curtain and was busy modeling the flowered dress for Steve, twirling around, causing the wide skirt to flare out from her tiny waist. She, too, looked darling.

But when I went over to ask Carolyn about Nanette's recent purchases, she said she knew nothing about them.

"Satin, pearls, perfume...Carolyn, do you have *any* idea where Nanette would wear such a special get-up?" I asked. "I thought she and Dr. Paulson did not go out much."

"Great question," Steve murmured.

I was glad he thought so.

Carolyn gave her dress another twirl. "That's easy. The club."

"The club?" I'd only seen members there in bathing suits, tennis whites, and golf duds.

"Yes. We have lots of parties there in the evening." Carolyn walked over to the bracelets on display at the counter and slipped a sparkly silver one on her wrist. "Charity fundraising balls, cocktail hours, lady's night..." She turned and looked at Steve and then at me. "Hey, tonight is gentlemen's night. When the ladies buy the men drinks. We should go."

I suppressed a sigh. Back to the club? Oh, goody, goody. "On a Sunday night?"

"Yes, where else can you go get a drink on a Sunday around here? Yes, we definitely should go. I can introduce you to people you didn't meet yesterday, Story. You never know. Someone might know something. It's worth a try."

I nodded. It certainly was. And I had nothing to lose at this point, although I had nothing suitable to wear to what sounded like a fancy event.

I glanced at Steve. He'd be going with us, of course. And wouldn't he look impossibly handsome in evening clothes?

Suddenly, it was important that I look really pretty.

Damn him.

NINE

I was in a dazzling fairyland.

A low moon cast soft light on the country club lawn. Golden fire torches lit the path to an outdoor bar. Tiny lights strung in trees around the patio and pool twinkled and glowed.

I walked up to a crush of boisterous partiers and scanned the crowd, looking for Carolyn and Steve.

I felt self-conscious among the well-and-expensively-dressed, but I assured myself I fit in just fine in a dress I'd dug out of the back of my closet. Which I'd forgotten I owned.

Fortunately, Alec didn't plan to attend Gentlemen's Night, according to Carolyn, who'd left my name at the door as her guest. Hooray! It meant I wouldn't have to dodge him. A huge relief. Though I did think it odd he'd insisted his wife and Steve go together. Like a couple?

"Hello, gorgeous."

I whipped around. A man with the whitest teeth I'd ever seen flashed me a flirty smile. The rest of him was just as impressive. Tall, with thick auburn hair, his slim physique did his tan linen suit justice, and his penetrating eyes reminded me of a lion's.

"Hello," I said, keeping my tone coolly polite. Nothing wrong with him being flirtatious, given the event's theme, but I wasn't there to buy a man a drink. I hadn't planned to, I couldn't afford it, and I hadn't brought any money.

"I'm Greg," he said. "Greg Satterfield. And you are...?"

"Story Smith, private investigator. I'm looking into the disappearance of Nanette Paulson. Did you know her?"

That threw him off his game. For a moment, at least. His flirtatious grin faded. And his big lion eyes glinted as he held my gaze. "Sure...of course. Everybody here knows everybody here. Such a mystery, what happened to her..." He leaned closer. "But honey...did you say you're a private detective? How amazing. And..." He lifted an eyebrow. "Alluring."

I didn't know whether to be amused or annoyed. Or both. I went with neither, deciding to stick with politely professional. "You heard me right." I kept my tone even and matter of fact. "How well did you know Nanette?"

"Not as well as I would have liked." He shrugged. "I don't play tennis well, or golf at all, so I wasn't in her orbit."

"So, you knew her from a distance?"

"Sort of, yeah."

"What did you make of her disappearance?"

"What do you mean?"

"Do you have any theories about what happened to her?"

He shook his head. "Sorry, I wish I did." He sounded sincere, pointed to the bar. "Say, can I buy you a drink? To make up for my lack of helpfulness?"

He wanted to buy me a drink? I didn't see the harm. I looked around for Carolyn and Steve, but still didn't see them, so I turned back to him and cocked my head. "Is that permitted at Gentlemen's Night? I mean...I thought the ladies..."

He laughed. "I make my own rules, Miss Story Smith. And, I want to help you. Let me get us both drinks and then I'll take you around and introduce you to some of my friends. Maybe one of them will give you a clue that breaks your case wide open. Or, maybe not. Anyway, I'm here by myself because my fiancé just broke up with me. And I couldn't help noticing you're the prettiest girl here—detective or no detective."

Okay. Now I felt sorry for him. And he was flattering me, sort of, but it was working. I glanced down at my dress, which I'd last worn to a dinner dance in my college days. Pearl-white, it had a scooped neckline, lacy cap sleeves, and a baby-blue belt. I was wearing my flat white pumps, and had twisted my hair into a topknot bun, tying it with a ribbon that matched the belt.

I'd replaced the hospital bandage on my hand for a couple of Band-Aides, much less noticeable.

And I'd dabbed makeup on the bruises on my neck, which Greg didn't seem to notice at all.

I did feel pretty.

"I'd love a drink, and to meet your friends," I said. "I can use all the help I can get."

"Swell." He grinned and motioned for me to follow him to the bar. He ordered me a martini and himself a beer, then, drinks in hand, we headed over the pool area, where another crowd mingled.

Wandering onto the deck, heads turned to look at us, everyone probably wondering who Greg's new date might be.

He steered me over to two couples and introduced them as his good friends, Hal and Mary and Pete and Shirley. "This is Story Smith, who Martin Paulson has hired to find Nanette," he announced. "She's hoping someone here can provide information that will help in her search."

"That's right," I added quickly. "I'm looking for anything unusual you might have noticed about her or heard about her or knew about her. Anything at all."

For a moment, all four just stared at me, then Mary, a petite brunette, grabbed my arm. "I think she was abducted," she whispered loudly. "It's the only explanation that makes sense."

Hal blinked at me from behind black-frame glasses and nodded. "Could have been revenge."

"Revenge?" I hadn't heard that one. "For what, do you think?"

"I don't know. Martin's a nice guy," Hal said. "But you never know what's really going on in somebody's life. What secrets they might have."

"Maybe Doc Paulson botched a baby delivery?" Pete, balding, and looking slightly tipsy, waved his drink. "That could be a motive. Right?"

It could, but it was pure speculation at this point, although worth investigating.

I felt like I was in a play, me among the rich and sophisticated, carrying a martini as a prop.

I took a sip. It was stronger and more sour than I'd expected. I barely managed to swallow without gagging.

"How often have you seen Dr. Paulson at the club?" I waved my glass at the group. "Did he ever come here to socialize? Sometimes with his wife, or was she usually alone?"

"Usually alone," Shirley, a statuesque blonde shot out. "But Nanette never seemed to mind. Martin would make it here occasionally, maybe once a month if Nanette was lucky, and when he did, she'd fawn all over him. But when she came alone, she'd just brag about him and about how successful he was. Blah, blah, blah."

Clearly, Shirley was no friend of Nanette's. But then, a lot of women don't like women who flirt with their men.

"I heard she dated a guy in the Mafia before she married Martin," she added. "It's a rumor I've heard, and you never know, so check it out."

I assured her that I would look into that, but I doubted it was true, given what Dr. Paulson had told me about how he and his wife had met. In any case, it was time to move on.

After thanking them all for their time, Greg and I continued our stroll around the pool. Greg introduced me to everyone there, but unfortunately, all I came up with was more of the same. Gorgeous woman. With a happy life. With no reason to just leave. At least as far as anyone here knew.

"I must be boring you," I told Greg, then drained the last of my drink. Bad idea. It made my head buzz. "You came here to have fun, meet women, and all you're doing is helping me work."

"Not at all." He reached for my glass. "Let me get you another."

"No thank you." I shook my head and pointed to the clubhouse, where a live band was playing, its rock and roll sounds spilling out onto the lawn. "I'm going to head in there. You don't need to come with me."

"But I want to." He took my arm. "Come on, let's go."

I let him lead me inside, where it was much warmer, and the music much louder. The place was jammed. Men and women sat around tables, danced in the center of the room, crowded around a bar along a far wall.

Greg was still holding onto my arm and I didn't want to give him or anyone else ideas about us, so I pulled away. "I think I'll go over there and talk to some folks." I gave him an appreciative smile. "Again, you don't need to come with me. Thanks for your help, but I'll be fine."

"Story, there you are!"

I turned. Finally, Steve. But no Carolyn.

"Hi, Steve. Where have you been?" I looked around, confused.

"Where have *you* been?" Steve glanced at Greg, then back at me.

"Outside." I turned to introduce Greg. "With—"

"Greg Satterfield...I know." Steve gave him a look that bordered on a scowl. "How you doing, Greg? Where's Bitsy?"

Greg shrugged. "We broke up. So...you know Story?"

"I sure do."

"Greg's been introducing me to people, Steve," I said, not even trying to keep the irritation out of my voice. "Lucky for me that I met him, since I couldn't locate you or Carolyn anywhere."

Steve looked as good as I'd suspected he would in a suit and tie. Only better. I felt my face grow warm and I turned away from him to look around the room. "By the way, where is Carolyn?"

"Over at the bar. She's fine."

"It's awfully good to see you again, old chum." Greg's tone was as smooth as Steve's was tense. "So, *how* do you know Story?"

"We're working together—not that it's any of your business, Greg. And I can take it from here."

"I get the message." Greg shot me a disappointed pout. "I've enjoyed our time together, Story. I hope to see you around."

I smiled. "Likewise. And thank you again."

Steve took my arm and steered me away.

Blast it. Was I going to allow myself to be led by a man? Again? I pulled away. "Where are we going?"

"I need to talk to you."

"Where?"

"It's loud in here. Let's go outside."

"But what about Carolyn? You can't let her out of your sight."

He gave an exasperated sigh. "You sound like Alec."

"I don't want you to get in trouble because of me."

"Stop worrying about that." He took my arm again. "Let's go."

Outside, the cool and quiet of the night came as a welcome relief. My nerves were a-jangle, and now my face was burning up. Actually, all of me felt uncomfortably on fire. "What do you want to talk to me about, Steve?" I jerked away from him again.

I needed to be doing my job, talking to people who knew Nanette, not letting myself get caught up in an intimate tete-a-tete with a man who was making me feel things I shouldn't. I'd never felt this way with any man.

Certainly not with Dean. Sadly. Maybe things wouldn't have ended the way they did for us if I had.

Steve pointed to the lawn leading to the tennis courts. "Come on, this way."

I trotted behind him. "Okay, okay. But would you tell me what's going on?"

"Nothing important. I just wanted to get you away from Satterfield."

"Really? That's why you're dragging me out here? He was harmless. Quite nice, actually."

"That's what you think."

I stopped. We'd walked far enough to get some privacy. I squinted at Steve in the dark. There were no lights out here and I could barely see his face. "What are you talking about? Greg was very helpful to me. He introduced me to some of his friends."

"Satterfield's a womanizer. We went to school together, and I won't burden you with the details, but I didn't like seeing you with him. I don't trust him."

Satterfield—a womanizer? I laughed. "Maybe it takes one to know one," I blurted out. "According to my brother Rob, *you* have a wicked reputation as a lady's man, Steve. He told me to watch out for *you*."

Steve stepped closer, close enough for me to see his eyes. He wasn't amused. "What are you talking about?" He sounded hurt, in a "what-me?" kind of way. "Do I know your brother?"

"Rob Smith, he's a P.I., too. In Philly. Although he just took a job with the FBI."

"Rob Smith...he's your brother? I didn't make the connection."

"Smith's a common name."

"Right...sure. Anyway, I don't know him well, and he doesn't know me. I will admit to having dated a lot of women though. Although none like you."

I sucked in breath. Oh, he was good. And I didn't even want to know what he meant by that. Now was not the time, nor would any time be the time. "You didn't need to steer me away from Greg Satterfield," I said, changing the subject. "Unless you think Greg had something to do with Nanette's disappearance, and that he's dangerous. Which strikes me as unlikely."

"Stay open minded, Story. Don't be fooled by a handsome face."

"I'm trying not to be. Trying not to be fooled by yours."

I shouldn't have said that. It was that stupid martini talking. My cheeks burning up, I went over to a bench under a tree and sat down.

Steve followed and lowered himself down beside me. "You think I'm handsome?" There was a catch in his voice, like he sounded surprised. And pleased.

I glanced at him, then looked away. "There's nothing wrong with my eyes."

"No, you have gorgeous eyes."

I laughed. "You sure know how to charm a woman."

"I'm not saying it to charm you. It happens to be true."

"Look," I said, exasperated. "I'm not sure what we're accomplishing out here. Greg's not my type. And I'm not easily fooled by a handsome face, so give me some credit. I let Greg help me because I couldn't find you and Carolyn. Unfortunately, I don't think I learned much that I can use. Nobody here seems to know anything."

He grunted. "Sometimes that's the way it is in this business." He turned to look at me, compelling me to turn my eyes back to him. He was close enough for me to feel his body heat. Or maybe it was my too overactive imagination. I forced myself to disregard whatever was going on with me, real or imagined.

"I'm learning." I blew out a breath.

"How'd you get into this business anyway?" His voice was soft. "It's a dangerous game, especially for a woman."

"Now you sound like my parents."

"You didn't answer my question."

I sighed. "I was inspired by Rob. Last Christmas, I helped him with an assignment. I went undercover as his wife to investigate the fiancé of a pretty heiress. We saved her from a fate worse than death—because her fiancé was an awful man, who turned out to be a murderer. I'd been working as a newspaper reporter, but I fell in love with being a private eye. And Rob fell in love with Piper, the heiress. They just got married a few weeks ago."

"Wow. That's quite a story, Story."

"Thank you." I was tempted to ask him if he knew Piper's friend, Claudia, but though better of it. Didn't want to ruin the moment. "What about you, Steve?" I asked. "How did you get in the business?"

He cleared his throat. "I grew up wanting to be a private eye. Much to my father's disappointment. He wanted me to be a lawyer."

"And here you are, playing bodyguard."

"Ouch, that hurts. Thanks."

"It's an important job." I poked him in the arm. "Kidnappers might be infiltrating Gentlemen's Night."

"Not funny."

He was right. It wasn't funny. And I was keeping him from his job. I stood up. "I really should get back to work, to the party. There are plenty of people I haven't spoken to—"

"Have you gotten yourself a gun yet?"

I froze. "What?"

"Do you own one? Do know how to use one? Because you need one."

I slowly turned back to him. "Why do you care?"

"Again, you're not answering my question."

"Okay, no. Not yet. It's on my list. But I haven't had time to go gun shopping."

"You need to make time. Soon."

"I will. But *you* didn't answer my question, Steve. Why do you care?"

He didn't answer. He just sat there, still as a statue in the inky darkness, as music from the party drifted over, muted snatches of a melody about longing and love.

Which I did not need. I did not need longing and I did not need love and I did not need Steve Evans telling me what to do.

"See you later, Steve," I said over my shoulder as I headed back toward the clubhouse. "I need to get back to work and so do you."

———

I found Carolyn in the clubhouse. She was perched on a stool at the bar, chatting with friends. And, as Steve had said, she was just fine.

I was heading over to her when someone tapped me on the shoulder. "Excuse me."

I whirled around. A fresh-faced young woman with silky brown hair and worried eyes met my gaze. "Are you the detective looking for Nanette Paulson? My husband said you were asking around about her."

My heart did a thump-thump. Did she know something? "Yes, That's me."

"I have information you might be interested in." She gnawed her lower lip, then looked around to see if anyone else was listening.

No one was looking our way. And I doubted anyone could hear us anyway, with the loud music and laughter reverberating around the room.

"What is it?" I held her gaze. "I'm very interested."

She hesitated. Then put her lips to my ear. "I think Nanette Paulson and Alec Lowell might have been having an affair."

My heart slammed against my chest. My breath caught in my throat. Was I dreaming?

I pulled back and looked deep into her eyes. "What did you say?"

"I saw Alec and Nanette together. A few weeks ago." She eyed the crowd to be sure no one was listening, then leaned closer toward me. "They were having dinner, just the two them, very cozy-like." Her voice was tense, rushed. "They were at an out-of-the-way restaurant that my uncle owns. It's in the country. Very secluded. I'm sure it was them."

My blood surged through my veins. Finally, another crack in Nanette's nearly perfect façade. "Did they see you?" I hiss-whispered.

"No. And I never told anyone that I saw them together. Not even my husband. I didn't think it was any of my business. Except now... now that Nanette is missing...I needed to tell someone. In case it's important."

It sure could be.

I glanced over at Carolyn. She was smiling at me and eagerly waving me over. I held up a finger to let her know I'd be right there.

I couldn't let on to her what I'd just heard. She couldn't know anything about this. Not now. Maybe not ever, because it might not be true.

I couldn't tell Steve, either. I needed to investigate this interesting tip on my own.

Lightly touching my informant's arm, I asked, "What's your name?"

"No, this didn't come from me. You didn't hear this from me."

"Sure," I said, nodding. "I understand. Can you tell me the name of the restaurant?"

"The Old Barn Inn. It's about an hour and a half drive from here. Near Lancaster."

"You said you witnessed this rendezvous a few weeks ago?"

"Maybe a month, I'm not sure."

"By any chance, do you remember the exact date?"

She shook her head. "No. But I do remember the day of the week."

I held my breath. I knew what she was going to say. I just knew.

"It was a Monday," she whispered. "I know it was a Monday."

TEN

The next afternoon, I drove—top down, sun on my face—to the Old Barn Inn. Cruising along back country roads on the way, I mulled over my informant's tantalizing tip.

It was intriguing. Intriguing enough to get me to make the trip to Amish country. Not to mention that investigating a rumor about Nanette and Alec having an affair also seemed a more promising lead than investigating Nanette's possible Mafia ties, or a patient's possible revenge against her husband.

It could also explain why Alec had seemed to resent me the minute he met me.

Could it be true that he and Nanette had been having an affair? It didn't seem implausible. My informant insisted she'd seen them dining together, and she sounded certain. She knew it was on a Monday, because she'd gone to the restaurant for one of her uncle's Monday night specials: Pennsylvania Dutch Chicken Pot Pie.

Sounded yummy, and easy to check out.

In any case, the scenic drive made me feel like I was doing something useful. And it wasn't exactly a hardship.

I love Amish country, where people live as if back in time, more like the 1850s than the 1950s. With no electricity or automobiles, farming the land.

I passed men in straw hats tending their fields with horse drawn plows. Women, in bonnets and ankle length dresses, hanging laundry on the line. Brown and white cows, grazing in fields, lazing under trees, watching me as I motored by.

As a child, envying their old-fashioned lifestyle, I'd asked my mother if I could become Amish. She said, no, it was something you had to be born into.

Which I now realize was just as well, because I probably wouldn't have lasted more than a day milking cows, canning vegetables, and scrubbing clothes by hand.

Anyway, the life I was living now was much more my idea of fun. Unraveling people's secrets and hunting down the truth.

I winked at a cow watching me with languid eyes and gripped the steering wheel with a contented grin. I was enjoying this hunt. It was the reason I'd become a private investigator. I was doing what I'd been born to do. No matter what Steve Evans, my parents, or anyone else thought.

And, since I was such a crackerjack gumshoe, I had no problem finding The Old Barn Inn.

It was tucked away, shaded by a strand of oak trees, just off Lancaster Pike. And quite charming. Cedar-shake white, many chimneys, a wide front porch lined with rocking chairs.

An out-of-the-way place, for sure. And far enough from Philadelphia that two people having an affair could believe they would not be spotted by anyone they knew.

It was lunch time when I arrived. It was a Monday and there weren't many cars in the parking lot. When I walked in, I was greeted by a male waiter, with the wholesome, rosy cheeked appearance of a young man who spent a lot of time outdoors.

"Table for one?" He peered behind me, then met my gaze with an expectant smile.

"Actually, I'm not here for lunch." I looked around the dining room, decorated in typical Pennsylvania Dutch style. Homey paintings of farm life on the walls. Tables covered with checked tablecloths. Matching red and white curtains on the windows.

So far only three tables were occupied.

The waiter looked disappointed. "You're not here for lunch? How can I help you, then?" He frowned. "You're not here for a job, are you? Because we don't have any openings."

"Oh, no, no." I gave him a reassuring smile. "I'm actually looking for some friends. I heard they might be here." A small lie. I'd heard Nanette and Alec had been there. Once. Maybe?

I described them in as much detail as I could, hoping he'd say he knew them, as regulars, or maybe big tippers.

No such luck. He waved a hand at the two elderly couples at one table, then to what looked to be small groups of vacationers at the other two. "If you don't see them here, miss, they're not here."

I gave a disappointed sigh. "Okay. I guess I was mistaken. Thank you."

When I didn't turn to leave, he expectantly held my gaze, maybe hoping I had changed my mind about eating there.

"You know, perhaps I can order something to go," I said. I was hungry and I did have to eat.

He smiled. "Let me get you a menu."

"Wait. Before you do, I have a question. Do you happen to work here on Monday nights?"

He furrowed his brows. "Yes, most weeks. Mondays are long days for me. Why?"

"Do you recall seeing a man and a woman having dinner together about a month ago, on a Monday night, who resemble the couple I just described?"

He gave me a what-are-you-talking-about stare. "You mean your friends?"

"Yes."

"No, can't say I have. Sorry."

I reached into my purse and pulled out Nanette's photo. "This is the—"

"Waiter!"

A gray-haired customer was waving his glass in the air. "Could I get some more water, please?" He sounded impatient, like his thirst was an emergency.

"Yes, sir!"

The waiter took a quick squint at the picture in my hand, frowned, and shook his head again. "I've never seen this woman before. Now, if you'll excuse me..."

I let him go wait on Mr. Thirsty. I pulled a chair out from one of the empty tables and sat down. I didn't see anyone else working there but needed to ask.

Rosy Cheeks hurried back to me with a menu. "I think you'll be pleased with some wonderful lunch specials."

I took a quick glance and ordered chicken and waffles and an apple dumpling. I was stretching my budget, but I told myself I deserved it. "While I'm waiting, would it be possible for me to speak to your manager, or any other folks who work here?" I asked, holding up Nanette's photo again. "To see if they have ever seen her."

"My manager?" He turned to look toward the kitchen. "He's also the owner. Let me see if he's with the cook."

He returned a minute later with a man wearing a red apron over black dress clothes, the sleeves of his shirt rolled up to his elbows.

"Hi, I'm Bill Guenther," he said. "Jimmy says you want to speak to me?"

Jimmy hurried back to his customers, and I nodded and stood up. "Yes, thank you. Are you the owner?"

"I am."

He had to be my informant's uncle. I wished she had given me her name but since she hadn't, I'd just have to wing it.

I showed him Nanette's picture. "I was wondering if you've ever seen this woman before?" I also wished I had a photo of Alec, but I'd start with her.

He reached for the picture, studied it, then raised his eyes to mine. "Why? Why are you asking about her?" His tone was cautiously suspicious.

"She's missing, and I've been hired to find her, and I heard she dined here recently on a Monday night."

He widened his eyes. "You think she's hiding out around here among the Amish? They don't take in—"

"No, I'm sorry, I didn't mean that. I mean she was seen here maybe a month ago, before she went missing. On a Monday night."

He narrowed his eyes. "Who told you that?"

I hesitated. I'd hoped to keep my informant out of it. "Your niece. She said she was here for your chicken pot pie."

That brought a smile to his lips. "Oh, Ellen. Yes, she sure does love my chicken pot pie. I serve that one Monday of every month. Serving it tonight, actually." He examined Nanette's picture again, then handed it back to me. "But this woman, she doesn't look familiar. So, I'm sorry I can't help you there. She's not a regular, if that's what you're wondering. I know them all."

"Perhaps she just ate here that one time, then."

"Perhaps."

I tucked Nanette's picture back in my purse and squared my shoulders. "Thank you for your time."

I would have liked to have ordered a bunch of food to go. The yummy smell of freshly baked bread, along with something sweet wafting from the kitchen made my mouth water. I bet they made a heavenly shoofly pie.

But I couldn't afford that expense. I needed to put gas in my T-Bird for the ride home.

"Come back and see us again." Bill Guenther gave me a friendly smile.

"Oh, I'll be back," I said. I meant it, too. I'd come back someday.

After I found Nanette. To celebrate.

Eleven

The last person I expected to see that afternoon, when I got back to Philadelphia, was Dr. Paulson.

I'd gone straight to my office after leaving The Old Barn Inn to type up some notes about what I'd learned there—sadly, not much—when he rushed through my open door, looking much the same as the day we'd met.

Emotionally fraught. But this time, more angry than distraught.

Actually—he was furious.

"Where is she? Where is my wife? Why haven't you found her yet?" Red-faced, he slapped his hands on my desk, leaned forward, and glared at me over my typewriter. "Your time is just about up."

Like he was telling me something I didn't know? I forced myself to stay calm and met his gaze. "I'm aware of that."

"What?"

"I'm aware that my time is almost up. But please, I've been

working hard to find your wife. And if you could just give me a little more time, I will."

I stood to face him. Maybe it was good that he'd come to see me. Rather than me going to him to ask for more time. Problem was, he didn't look in the mood to give me one more single minute.

I pointed to my typewriter. "I've just been compiling today's notes. I've been keeping daily reports, which I plan to give you."

I would have reported to him every day, up to this point, if what I'd uncovered so far about his wife wasn't so potentially upsetting to him. That Nanette might have been having an affair. With his so-called best friend. Who also happened to be the husband of her so-called best friend.

He jabbed a finger at the paper sticking out of my portable Under-wood. "Why haven't I seen any of your so-called reports yet?"

"Because I've got nothing solid to relay. Yet. But, as I said, I if I could have—"

"One more day, Miss Smith, you have one more day. And then I'm hiring someone else. And you better be prepared to give him those reports."

Him. Of course, he would hire a man to replace me. Staring at my raging client, I felt my face flush with frustration.

He waved a hand. "Have you found anything useful to this point? Anything, anything?"

I desperately tried to think of something that I could tell him that wouldn't get me fired immediately.

But, what?

I needed my one more day. And more. I understood his grief-fueled anxiety. But even a man with extensive private eye experience could not have solved this case in a week. I knew that because I had one secretly assisting me.

"Doctor, I do have some leads." I sat back down, then pointed to the client chair beside my desk. "Please, have a seat, and I'll share some of what I've found."

He must have heard something in my tone that gave him hope. He yanked the chair around and plopped into it, folding his arms across his chest. "I'm listening."

"I've visited your country club, twice." I kept my voice calm and even. "I learned that Nanette played a lot of tennis and golf and that she was quite good at both. And that she really enjoyed it when you accompanied her, but that your busy schedule—"

"Yes, yes, yes. All true. But who cares? So what?"

"I was also surprised to learn that she and Alec Lowell often played tennis together. That she and he were frequent doubles partners."

I waited. Held my breath. It was the least upsetting thing I could report on what I'd learned about his wife and Alec Lowell.

How would he react?

He exploded. Like a volcano spewing lava. Eyes bulging, chest heaving, nostrils flaring. "Again...so...what? What exactly are you getting at?"

"I don't know...yet...actually." That was sadly true. "I've been gathering facts, interviewing Nanette's many friends, trying to discover if she had any enemies. But, as far as I can tell, everyone loved her."

"Yes, of course. Such a great detective you are." The sarcasm in his voice felt like a knife to my gut.

I acted like I didn't notice it. "There is something I need to ask you about, Doctor. At Gentlemen's Night at the club—"

"You went to Gentlemen's Night? At the club?"

"Yes. I told you, I went to your club twice. Once in the day and again in the evening."

His expression softened. He looked mildly impressed. "Well, how did you get in there, then? It's private."

"Carolyn Lowell. She wants to find Nanette as much as you do. She's been helping me."

He rubbed his chin with a shaky hand. "Oh. That's good to hear. What did you find out at Gentlemen's Night?"

"I heard some rumors. That I need to ask you about. But first, are you aware that Alec has hired a bodyguard for Carolyn? He believes Nanette could have been involved in something dangerous."

He stared at me. "Bodyguard? No. Something dangerous? That's ridiculous."

"One of the rumors going around is that Nanette used to date someone in the Mafia. Before she met you."

"Outrageous. Not true. I told you, we met while she was in nursing school. She never dated anyone before me."

"That's what I thought you said. Another rumor: do you believe anyone could be out for revenge against you? For any reason, maybe a birth that went wrong, ended tragically?"

He didn't say anything for what seemed like forever, as if genuinely considering the possibility. Then finally, he said, "No. I can't honestly think of anything like that."

I nodded. "Alright then, I would like to dive a little deeper into Nanette's background. Her life before she met you. Starting with the orphanage where she grew up. Do you happen to know the name of it?"

He squinted at me. "No. But why do you want to go there?"

I wasn't sure myself why I wanted to visit that orphanage. Just suddenly had a feeling it might be important. There were many things my client didn't know about his wife. She had secrets. Secrets I needed to keep to myself for now. And possible secrets I hadn't uncovered yet.

When I didn't answer his question right away, he leaned forward. "Nanette didn't like to talk about the orphanage. The only thing I know is that it was somewhere in New Jersey farm country. In the middle of nowhere, is how she described it. Outside Vineland, I think."

"That's a start," I said. "It shouldn't be hard to find, if it still exists."

Anger crept back into his face. His cheeks turned red and splotchy. His eyes were hard. "You can go visit any place you like on your one more day of working for me, Miss Smith." He stood up. "But I sincerely hope you find Nanette while you are at it. Because after tomorrow, your time is up."

———

Martin Paulson's visit left me rattled.

But minutes after he left, Steve walked into my office, which made me jump. Up and out of my chair.

I ran around my desk to greet him.

"What are you doing here?" I peered over his shoulder, expecting to see Carolyn trailing behind.

No Carolyn.

He gave me a tight smile. "I need to talk to you."

Dressed in shorts, a T-shirt, and sneakers, he looked as if he'd been spending time outside. Sunburnt. Sweaty. I shook my head, confused. "Talk to me about what?"

He stepped further into my office. "I was worried about you. You left Gentlemen's Night in a hurry, didn't even say goodbye."

Goodbye? It hadn't even occurred to me to let Steve know I was leaving. My tip about a possible secret rendezvous between Nannette and Alec had caught me so off guard that all I could think about was getting out of there fast so I could plan my next move.

Steve gazed around my office. "Nice place. Small. Modest. But a start."

"Gee, thanks." I waited for him to say more. What was the real reason for his visit? Curiosity? To scope out the new competition? Was he really that concerned about my wellbeing? Just because I had left a party without saying goodbye?

"Uhm, Steve...where's Carolyn?"

"I knew you would ask that." He gave me a wry grin.

"And...?"

"She's at Freddie's swim meet. It's in Wynnewood, and don't worry, she's safe. Sitting in bleachers, surrounded by scads of other parents." He winced. "Loud, cheering parents, I might add. No one could possibly get at her there, or if they tried, they'd be extremely noticeable. Truth is, I needed a break."

"So, you left to come see me?"

"Why not? Like I said, I was worried about you. You disappeared so suddenly from the party that I was wondering if you'd gone back to that snake, Greg Satterfield."

Huh. Was Steve truly jealous of that man? That was flattering. Sort of. Except, I sensed there was something else.

I backed up and sat down again behind my desk. "I didn't see Greg anymore that evening, if that's what you're asking. And here I am, safe and sound, and hard at work." I tilted my head. "How did you find my office?"

"When Carolyn came to see you a few days ago, she had me wait in the car. I took note of the address."

He stood there, with his hands in his pockets, and an aren't-you-going-to-ask-me-to-have-a-seat grin on his face. I waved him into the chair vacated by Dr. Paulson only minutes before.

So far, it had been a whirlwind of a day.

"Any new developments on your case?" Steve leaned forward. "Come on, you can tell me. I think maybe you left Gentlemen's Night so fast for a reason."

Damn, this cool cat was perceptive.

"My client was just here." I lifted my chin. "He came to remind me that I only have one more day to find his wife. Because he only paid me for a week."

"Oh. Poor Story. What are you going to do?"

I hesitated. How much should confide in Steve? He'd saved my life, and he was helping me, sort of, and I liked him—he was hard not to like. Even though I was trying hard not to let myself feel any more than that.

But what if Dr. Paulson wanted to hire Steve to replace me? Would he turn down the offer? Probably not. And would I blame him? No. It would be much more interesting than playing bodyguard.

"What are you going to do?" Steve leaned forward. "With your remaining day? Any leads from Gentlemen's Night panning out?"

Gentlemen's Night again. "I've got a few." I shrugged. "I'm working them."

"Good girl. Did you get yourself a gun yet?"

Good girl? And more pestering about a gun? "Not yet." I left it at that. I was pretty sure I wouldn't be needing a gun at an orphanage. Although the way this case was playing out, I shouldn't assume anything.

"I want you to succeed, Story, you've got to know that." Steve flashed me a crooked smile that—damn it—sent my heart racing. "I want you to succeed for my sake, as well as yours. The sooner you find out what happened to Nanette, the sooner I can quit my bodyguard job and get back to my real life."

So that was the true reason he'd come to see me. He wanted to find out what I knew. Or if I was close to knowing anything. So he could get back to acting like a real P.I.

"Do you think Nanette is still alive, Steve?"

He pressed his lips together. "No idea. What do you think?"

I shrugged, wishing I could tell him more, knowing I shouldn't. "What about Carolyn? Do you think she really is in any danger?"

It was his turn to shrug. "No idea. Whether she is or whether she isn't, I'm just doing my job."

I thought about his easy camaraderie with her at the club.

"How did Alec happen to hire you, Steve?" I asked. "Why you?"

"Oh, that's easy." He leaned back and propped his right ankle on his left knee. He grinned. "Carolyn and I met at a party last fall. We hit it off. And apparently Alec noticed."

That shocked me, and I didn't try to hide it. "Hit it off? What do you mean, you hit it off?"

"We were at a Halloween party, at the estate of a mutual friend.

Lots of music, dancing, booze. Carolyn looked so lonely, and lovely, dressed as an angel, that I went over and asked her to dance. We ended up talking half the night."

I stared at him. Then realized my jaw was hanging open. I felt blind-sided. I had expected him to say that Alec got his name and number out of the phone book. I closed my mouth and swallowed hard. "Oh."

"You seem surprised." Steve looked amused.

"I am." I cleared my throat. "And I have so many questions."

"I bet." He waved a hand. "Shoot."

"Okay, first, why was Carolyn looking lonely? Wasn't Alec there with her?"

"Oh, he was, but he wasn't paying her much attention. It took me a while to realize he was her husband. I wouldn't have asked her to dance if I'd known she was married."

"Was Nanette there?"

As soon as I asked the question, I knew I shouldn't have. Steve blinked and blinked again. "What? Nanette? I have no idea. Remember, I never met the woman. That I know of. I've only seen her photo. She may have been there, but if she was, she didn't stand out to me. There were lots of pretty women there, and besides, people were in costumes."

"Oh, right." I took a deep breath to get a hold of myself. I didn't want to know, but I had to ask. "So, you and Carolyn...? You two are not...uhm...?"

"We're not what?"

"You know..."

His eyes went big. "Of *course* not. I don't fool around with married women. No matter what you've heard about me from your brother, I don't do that..." He shot me a curious look. "But why did you ask about Nanette possibly being at the party? Do you know something about her and Alec?"

Yes. I swallowed the word before it could escape my lips. "I might..." I blurted. Blast it all. I couldn't help it. There was something about the way he was looking at me and those words just slipped out. "But it's not anything I wish to talk about. Yet. Please...let us just say I'm looking into it."

"Story..."

"Steve..."

"What? You're really not going to tell me?" Steve looked hurt.

"I'll tell you more when, and if, I learn more, but in the meantime, say nothing to Carolyn. Please, please."

"Of course, I won't."

Quick. I needed to change the subject. "You said Alec noticed that you and Carolyn hit it off. So, wouldn't that make him jealous? Why would he hire you, of all people, to guard her day and night?"

"*Great* question. One I've been asking myself again and again."

"Carolyn's been questioning it, too," I said. "She was wondering why Alec didn't hire somebody ugly to be her bodyguard."

Steve grinned. "She said that?"

"Yep. So, did you ask Alec? I mean, not in so many words, but... you know..."

"Of course, I asked him why me. He just said he'd noticed Carolyn and I clearly had a bond, and that's why he wanted me, because she trusted me. He said that's why he was willing to pay me extremely well to keep her safe. I believed him...but now, I'm beginning to wonder."

"A bond," I whispered. "How odd."

"Exactly." He stared at me. "It's almost like Alec is pushing us together. Like, he wants us to be together. But why?"

I could think of a reason. So, he could be with Nanette. Who was —where? But why wouldn't Alec just ask Carolyn for a divorce?

My head was spinning with too many questions. And zero answers.

Steve and I sat together in silence, gazes locked. It was like I was trying to read his mind while he was trying to read mine.

"How does Carolyn feel about you, Steve?" I asked. "Because, if Alec does want you two to get together...?"

He pressed his lips together, looking pained. "I think she really likes me, which is scary. She's needy and vulnerable because she's lonely. She puts on a brave face. For herself and for Freddie. But I'm starting to feel like a pawn in some unknown game. One I don't know the rules to, and I don't want to play."

"I don't blame you."

He stood up, suddenly looking uncomfortable that he'd shared so much with me. "So, what's your next move, Miss Lady Detective? You've got one more day, and then what? I'm asking for both of us. Because I think our fates are somehow linked. Don't you?"

I did. But I wasn't ready to admit how much it seemed so. It was too crazy.

"Tomorrow, I'm going to dig more into Nanette's past." I stood to face him. "And then, I'll let you know what I learn. Because I'm not giving up on this case. No matter what, I'm going to find Nanette Paulson."

"I believe you. I really believe you will." Steve pointed to the pad of paper beside my typewriter. "I want you to keep me updated, but it would be awkward for you to call me at the Lowell residence. It's not my job to answer the phone and there's no telling who would. Instead, let me write down my office address and phone number, and you can deliver messages to me there. You can leave them with my receptionist, Alice."

"Okay, good idea." I ripped off a piece of paper and he scribbled his contact information and handed it back to me.

"Wait, you have a receptionist?" I grinned. "How will I know when she'll be there?"

He returned my grin. "She's always there. Alice Monroe is a retired secretary who acts like she's my adopted grandmother. She claims she has nothing better to do than hang around and answer my phone."

"Lucky you."

His grin widened. "Lucky me."

Okay, so Steve charmed the older women, too. Not surprising. The way he was looking at me now suddenly made my knees go gooey. His eyes held a glint that whispered...something.

He didn't appear to be in any hurry to leave and I suddenly needed him to. "Don't you have a swim meet to get back to?" I asked.

"Do I?"

"You tell me."

"Okay, I think I do."

"I'll get in touch after tomorrow," I said, managing a smile. I was trying for cool, calm, and collected. I think what I managed was goofy as all get out.

"Okay," he said, flashing me that crooked grin of his that always grabbed my heart. "Please do keep in touch."

TWELVE

There was only one orphanage in the Vineland, New Jersey area, according to the helpful woman who answered the phone at the Cumberland County Courthouse.

She told me that the Southern New Jersey Home for Children had been in operation for decades, so it had to be the place where Nanette grew up.

Or so I told myself while driving there the next morning.

I wanted to go in person because I didn't expect to get far asking questions on the phone. For all I knew, their records were confidential, and it might take some schmoozing to get any information from them regarding a child named Nanette. Whose maiden name I unfortunately did not know.

I could have kicked myself for not asking Martin Paulson her maiden name. Clearly, I was not yet the crackerjack private eye I wanted to be. But I had to give myself a break, I was learning.

The southern New Jersey countryside wasn't as scenic as Pennsylvania Dutch Country. It was flat, no rolling hills, but I still found the drive enjoyable. Fields of corn. Farmhouses, some quaint, some weathered. Old wooden barns. Cows. Horses. Occasional flocks of sheep.

According to my contact at the courthouse, the orphanage was also a working farm. Which made sense, given where it was located, and who it served: children of all ages, from babies to teenagers, who needed a safe place to live. On a farm, they could contribute to their upkeep by doing chores, while learning practical skills.

Only the adult Nanette I had come to know would not have been thrilled about farm work.

Pulling into a small, unpaved parking lot next to a modest red brick building marked "Office," I could see right away she'd come a long way in life. From poor orphaned farm girl to rich doted-on wife.

Not bad. The question was how had she done it? And did it have anything to do with where she was now?

It was shortly after ten a.m. when I opened the office door and walked in.

Bells jangled, announcing my arrival, which startled a stout gray-haired woman behind a reception desk, who appeared to be reading a book.

"Goodness," she tittered in a high-pitched voice, glancing up. "We have a visitor so early in the day. Can I help you?"

She looked in need of company and pleased to have some. A good sign.

"Yes, I hope you can help me." I gave her a hopeful smile. "I'm looking for information about a girl I believe grew up here, her name was Nanette."

At first, she looked disappointed, almost as if she'd been expecting me to announce that I'd come to adopt a child. Then she drew her brows together and frowned. "Grew up here? You mean she's not living here now?"

"No, she's an adult, in her thirties. A married woman, she actually went to nursing school and married a doctor. Her name is Nanette Paulson. Unfortunately, I don't know her maiden name."

"Nanette Priestly!" Her eyes grew big and misty and for a moment I thought she might cry. "One of our stars." She waved me over to her desk. "Tell me, how is she? We miss her so. I'd heard that she married a doctor. She made us all so proud."

I was glad Nanette was an uncommon name, and hopeful we were talking about the same person, although I was surprised—and relieved—that I didn't have to beg for information.

"And your name?" I asked.

"Louise Brandywine. I'm the director. I've worked here most of my life, started out as an assistant house mother. I was here when Nanette arrived." She stared at something unseen beyond my shoulder, as if remembering that day. "As I recall, she was around five. Her mother couldn't keep her anymore. Such a shame it was, and so very sad. But typical for us, you see. Many of our children are not orphans in the traditional sense. Her mother was alive when she brought her here. But she died soon after. Tuberculosis, I believe."

I couldn't believe my luck, that Louise Brandywine was so chatty. Mesmerized by what she was so breezily telling me, I'd just let her talk. She hadn't even asked my name.

"And her father?" I hoped to keep her talking.

Her face darkened. "No father. He abandoned her mother, another typical story here."

"But Nanette wasn't typical...you said...she was one of your stars?"

"Oh, my, yes. She was so bright. Loved school. Took to it like a butterfly in a field of flowers, with such enthusiasm and delight. She was a joy to teach, her teachers said. She went to the public school, down the road, like all our children."

"Is that how she ended up going to nursing school?"

"Yes, indeed. She so impressed her high school teachers that they banded together and landed her a full scholarship to a three-year hospital nursing program. Tuition, plus and room and board." She beamed. "Like I said, she made us proud."

I nodded. "I bet she did."

I smiled, wondering if they knew she'd never actually worked as a nurse. But before I could decide on how to go about asking about that, and more sensitive questions, Louise Brandywine finally asked my name and the reason for my visit.

When I gave her the bad news that Nanette was now missing, she gasped.

"I can't believe it," she whispered. "How terrible for her husband. I do hope you find her soon, dear."

"Yes," I said. "That's why I'm here. To find out more about Nanette's past. Because I can't find anything in her recent life that would explain what happened to her."

I didn't believe there was anything to the Mafia rumor, but I saw no harm in inquiring. "Before she went off to nursing school, did she date any boys?"

She laughed. "Goodness, no."

"Why do you put it that way?" I pressed. "It's my understanding that she was quite pretty."

"Gorgeous, yes, a beautiful girl." She looked at me like I hadn't been paying attention. "But she was one hundred percent focused on her schoolwork. It was like she had no time for anything else but getting all A's. And that included farm chores, which all the children are expected to do. No, Nanette had her eye on her future. And sadly, when she left here, she never looked back."

"Sadly?"

She gave a deep sigh. "Yes. Once she left here, at eighteen, to go to nursing school, she never came back to visit. Not once. Not even to see her sister, Dora, who was heartbroken."

Wait. *Sister?* What sister? Dr. Paulson had told me Nanette had no siblings.

"Sister?" I didn't even try to keep the surprise from my voice.

I suddenly needed to sit down. I pulled a wooden chair away from the wall and dragged it over to face Louise Brandywine's desk.

"I didn't know Nanette had a sister," I said. "Her husband doesn't know she has a sister. He told me she was an only child."

"Oh, dear." The headmistress shook her head. "I'm not surprised, though. Like I said, Nanette never came back here. To see Dora, or anyone else. It was like she left her past behind, all of it. She made a complete break."

I felt a sudden chill. How could anyone be so cruel to their sister? I felt profound pity for a child I never knew.

"How old was Dora?"

"Two years younger than Nanette. Dora was three when the poor little darling's mother brought them here. And growing up, they were close. Although very different. Dora didn't like school much. She preferred mucking horse stalls, milking cows, gathering eggs. Nanette hated getting her hands dirty."

I was flabbergasted, I didn't know what to say. Another secret

Nanette had managed to get away with, until now. This was information I could and would definitely present to Dr. Paulson.

I couldn't prove that Nanette had not really volunteered to help the poor on Monday nights. How could I prove anything about something that had never happened?

And I couldn't prove that Nanette had been having an affair with Alec Lowell. All I had was one eyewitness sighting of them dining together in a secluded restaurant far from home.

I could, however, prove that she had a sister growing up in the Southern New Jersey Home for Children. There had to be written records. To be sure, I gave the elderly director Nanette's birthdate and asked her to check her files.

She got up and went over to a gray metal filing cabinet in the corner and came back with a folder. "Yes, that's correct."

"Mrs. Brandywine," I said, my heart racing, "where is Dora now? She must be what, around thirty-two?"

Her face brightened. "Yes, she is, and she's doing quite well. Married, with I believe three children. She and her husband live on a small farm not ten miles from here. She comes back to visit often, bless her heart."

"Oh, isn't that nice. Bless her heart."

Her face brightened even more. "Say, something just occurred to me, Miss Smith."

"What is it?"

"Maybe, just maybe, that's where Nanette is right now. Perhaps she needed to get away for a while. Perhaps she missed her sister and is staying with her. Wouldn't that be wonderful?"

I smiled. It sure would. Not a chance in a million, I was pretty sure. Still, worth investigating.

"I would love to think Nanette is visiting Dora," I said. "What's her last name now?"

"Macy. Dora Macy. And her husband's name is Charlie." She wrote down their address and drew a crude map on a piece of paper and gave that to me. "It's an easy drive, turn left out of our property and then after about five miles, bear right on Mill Road and keep going another five miles. Look for their mailbox out by the road. I'm sure Dora will welcome you. She's a sweet woman."

I studied the map, excited. This felt like a real lead, at last, although I had no idea where it might take me. "You said Dora was heartbroken that Nanette never came back here to see her. Do you happen to know if the two have connected since?"

"I don't think so, I think Dora would have mentioned it to us if they had. Dora cried after Nanette left to go to school. She felt abandoned, and wrote many letters to her sister, which were never answered, to my knowledge. More's the pity."

"So, Dora gave up trying to contact her?"

"As far as I know. She married Charlie, a local boy she met in high school, shortly after their graduation. Which was fortunate, because legally she had to leave here at eighteen. She invited Nanette to her wedding, but Nanette didn't come. I know because I was one of the guests."

I nodded, suddenly at a loss for words. I found myself overwhelmed with sadness at Dora's story, while at the same time not surprised, given everything else I had learned so far about her sister.

Nanette's life was layered with secrets, and her husband thought she was a saint.

I couldn't wait to meet Dora Macy.

Thirteen

The Macy homestead was ramshackle modest.

The house was missing a few shutters and could have used a coat of paint. The front yard, which was weed strewn, would have looked neater without all the children's toys and bicycles lying about.

A half-rusted mailbox out front had "Macy" painted on it in big black letters, so I knew for sure I had come to the right place.

When I turned into the dirt drive, with my top down, two little girls ran out to greet me.

"Can we get a ride?" the taller one, who looked about the age Nanette would have been when she was orphaned, squealed. "Can we, lady? Can we, can we?"

"Molly!" A young woman in a plain brown dress and lace-up black shoes came running out of the house. "Where's your manners?" Grabbing Molly's hand, she reached for the other child and pulled both girls close. She stared at my car, then at me. "Can I help you, miss?"

"Are you Dora?" I gave her a friendly smile.

"Yes."

"Then, yes, you can help me. I happen to be looking for your sister, Nanette, and I was hoping to ask you some questions." I opened my door and hopped out without waiting for a reply.

She didn't look capable of giving one, anyway. As I slowly walked toward her, she gawked at me, wide-eyed, unblinking, as if I had come from another planet.

I kept smiling. "You do have a sister named Nanette, right?"

She finally blinked. "Yes."

"Then, I've come to the right place." I pointed toward the house. "Do you mind if I come in? I've just been to the orphanage where you and your sister grew up, and Mrs. Brandywine gave me your address. She seemed to think you could help me, and I sure hope you can."

Dora Macy continued to stare at me, not saying a word.

She looked like her sister. Although not as pretty. Thin wrinkles around her eyes, likely from squinting so much in the sun, caused her to look worn and tired. Understandable, since she was working on a farm while raising young children. And to be fair, she wasn't wearing any makeup. In her photo, Nanette was made up like Marilyn Monroe.

"I used to have a sister. Named Nanette. But not no more." She spat the words.

Hugging her children closer, she held onto them, as if for dear life. "Nanette left me years ago and I ain't seen her since. So I cain't help you, lady. Sorry."

I nodded. "I understand. And...I'm sorry for your pain. For what your sister did to you. Mrs. Brandywine told me how you ended up abandoned. Still, I'd like to talk to you. I need your help."

She cocked her head, looking at me like I was nuts. "Why?"

"Because Nanette is missing. And her husband has hired me to find her."

She narrowed her eyes to slits and stared at me in awkward silence.

Birds twittered in a grove of nearby trees. Off in a far field a tractor noisily plowed the soil.

Molly sniffed, sniffed again. She looked about to cry. Her sister tried to wiggle out of her mother's grasp but was pulled back.

"Missing? What do you mean missing?" Dora sounded confused and indignant. "I don't know what you're talking about."

"She disappeared one day, not long ago. From the Ocean City boardwalk. Vanished into thin air. No one has seen her since."

She scrunched up her eyes. "Ain't nobody called the cops?"

"Yes, they are looking into it. But they are not totally convinced she didn't disappear on—"

"Maaaah...maaah..." The younger girl started to cry, then struggled to pull away and began wailing. "Aaaahhh...aah...I don't wanna..." Her face splotchy and smeared with tears, she twisted to escape her mother's grasp, then screamed as if someone was murdering her.

"Linda, hush." Dora shook her head at me. "I'm sorry, like I said—"

"Please..." I extended my hands, palms-up, in an I'm-begging-you gesture. "Could we just go in the house? I need to talk to you. It's really, really important."

Linda stopped crying and stared at me.

Molly whimpered.

The children were frightened, I could tell. Mommy was talking to a strange lady. Mommy was raising her voice. Mommy was shaking.

"Please…" I whispered, then smiled at the girls. "I'm friendly. I'm really nice. You'll see."

"Okay." Dora pressed her lips together, hard. She gave a loud, exasperated sigh, then hitched her chin toward the house. "I guess you can come in for a minute. I don't expect I can help you, but I'll try." She squeezed her daughters' hands. "You two go on to your room, play with your toys. You both be good while I talk to this lady, you hear me? If you're quiet and don't give me no trouble, maybe there'll be cookies."

"Cookies, cookies!" Molly stopped sniffing. Suddenly joyful, she ran toward the house, her sister close behind, as Dora and I followed.

We entered the front door and walked into a small living room, messy with toys much like the yard. The girls disappeared as directed, and Dora and I went into the kitchen. She waved for me to take a seat at one of the mix-matched chairs around a wooden table as she went over to the ice box. "Would you like a Coke?" She held up a bottle.

"Sure." My mouth was parched, and I welcomed her hospitality. Mrs. Brandywine was right. Dora did seem to be a sweet woman, just somewhat overwhelmed by her life, and my surprise appearance.

With hands I noticed were still shaking, she fished a bottle opener out of a drawer and popped the cap off my bottle and one for herself.

She took a sip and sat down across from me. "Okay." For the first time, curiosity glinted in her eyes. "You said Nanette disappeared on the boardwalk. And that her husband hired you to find her?"

"Yes, I'm a private investigator." I took a business card out of my purse and handed it to her.

She glanced at it, then took another sip of her Coke. "Okay, well, I guess that don't surprise me. He's rich. Got the money. Still..." she tossed my card on the table. "Were you saying the cops think she left on her own accord?"

I nodded. "That's right. But her husband doesn't believe that. He said they were extremely happy together and that she was a devoted wife."

"Poppycock." Dora set her bottle down with a thump. "The cops are probably right. Nanette left on her own. She's good at that. Leaving is what she does. Take it from me. When she left me, alone in the world at the age of sixteen, she never looked back. Never came back. To get me or visit me. Not ever."

The bitterness in her voice made me cringe. I felt sorry for her and didn't try to hide it. I couldn't imagine being abandoned the way Dora had.

"Why do you think she did that to you?" I asked, hoping for some penetrating insight. "I mean, why did Nanette just leave and never come back?"

"She planned it." Dora took a big swig of her Coke. "The day she left for nursing school, she told me goodbye. Said she wasn't never coming back. Said she was off to a whole new life. Said that from then on, she was going to be a whole new Nanette. I think she was hurt real bad by the way our mother left us. When Mama left, she never came back, neither."

"But your mother couldn't care for you. And she died shortly afterward. That's what Mrs. Brandywine told me."

"Yes. That's true." Dora's voice was a hoarse whisper. "But that didn't matter to Nanette. I was too young to remember much. But Nanette...when Mama left us, I think it broke her. At least that's what I tell myself. I have tried and tried to forgive Nanette for leaving me.

But now, with you coming here…" She leaned forward and covered her face with her hands. She shook her head back and forth and I wondered if she was crying.

"I'm sorry. I'm sorry that my questions are bringing back painful memories for you, Dora. I feel terrible about that. But I'm learning that your sister had secrets. And you are one of them. To tell you the truth, I was hoping that maybe she was staying with you."

She made a sound in her throat that sounded like a choked-off laugh, then raised her head and looked at me, her eyes surprisingly dry. "She's not here. And if you must know, I'm glad. Did you know that I could have been adopted if it wasn't for her?"

"What?"

"Yes. Shortly after we ended up in the orphanage, a woman came to adopt a child, and she wanted me. Until Mrs. Brandywine told her about Nanette, and that we couldn't be split up." Dora's mouth turned down in a bitter frown. "The woman didn't want two kids, so she adopted one of the other little girls. Who didn't have a sister that had to come with her. And that was that."

"I'm sorry," I said again. "Mrs. Brandywine said you wrote to Nanette, but that your letters were never answered?"

"No. But I wasn't surprised. Because Nanette told me not to write to her or try to find her. I didn't listen. I thought she didn't mean it. But she did. I stopped trying to contact her after my wedding."

"You mean you never tried to contact her after that? At all? No letters, no phone calls?"

"No. Nothing. Mrs. Brandywine told me she read in the paper that Nanette had got herself married. To a doctor." Dora gripped her Coke with both hands and looked away. "Which told me that Nanette got the life she wanted. Nanette always got what she wanted."

"Dora!"

A man burst through the kitchen door, slamming it behind him. "Who's here?" He halted, ogling me. "Who's this?"

"This is Miss Story Smith," Dora said. "And Miss Smith, this is my husband, Charlie."

Charlie looked none too pleased to see me. He was dressed in blue denim farm overalls, which were streaked with dirt, as were his face and arms. He had short cropped black hair and small dark eyes which were regarding me with suspicion. "That your fancy car out there?"

I nodded. "Sure is."

"Miss Smith is a private detective, Charlie." Dora sounded oddly defensive about that, like he wouldn't be pleased.

He wasn't. "You don't say." He glared at me. "What you want with us, lady? We got no need for—"

"She's here about Nanette. She's missing." Dora rushed the words, but I heard hesitation in her voice, like she was afraid of how he'd react to that news, or just the mere mention of Nanette's name.

"Nanette." He practically growled his sister-in-law's name. "We ain't seen her in years." He looked at me with faux pity. "You come to the wrong place, lady, if you're trying to find her."

He'd said "we." I jumped on that. "Did you ever meet Nanette, Mr. Macy?"

He scoffed. "Sure, in high school. She was two years ahead of Dora and me. A long time ago. What of it?"

"What did you think of her?"

He folded his arms and took a stance that said he thought my question was stupid. "I didn't think nothing of her. She was Dora's sister, was all."

"And now?"

"Now what?"

"How do you feel now about the fact that Nanette abandoned Dora?"

"I think it stinks." He smirked. "Tell her, Dora. Tell her how much I think it stinks."

Dora slid a sideways glance at Charlie, then gave me an embarrassed press-of-the-lips, like she had hoped to avoid the subject. "Charlie's been wanting me to ask Nanette and her rich doctor husband for money. Been pestering me for years to do it. But I always refused. How was I supposed to ask a sister that disowned me for money?" She turned to glare at her husband. "No, sir, I was never going to do that. I got pride."

"Pride, pride, pride." Charlie barked a laugh. "That don't get you nowhere in life, now do it?"

Dora's face flushed. She looked like she wanted to crawl under the table.

I was feeling even more sorry for her. But this conversation was getting interesting. Nanette had an enemy no one knew about. Maybe not even Nanette.

"Why did you need the money, Mr. Macy?" I asked.

He looked at me like I was an idiot. "Bills. Bills we can't pay. Life's hard on this farm. We got a mortgage on it and there's been times we couldn't pay. I didn't see the harm in asking Dora's rich sister for help."

"And I did see the harm," Dora murmured.

He didn't say anything, and I let him stew, hoping he would blurt out something revealing. Was it possible, just possible, he'd plotted revenge on Nanette and Martin Paulson? Or maybe carried out a kidnapping that went bad? Maybe he'd snatched Nanette and then accidently killed her. Maybe that's why Dr. Paulson never received a ransom note.

The possibility made me go numb.

Charlie Macy took two steps toward me, which suddenly felt menacing. "You're wasting your time here, Miss Smith. We ain't seen Nanette in years and I don't like talking about her." He put one hand on his hip and jerked the thumb of his other hand at the door. "Maybe it's time for you to leave. If you get my meaning."

I got his meaning. But I wasn't ready to leave.

I took a sip of my Coke and stayed right where I was. "What do you think could have happened to your sister-in-law, Mr. Macy?" I kept my voice casual, as if I was inquiring about the weather.

Eyes wide, he stepped back and looked at me with anger and annoyance. "What do you mean? How would I—?"

"I told Miss Smith I thought Nanette probably left on her own." Dora shot her husband a pleading look. Pleading with him to be nice? Or to shut up? Or both?

"To start a whole new life—that's what I told her," Dora said. "Because that's what Nanette does. She's good at it."

"Do you think there is a possibility she could have been kidnapped?" I looked at Dora and then at Charlie, watching for his reaction.

To my surprise, he laughed again. Louder. "Who the hell would want to kidnap *her*?" But there was tension in his tone that made his laughter sound forced. Narrowing his eyes, he jabbed a dirty finger at me. "Oh, I get it. You're saying maybe I *snatched* her? For ransom? Hey, you know, that would have been a good idea. Why didn't I think of that?"

"Charlie!" Dora looked stricken.

"Calm down, Dora," he growled. "You know I didn't kidnap your stupid sister." He looked at me and jerked his thumb at the door again. "You heard me, lady. I got nothing more to say. So... get... out...Now."

Okey-dokey. I was done. Didn't see any point in arguing. Or in telling them they would probably be hearing from me again. Depending on how my client reacted when I told him about Dora.

Which I planned to do the minute I got back to Philadelphia. I finally had some concrete news, and I had to play my cards right. Convince him I had more investigating to do, and that I deserved more time.

I stood, politely thanked Dora for the Coke, then headed for the kitchen door. Might as well go out the back.

Then I heard soft giggling and turned. Molly and Linda had tiptoed into the kitchen.

"Is it time for the cookies yet, Mommy?" Molly grinned.

"Yes, honey," Dora said, then shot me a look that said *please go. Now.*

I nodded.

Once outside, I half-ran to my car.

Charlie Macy was an interesting character. Somebody I didn't want to mess with. But did he have anything to do with Nanette's disappearance?

I had to convince Dr. Paulson that we needed to consider it, and that he needed to give me more time.

FOURTEEN

It was almost two o'clock by the time I got to Dr. Paulson's office. And learned, to my disappointment, that he was not in.

One of his patients had gone into labor and he was delivering a baby.

"No telling how long he will be," his nurse told me. "You never know with babies, could be an hour, could be twelve, or God help the new mother, could be tomorrow."

Great. Just what I wanted to hear.

I wondered if I should I head over to my office to type up my notes about the orphanage and the Macy interviews.

Or go find Steve's office? He'd asked me to keep in touch.

Steve's office sounded much more appealing.

I was dying to see his place, wanted to meet his receptionist, and since I needed to run my thoughts by him, I could give her a message for him to call me.

At this point, I had two theories about Nanette that needed further investigating.

One, a possible kidnapping by her brother-in-law. Which meant she must be dead. Charlie Macy was mean and motivated enough to commit such a crime, but I couldn't picture Nanette being held captive in a barn somewhere on his farm, bound and gagged. If that was the case, wouldn't he have sent a ransom note by now?

The other theory was that she'd been having an affair with Alec Lowell. Meaning she could still be alive. Or not.

I fished Steve's address out of my purse, and since I knew Philadelphia well, his office wasn't hard to find. Unlike mine, it was in a respectably ritzy area, in an impressive high rise, a few blocks from the Delaware River, not all that far from Independence Hall.

I went into the lobby, located his name on the list of occupants next to the elevator, and pushed the button.

To the top floor. Wow. Even more impressive. He probably had a grand view of the river.

Pushing open a glass door bearing the words "Steven Evans, Private Investigator," I found his receptionist sitting behind a massive desk. Behind her was Steve's office, and yes, he had a marvelous view of the river, thanks to a floor-to-ceiling window that looked out on water sparkling in the sun, framed by tall buildings in the distance and a baby-blue, cotton-cloud-dotted sky.

The woman I assumed was Alice Monroe had snowy-white hair, arranged in a tight bun. Her oval-shaped silver eyeglasses added to her an elderly, matronly appearance. Grandmotherly, as Steve had said.

Her smile, though, took ten years off her age. It was welcoming, and genuine.

"Good afternoon." Pecking on a huge black typewriter, she looked up at me. Her eyes sparkled. "Can I help you?"

"Yes," I nodded. "My name is Story Smith and—"

"Why, of course you are." The cheery enthusiasm in her voice caught me by surprise. "And you are even prettier than Steve described. He told me you might be stopping by and warned me to be nice."

Oh. That was clearly a joke. I couldn't imagine the woman before me being anything but nice. But he'd described me as pretty? I flushed. I had no idea what to say to that.

She stood up to shake my hand. "Wavy dark blonde hair, he said. Big hazel eyes. Slim, like a fashion model." She nodded. "Yes, that's you. And it's so nice to meet you."

"Nice to meet you, too. Alice, right?" My voice sounded strangled. I cleared my throat. "Alice Monroe?"

"That's me, and please call me Alice, not Mrs. Monroe." She sat back down. "I assume you are here because you have a message for Steve? You know he's presently working a case that involves being out of the office most of the time?"

"I do, and that's why I'm here. I need him to call me when he can."

"Is it an emergency? Because it might be a while before I hear from him. He calls me when he's able, but he's pretty tied up most of the day, and into most nights."

Boy, did I know that. "No." I shook my head. "This is not an emergency, but it is urgent. So, I hope he calls you soon."

"I do, too." She folded her hands primly and gave me a serious look. "You are not the only person who wants to talk to him. A potential new client is extremely eager to speak with him."

"Oh?"

"Yes, an important professional. Who says his wife is missing." She gave a loud sigh. "He's desperate to find her, and he hears Steve is one of the best in the business."

I stopped breathing. My entire body went numb. Then cold. Was she talking about Martin Paulson?

"Uhm...that's interesting," I said, trying and failing to sound casual because my voice was suddenly way too squeaky. "Who might this professional be?"

Alice tilted her head. "I really shouldn't divulge that, dear."

"I won't tell anyone," I said. "I promise."

She pressed her lips together, took a deep breath, then let it out while holding my gaze. "Well...he's a doctor. But that's all I can say. I'm sorry, but it's confidential. I shouldn't even have told you that."

She'd told me enough. Dr. Paulson wanted to hire Steve to replace me. Hearing one of my biggest fears confirmed made it horribly real.

I swallowed hard, unable to speak, and just nodded. Apparently, Alice did not know anything about the case I was working on. Steve hadn't told her. Why would he?

She held out a piece of paper. "If you give me the number where you want Steve to call you, I will get it to him as soon as I can, dear."

I hoped she didn't notice that my hand was shaking as I reached for the paper. I jotted down my office number, my home number, and Wendy Castillo's office number. "He might have to try several places to get me," I said. "I'm working a complicated case and I'm not sure where I will be."

She took the paper from me. "I understand."

"Tell me..." I struggled to keep my voice even. "When did the doctor call?" Alice probably thought it wasn't any of my business, but I had to ask.

"A couple of hours ago." Her polite, grandmotherly smile faded, and she looked at me, puzzled. "Why?"

"Oh, just wondering." I glanced out Steve's window. A large ferry boat steamed by. A sailboat floated past it, going the other direction, bobbing up and down in the larger vessel's wake.

The world was spinning on, while I stood frozen in place. Forcing back tears.

"Miss Smith?"

I turned back to Steve's receptionist, who was looking at me with a puzzled expression. "Are you alright?"

"Oh, yes, certainly." I took a deep breath. "I was just thinking... wondering...when it was the last time you spoke to Steve?"

"This morning. But don't worry, I'm sure he'll get in touch with me soon. He seemed eager to hear from you."

And now I really needed to talk to him.

But first I had to go find Dr. Paulson, who was probably in the middle of delivering a baby.

No matter. I'd wait.

Fifteen

When I got to the University of Pennsylvania Hospital maternity ward, I discovered that Dr. Paulson was indeed still in the delivery room.

A soon-to-be new father was pacing back and forth in the waiting room, hands behind his back, muttering to himself, when I rushed in.

"Damn. What in tarnation is taking so long?" The anxious man stopped and stared at me, frustration etching his long, thin face. His gaze turned hopeful. "Hey, are you Doc Paulson's nurse? Any news about my wife and baby?"

Did I look like a nurse, in my navy-blue dress, sheer stockings, and heels? I'd stopped home to change clothes after leaving Steve's office, wanting to appear professionally polished for what I expected would be an emotionally tense meeting. One in which I needed to convince my client to give me at least another week.

I shook my head. "No, I'm sorry. I'm not a nurse. I'm just here to talk to Dr. Paulson, whenever he becomes available. Have you been here long?"

He made a sound in the back of his throat that sounded like a combination of a grunt and a grown. "Twelve hours. With no news. You might have a long wait, lady."

He was alone in the sterile, tile-floored room, lined with plastic chairs, and devoid of windows, not a comfortable place to wait for a baby to be born. But, by the looks of him, even soft comfy sofas and chairs, and windows with picturesque views like the one in Steve's office wouldn't have done much to sooth his nerves.

The only thing he could do was wait.

Which was clearly my only option, as well. I sat down and watched the man resume his pacing.

I decided I might as well make conversation. "I'm sure you'll have some good news very soon, sir."

"I hope so...hope so..." He stopped and slump-walked over to the chair next to mine and half-fell into it. Hanging his head, he peered at me out of the corner of his eye. "Uhm...why do you need to talk to the doc? You don't look like you're in need of his services. Or, at least not anytime soon...if you know what I mean. I mean..."

I bit back a laugh. "Yes, I know what you mean. And no, I'm not in need of his services as an obstetrician. I need to speak to him about something urgent."

"No telling how long you'll have to wait." He gave a loud sigh. "Could be till tomorrow the way things are going with me. With me and my wife. Poor Betty. I hope she's not in too much pain."

"I hope not."

He pointed to double doors along one wall. A large sign across them warned, in huge red letters: No Admittance. Medical

Personnel Only. "Wish I could be in there with her, but they say fathers aren't allowed. Might get in the way. Might faint, which I probably would. So, I'm just waiting and waiting and waiting out here."

"Is this your first child?"

He gave a proud sniff. "Sure is. If it's a boy, he's going to be named William, after me. Billy, we'll call him. I go by Bill."

"And if it's a girl?"

"Susan. We'll call her Susy." He grinned. "I can't wait to find out—"

A nurse in starched white burst through the double doors. "Mr. Allen? Mr. William Allen?"

He jumped to his feet. "Yes?"

"Congratulations. It's a boy."

"Oh-wow-oh-wow-oh-wow!" Beaming, he clapped his hands and jumped up and down. "When can I see him, when can I see him? When can I see Betty?"

"Soon." The nurse gave him a patient, lips-pressed-together smile. "Just as soon as the doctor finishes up, he'll be out to see you, and let you know how it went. Although I can assure you that your baby is healthy. He's got a very healthy set of lungs."

"But how come I couldn't I hear anything that was going on in there?" He nodded toward the double doors. "I was waiting to hear a baby cry."

She smiled again, even more patiently. "The delivery room is down the hall, Mr. Allen. Behind more doors. Sound proofed, for patient privacy. You understand."

She looked at me, as if noticing me for the first time. "Are you a family member?"

I shook my head. "My name is Story Smith and I need to talk to Dr. Paulson about an urgent personal matter."

She blinked. "About…?"

"I'd rather not say right now, but he'll know my name. When he learns I'm here, he'll want to speak to me. I wouldn't be here if it wasn't extremely important."

I could tell she wasn't used to dealing with someone like me. Someone who was waiting for a baby doctor to deliver a baby, but not really waiting for the baby.

"Alright. I'll inform him you are here." She stiffly turned her attention back to Mr. Allen. "The doctor will be out to see you soon."

"Thank you, nurse."

"Congratulations," I said after she left. "I'm happy for you."

"Thank you. This is so exciting. A son. I can't believe I have a son."

I nodded. I was thrilled for him. Relieved that everything had gone well. That his long wait was over. That it had a happy ending.

I could only hope that my wait would end as happily.

I had my doubts.

———

The new father and I didn't have long to wait.

Minutes after the nurse had disappeared behind those double doors, she and Dr. Paulson came back out.

The doctor glanced at me and held up a finger to signal that he'd be right with me.

Then he arranged his lips into a congratulatory smile and hurried over to Bill Allen and shook his hand. "Your wife is doing great, she's a trooper. And your son is a fine little lad. Eight pounds, two ounces. Congratulations." He turned to the nurse. "If you're ready, Miss Johnson will take you back to see them now."

"Am I ready, doctor? I am more than ready!"

I watched him and the nurse leave. Then I turned to my client, who looked as anxious as the new father had waiting for his news. And as exhausted. He hadn't taken the time to change out of his scrubs, which I couldn't help noticing were spotted with blood.

"Have you found Nanette?" His voice was terse, tense, hopeful. "Is that why you're here?"

"No. Not yet. But I have news. Important information."

"What? What?"

I hesitated. It felt awkward, standing there facing him in the middle of that cold, sterile room. "Let's have a seat, doctor." I pointed to the chairs.

"I don't want to take a seat...out with it now, Miss Smith." He folded his arms across his chest and glared at me. "Tell me what is so important that you had to come here and wait until I finished delivering a baby. I'm all ears."

"Okay." I took a deep breath, put my hands on my hips, and stared at him. "You're probably not going to like some of what I am about to say. Which is why I thought maybe we should sit down."

"Spit it out!"

I shrugged. "Okay. First, I've discovered Nanette has secrets. That may or may not have anything to do with her disappearance. Although there's a good chance. Which is why I need you to give me more time."

"Secrets? What are you talking about? What secrets?"

"To start with, there's no evidence she ever really volunteered to help the poor on Monday nights."

"What?" He shook his head. "What do you mean?"

"I visited all the soup kitchens in Philadelphia. Canvassed the entire skid row district. No one recognized her picture. She must have been doing something else on Monday nights. I need to find out what."

"No..."

"Yes, doctor. But there's more, which could also be important."

He walked over to a chair, staring straight ahead, looking like a zombie, and sat down. "Go on."

Relief washed through me. Was he actually ready to listen?

I took a deep breath and braced myself. "I've heard from multiple people that Nanette was extremely flirtatious. Which means—"

"Which means nothing. Why do you keep harping on that?"

"I'm not harping. I am trying to figure out whether it might—"

"It means nothing, I tell you." He stood up and shook a fist. "And you know what? You're a pathetic detective. You're fired."

I ignored my sinking heart. "You might think again about firing me when you hear what else I've discovered, doctor."

"I doubt it. I've already lined up another P.I. One with experience. To replace you."

"Steve Evans?"

He widened his eyes. "How did you know?"

"I'm a better detective than you give me credit for, doctor. Which means I know that you haven't actually spoken to Steve yet, let alone hired him. So, give me another week. Please, give me at least one more week."

"Why should I?"

"Because I've uncovered something else about Nanette. She has a sister. A sister I bet she never told you about. A sister who's married, with three children. And a husband who's been angry for years that Nanette left her sister behind at the orphanage and never looked back."

He was staring at me as if I had lost my mind. Open mouthed, not blinking, not breathing. "What?"

"You heard me right. I know her name and where she lives, and I've been to her place, and I've talked to her and her husband."

"How? How do you know she's for real?"

"The orphanage. I went there first. They have records. She's for real."

He collapsed back into his chair. "What does this mean?"

"It means Nanette has secrets. Which I need to unravel to find her. Which means I need more time."

He bent over and covered his face with his hands. He sat motionless for a very long time, then lowered his hands and glanced over at me. Tears welled in his eyes. "The husband's been angry for years?"

"Yes. They've had financial challenges. He's been urging his wife for years to contact Nanette, to ask her for money, because they knew she married a doctor and figured she had plenty. But his wife refused. Because when Nanette left the orphanage, she told her sister to never contact her again. She was starting a whole new life and leaving her past behind."

"Do you think this husband might have wanted to take revenge? Against Nanette? Against me? Maybe he took her?"

"It's possible, doctor."

I was glad this stubborn, gullible man was beginning to see the picture. Willing to see that his wife wasn't perfect. Maybe far from perfect. That she'd by all appearances been playing him for a fool.

He was smart and successful, that was obvious. But when it came to his wife, he clearly saw only what he wanted to see.

"And this sister, what is her name?" he asked wearily.

I'd come prepared for him to ask me that. I slid him a tight smile. "I prefer to keep that to myself for now. And keep investigating. I've worked hard on this case, and I'm not willing to just turn all I've learned over to someone else. I deserve more time."

I waited. Held my breath. Kept my tight smile in place as my heart pounded away in my chest for what felt like a year.

Finally, he stood and looked down at me with surrender in his eyes. And a glint of defiance. "Okay, you win, Miss Smith. I'll give you more time."

Joy washed through me. Yes!

"You get one more week."

"Okay, okay...thank you."

"One more week, and you better find Nanette."

"I will." I stood and shook his hand. "I promise you, I will."

Sixteen

"Yoo-hoo, Story, I have something for you." Wendy's perky voice greeted me when I arrived at my office the next morning, more than a bit bedraggled. It was after ten o'clock, because I'd slept late—hadn't gotten home from the hospital till well after midnight.

Wendy waved what looked like a check.

Hey, it was a check. I made a beeline into her office.

It was from Dr. Paulson! My fatigue lifted, and I suddenly had the energy of a steam engine ready to charge down the tracks.

"Thanks," I said. "When did he bring this by?"

"About an hour ago."

"Nice."

"And I have something else for you. A personally delivered message—from a really good-looking guy."

My heart bumped. "Steve?"

She nodded. "Yep, that's his name. Steve Evans. He said to come to the mansion where he's working, as soon as possible, and that it's okay, and to not worry because today the coast is clear." She'd sounded as if she'd been reciting from a script and looked proud of herself for having memorized it all. She leaned forward, an eager grin on her face. "Does that make sense to you? Is he your boyfriend?"

I shook my head. "Not my boyfriend. But yes, thanks, his message makes sense. So...he came by here? When?" Hopefully not at the same time as my client. Heaven forbid Steve and Dr. Paulson should run into each other.

"About thirty minutes ago."

I sighed in relief. "Okay, thanks. I appreciate all your help, you're a godsend."

She sat back and folded her hands. "Glad to help somebody with such an exciting life. Glad to *know* somebody who lives such an exciting life."

Exciting? It was certainly shaping up that way.

I let myself into my office and plopped down behind my desk. I put my head back and contemplated the ceiling. Wasn't exciting what I'd been looking for? Yep. But this business was also kind of scary, and confusing. I had another week. But what was my next step?

My client's wife was still missing, and it looked like his best friend might have something to do with her disappearance, and I couldn't think of any other move but to track Alec Lowell. Tail him for a day.

It was either that or go back to the Macy farm and snoop around on the off chance I'd find Nanette tied up in a barn somewhere. Or worse, buried under a haystack.

No, Alec was my best bet. I'd have to follow him around. Literally.

Except, Steve was telling me that the coast was clear, meaning my target wasn't home, or expected to be home any time soon.

What did that mean?

I stood up, grabbed my purse, locked my door, and told Wendy I was going to see Steve.

Thirty minutes later, I was being escorted into the Lowell mansion by Carolyn, who looked surprised, but not displeased to see me.

"Steve left a message with my receptionist to come here," I told her. "He said Alec wasn't home, so I'm assuming it's okay?"

Dressed in pink shorts and a sleeveless white blouse, she had her hair pulled up into a high, perky ponytail, looking fresh and dewy. Ready for another life's-a-party day. She squinted at me. "You have a receptionist?"

I sighed. "A very part time one, it's a long story. But Alec's not here, right? He's not going to appear out of nowhere and toss me out?"

She shrugged. "No, he's not here. He's in Atlantic City, meetings all day involving some big, important deal." She rolled her eyes, made a face. "Said he won't be back till late tonight, and not to wait up for him. So, what's new with that?"

At first, her tone was neglected-housewife bitter. But then a dreamy teenage-girl-in-love smile lit up her face. "Who cares? Do I care? No...I have Steve now. And Steve likes me, and I like him, and now Freddie likes him, too. Freddie thinks he's a cool dude." She waved a hand at the staircase. "They're upstairs together."

I inclined my ear to the second floor. I could hear music, like they were listening to records or the radio. Interesting. And disturbingly odd. Alec had installed a man in his house who was so beloved by his wife and son that he was almost taking his place. But, why, why, why?

"Wonder why Steve wanted you to stop by?" Carolyn said.

"I'm sure it's to get an update on Nanette." I pointed to the stairs. "Can I go up?"

"Oh, sure...sure." She waved for me to follow her, then halfway up, turned and put a hand on my arm. "Wait. I want to know, too. What have you found out about Nanette? Anything new?"

I hesitated. I could at least tell her about Dora and Charlie. Just not the details. "Actually, I've discovered that Nanette has a secret sister. I don't know yet if it's relevant, but I met her, and her husband, and her children."

"What? A sister? Impossible! She would have told me."

"She never told anyone. Left the sister, and her past, behind when she left the orphanage. I'm looking into what it might mean."

Carolyn slowly lifted her hand off my arm and stared at me as if she had seen a ghost. Or at least the whisper of an idea that she'd never really known her friend at all. Shaking her head, she turned and bounded up the stairs, her ponytail flipping back and forth, me following.

The music grew louder once we reached the second floor, coming from a room at the end of a long hall.

"They're in Freddie's room." Carolyn gestured for me to follow her past two other rooms, one which appeared to be the master bedroom, then a smaller one next to it, which had to be Steve's.

Freddy's door was half ajar. Carolyn pushed it open.

Still wearing striped pajamas, Freddie sat cross-legged on his bed. A cowboy-themed bedspread had been haphazardly thrown over the sheets, and a pillow at the headboard was topped with a gleeful sock monkey.

On a poster above the bed, a rock and roll musician with sleek black hair and bedroom eyes was crooning into a microphone and clutching a guitar like the one in Steve's hands.

Steve, in jeans and a T-shirt, was sitting in a chair, strumming the guitar, and softly singing a cool, catchy tune when we walked in. He stopped and gave me a sheepish smile. "Story, you got my message."

"I did." I bit back the swooning, junior-high-girl grin that threatened to overtake my face. Damn Steve for having that effect on women. On me. Singing or not singing—but singing revved it up a thousand times.

He had a great tenor voice and I'd never heard his song before. Some amazing combination of Frank Sinatra and Bill Haley and His Comets. "What song were you just singing, Steve?" I asked. "I didn't recognize it."

"That's because he wrote it." Freddie swung his bare feet over the edge of his bed and let them dangle. Propping himself up on his hands, he gazed at Steve with admiration. "He writes his own songs. And some are even better than Elvis's."

"Elvis?" I frowned. "Who's Elvis?"

Freddie gave me a smug look and pointed to the guy on his poster. "Elvis Presley. A lot of kids don't know about him yet, but I do. He's gonna be a big star. Really soon. You wait and see."

Freddie looked different. More relaxed, confident. Also younger, less defensive, and genuinely happy. Spending time with Steve had clearly changed his attitude about having a private detective around. He had a hero in the bedroom next door.

What the hell was Alec thinking? Did it make him feel less guilty about neglecting his family? And where would this lead?

"Steve's a really good musician." Carolyn walked over and lowered herself down onto the bed next to Freddie. "If he ever wanted to quit being a detective, he could make it in showbiz, no doubt about it. He'd give Elvis and Pat Boone and all the rest of them a run for their money."

"Play something else," Freddie told Steve. "Play something for Miss Private Eye. Play that song you just wrote, you know—"

"No, not right now." Steve shook his head, looking uncharacteristically shy. For Mr. Unbounded Confidence, that was refreshing. He handed the guitar to Freddie. "Why don't you play that song you just wrote? I'm sure your mom would love to hear it. I need to talk to Story."

"Freddie, you can play, too? And write music?" I gave him an I'm-super-impressed look.

"Steve's teaching me." He strummed a few strings on the guitar. "I'm just getting started, but it's so fun."

Steve stood up. "Come on, Story, let's go into the hall and talk. Freddie, practice your awesome song. I'll be right back."

Steve whisked me out of the room so fast it was clear he didn't want Carolyn to follow. It worked. Freddie started playing and singing something simple and sweet that sounded like it had been written by a teenage boy in love. It was quite good, and his voice wasn't bad either.

"You're a man of many talents," I told Steve as he closed the door behind us.

"Thanks. Music's just a hobby. I love it, but don't worry, I'm not going to pursue a showbiz career any time soon."

"You could if you wanted to. You have the looks and the voice."

He took my arm and led me away from the door, acting like he hadn't just heard me say that. "I was worried about you. Thanks for coming over when you got my message. What's the news about Nanette? Uncover anything promising?"

"Yes. Lots. But I have no idea if any of it is promising."

"Quick. Tell me. I don't know how much time we have until Carolyn comes out and wants to hear it, too. Unless you want her to...? Anything that should stay confidential for now?"

"Yes, your P.I. instincts are right on the money. I told her a little, but some of this needs to be for your ears only." We were close and whispering. Which felt delicious. And unnerving. Was Steve my friend or my competitor or my assistant? I wanted to ask him that in the worst way, but now was not the time.

I took a deep breath. "First of all, it turns out Nanette has a sister, one she never told anyone about, including her dear doctor husband. The sister was younger, and she and Nanette lived together at the orphanage. When she went off to nursing school, Nanette told the sister goodbye. Permanently."

"Wow." Steve raised his eyebrows. "Interesting. Great work."

"Thanks. Even more interesting, this sister has a husband who's bitter toward Nanette for shunning them. I met the sister and her husband at their home."

"I'm impressed."

"Even better, Dr. Paulson was impressed enough that he's giving me another week. I'm depositing his check when I leave here. Then I need to find Alec Lowell and tail him. Hopefully today."

"Wait. Why tail Alec?"

It felt right to confide in Steve now. Now that I had that extra week.

"Because that's my other news. I have good reason to think Alec and Nanette were having an affair."

"What?!"

"Shhh...I don't want to go into it right now, but my next step is to follow him and try to find some proof."

"An affair? This is getting crazy. What about Nanette's sister?"

"I'm going to look into Alec first. It's a strong lead, and I can't ignore it."

"How strong?"

"Strong enough. That's all I'm willing to say just yet."

Steve stared at me with a frustrated frown. I knew he wanted to come with me. Too bad he had to play babysitter. Not that I wanted his company. Well, I did...and I didn't. Mostly didn't...

Down the hall, Freddie was singing and playing his heart out. Good for him. He had to be making his mama proud. Who knew Steve had so many talents? Including teenage-boy-tamer and music teacher.

"I'm not totally surprised by what you're telling me." Steve's frown turned pensive, his eyes went dark. He shook his head. "In fact, this is making the picture clearer for me. Strangely clearer."

"What do you mean?"

He raked his fingers through his hair. "I mean, I'm more and more convinced that Alec wants me and Carolyn to get together. Romantically. Now it seems it's not my imagination. Which is making me uncomfortable, really, really uncomfortable."

"If Alec was having an affair with Nanette, that might explain what's going on," I said. "Get his wife to fall in love with somebody else, so he could be with his mistress. Would make it easier and cheaper for him to get a divorce, too. A lot cheaper, alimony-wise."

Steve groaned.

"That's why I need to tail him," I said. "The problem is, how do I find him in Atlantic City? That's where he is today, according to Carolyn."

Steve gave me a crafty smile. "Maybe he's not really in Atlantic City. Maybe that's just what he told her."

"And?"

"If I were you, I'd head over to his office. Lowell Industrial Manufacturing and Machinery. It's on Market Street, next to one of the many factories he owns in Pennsylvania. Don't know why he'd be going to Atlantic City. He equips factories and businesses with industrial machines, and America's greatest resort is an oceanfront playground."

"Carolyn said he was involved in making some big, important deal."

"Maybe yes, maybe no. Anyway, I'd head over to his office. See if you can find out if it's true. You could check the phonebook for the exact address."

I pressed my lips together and nodded. "Thanks, Steve. I'm learning a lot from you."

"In the meantime, I'll keep my eyes and ears open here. Nose around when I can, see if I can find any evidence that Alec and Nanette were—"

Freddie's door opened. Carolyn came out, then stopped when she saw Steve and I with our heads together. She looked like someone who'd walked into a party to which she had not been invited.

Steve whispered, "Guess you better go."

"Yep."

Carolyn walked toward us. "You two look rather cozy."

"Just filling Steve in on some developments, which I'll let him explain because I've got work to do." I gave her an I-hope-you-understand smile. "By the way, Freddie sounds really great. I like his song. I think your son has some musical talent."

"Thanks." She clapped her hands and beamed. "He's blossoming, coming out of his moody teenage doldrums. Thanks to Steve." She reached over and patted Steve's shoulder, giving him a look that most men would have found sexy. Suggestive.

I'm sure he did.

Uh-oh.

Steve reacted by not reacting. Didn't move, didn't return her smile, didn't look at me, either.

Oh, boy. He had his work cut out for him. How was he going to play this? Was he attracted to Carolyn? At all? If he was, I couldn't blame him. She was a beautiful, vulnerable, wounded bird who needed care and protection. She was crying out to be loved.

It wasn't my business how Steve felt. He'd said he didn't go for married women. Still... I shouldn't be wondering with a chill in my heart what he would do. But I was.

I cleared my throat. "I'll be going now." I looked back and forth between frozen-faced Steve and flush-faced Carolyn.

Neither looked at me.

I turned, raced down the stairs, and let myself out.

SEVENTEEN

I took Steve's advice, looked up the address for Lowell Industrial Manufacturing and Machinery, and headed there after depositing Dr. Paulson's check in the bank.

I considered making a detour to my parents' house first to ask my father if he'd swap cars for the day, then thought better of it.

My Thunderbird was conspicuous, but was that going to change? No. And I couldn't expect Dad to willingly hand over his boring black Chevy every time I wanted to follow someone without being detected. He'd probably refuse. Even if he did agree, he'd probably fall in love with my car and want to keep it.

To ease my fears about standing out, I put the top up. That would have to do. Besides, I needed to learn how to follow a car and keep it in sight while staying several vehicles behind my target. To keep my distance, but not too far.

First, I had to find Alec Lowell.

I parked in the back of his company's lot, which fortunately wasn't gated or guarded.

But Alec had always parked his car in a garage behind his mansion, which meant I'd never seen it. Which meant I couldn't tell if he was at work or not.

First order of business? Find out. Because even if he did plan to go to Atlantic City, maybe he hadn't left yet.

As I approached the front entrance, I spotted a sleek, two-tone, green and white Pontiac Chieftain parked in a spot nearest the door, under a "Reserved for Company President" sign.

He was president, right? So, this had to be his car.

A receptionist inside confirmed it. With a snooty air that bordered on suspicious when I inquired if President Lowell was in.

"Who's asking?" She looked at me as if she were a queen and I was an annoying, groveling peasant. Haughty squint, frizzy hair, double chin. She obviously relished her role as gatekeeper of Alec Lowell's kingdom.

I didn't want to give my real name, so I made one up on the spot. Judy Jewell.

"And what is it you want, Miss Jewell?"

Not wanting Alec Lowell to catch sight of me, much less speak to him, I decided to have some fun.

"I'm here to apply for a job," I said. "I hear they're looking for a receptionist."

She gasped, then she swallowed her surprise by masking it with a tight smile. "I believe you are mistaken."

"I don't think I am. I read in the want ads that you're looking for a receptionist for the new Atlantic City office."

"We're not opening a new Atlantic City office." The look on her face said she wasn't entirely sure, and she clearly didn't like my presumption one bit. "That I know of, anyway."

"Uhm...well, you see the advertisement said interested applicants could apply for the position here or in Atlantic City and I didn't want to make the long drive to the shore for nothing and so is President Lowell here?" I stopped to take a breath. "Maybe I could talk to him here? If he's not here, I'll be glad to make the trip cause I really, really want that job."

I spoke rapid-fire fast, stringing my words together like a floozy. Harmless, and clearly not good receptionist material. Someone to get rid of, quickly.

She dismissively waved a hand. "President Lowell is busy with back-to-back meetings, and anyway, he does not personally hire new staff. Which we don't need, in any case, because as far as I know we are not planning to open any new offices. I do know that President Lowell is not in Atlantic City." She looked at me like the very idea was ridiculous.

I gave my best floozy-disappointed pout, but inwardly I was cheering. I had what I needed. Now all I had to do was wait for him to leave the building and get in his car.

All I had to do? No telling how long that would take.

I thanked Her Majesty and went back outside and settled into the driver's seat of my T-Bird, hunkering down to wait.

Two hours later, he finally came out. Alone. He made a right out of the parking lot and I followed at a respectable distance, as many cars back as I dared, in case he should glance out his rearview mirror and see me.

Two miles later, he parked in front of a brown apartment building in a block lined with brown apartment buildings and went in. It was a respectable neighborhood, with trees along the street and grass growing out of cracks in the sidewalk. Not everywhere, just in some places. Not fancy. But safe. The kind of community that wasn't much of one, where people didn't plan to stay long and kept to themselves.

It was lunchtime. I wondered what Alec Lowell could be doing here? Meeting someone? If so, who?

Or maybe he'd rented a secret apartment for himself in this building?

Whatever he was doing, this was far from where he told his wife he'd be spending the day.

He wasn't in there long. About thirty minutes. From a block away, I watched him get back in his car and drive off. Again, alone.

I followed him back to his office.

Five super long hours later, he came back out again and got back in his car.

Thank God.

It had been a hot wait, but fortunately there was a deli across the street where I'd been able to grab myself some lunch and use the restroom.

This time, Alec turned left when he pulled out of the parking lot. Traffic was heavier because it was rush hour, but I managed to keep him in sight.

Many miles later, I let myself fall further behind because we were heading into rural Chester County, with far fewer cars on the road. I was starting to get nervous about him noticing me in his rearview mirror, when he turned into the parking lot of a quaint little restaurant tucked under some oak trees.

It was a cozy place, with a French provincial cottage look and a French name: Café Louis.

Romantic. Alec had to be meeting someone. He wouldn't have driven all this way to have dinner alone.

My heart was hopping up and down in my chest like a bunny rabbit. I waited about five minutes before venturing inside, hoping against hope that the interior was dimly lit.

It was. Shutters covered the windows. Tall, elegant candles flickered in the center of each table, illuminating diners' faces with soft golden light. Just enough light. How lovely. How romantic. How private.

I held my breath and looked around.

There he was, just as I'd anticipated. Sitting at a table in a back corner. And he wasn't alone.

A woman sat across from him. Young. With dark hair. And an elegant profile.

She turned to speak to a waiter holding a wine bottle.

My heart stopped. My breath caught in my throat. I thought I might faint.

The light was dim. I couldn't be certain. But she sure looked like my picture of Nanette.

———

I didn't want Alec to see me. I had to get out of there, then wait for him and his date to leave.

Fortunately, no one had yet come over to seat me, so I turned and slipped back outside.

Darkness settled in as I waited in my car once again, top up, windows down. I was starving and had to go to the bathroom but dared not use the one in the café. Men definitely had an advantage in this profession, they could pee in a bottle. I wondered if I should I buy myself a bedpan along with a gun? Probably not a bad idea.

An hour later, my couple came out, arm-in-arm, so snuggly they looked like Siamese twins. Since it was a moonless night, and the parking lot unlit, I could barely see the woman's face.

Alec walked her to a black Ford sedan, the kind that had rolled off the assembly lines right after World War II. Boring, lumpy, hastily made to meet pent-up demand.

The type of car nobody would look at twice, parked on the opposite side of the lot from where I waited. Which was great. Hopefully, Alec wouldn't glance over and see my Thunderbird. Not that he had eyes for anything else but the brunette in his arms.

They kissed with the passion of two people about to hop into bed. Ugh. When were they were going to open the stupid car door? They pawed at each other and for a minute I thought they might climb onto the Ford's roof and go at it right there.

After what felt like forever, Alec finally opened the stupid door, helped the woman in, closed it, waved goodbye, then headed to his car a few feet away.

Was he going to follow her, or was she going to follow him?

He pulled out of the lot first, then took off down the road. Fast. Which meant they were not going to stay together. Which meant she was the one I'd have to tail now.

She waited about five minutes, then turned in Alec's direction, at a more leisurely pace.

I followed, feeling pretty confident. If this was Nanette, wonderful. It shouldn't be too hard to confirm, in which case I'd alert her husband along with the police.

If not, I'd at least discovered that Alec liked women who looked like Nanette. Which might mean they had been having an affair. Which meant what? That maybe he'd grown tired of her? And killed her?

Whoever this woman was, I couldn't lose her. There was an excellent chance that she planned to meet up again with Alec at another location. Which would account for her rather slow driving, like she was in no hurry to get wherever she was going, knowing that her lover would be waiting there.

Ah...love.

Ah, phooey. She started driving slower, which made it harder for me to follow because I had to slow down, too, which looked mighty suspicious. Had she noticed me? That was an old trick, if you think someone is following you, slow down and see if they would pass you.

I couldn't pass. The road opened up to two lanes each way. We were headed toward Philly, with traffic picking up. Cars zoomed past us.

I hoped like hell she hadn't noticed me. Maybe she was daydreaming about lover boy and what they were about to do to each other when they met again.

Which seemed likely when she pulled into the parking lot of a two-story Holiday Inn near the Philadelphia Airport. It seemed she had already checked in. Instead of going into the lobby, she drove around, parked, and disappeared into a ground-floor room on the side of the building.

I waited a few minutes, then drove toward her car, looking around for Alec's Pontiac. I didn't see it. I drove to the other end of the lot and parked far enough away that if he did suddenly appear he wouldn't see me.

It was getting late, and I was exhausted. It had been a long day and

I longed for my bed. I still had to find a bathroom but couldn't leave now.

Perhaps there was a way to learn the woman's name? Walking around to the lobby, I took note of her room number as I passed: 116.

After using the restroom, I went over to the clerk behind the counter, a bright-eyed young man with a shock of black hair and black-framed glasses to match.

"Looking to check in?" he asked, sounding way too chipper for the hour.

"No." I gave him a hopeful smile. "I'm looking for a friend. Nanette Paulson. She's supposed to be staying here, and I'm supposed to drive her to the airport tomorrow."

He nodded, pulled out a register, and ran his fingers down the page. "Nobody by that name here. Sorry."

Of course. I hadn't expected her to use her real name, although I'd figured it was worth a shot. "I think she said she's in room 116. Is that right?"

He glanced at the page again and shook his head. "That's not the name I have registered for 116." I waited to see if he'd tell me who was registered for that room, but no such luck there, either. And asking would have aroused suspicion.

"Maybe she checked in under her brother's name? I think he's paying for it. Alec Lowell?"

He shook his head again. "No. Sorry. And..." He ran his finger down the page again. "There's no Alec Lowell registered here for any room. Perhaps you have the wrong hotel? There are several in this area."

I shrugged. "Yes, I suppose you're right. Thanks anyway."

I trudged back to my car. Alec's was still nowhere to be seen.

I waited another hour, growing sleepier by the minute. It was becoming increasingly difficult to keep my eyes open, which would make it dangerous driving home.

Which was where Alec probably was at that moment, getting into bed with his wife, lying to her about his day.

It was well after midnight.

I looked over at room 116. The lights were off. My Nanette look-alike was probably also in bed, sound asleep. No point in me waiting around all night.

I drove off. I'd come back in the morning, nice and early. I'd just have to take the chance that she'd still be here.

EIGHTEEN

Lucky for me, the woman's car was still there when I pulled up just after six a.m.

Or maybe it wasn't luck. Maybe it was more like payback for being willing to sacrifice sleep. The sun was just beginning to rise, and I had that sort of sick, fatigued feeling that comes with not getting enough shut eye.

I parked where I had before and sipped my coffee. The caffeine perked me up, or maybe I was just imaging it, which amounted to the same thing.

Anyhow, setting my alarm for four-thirty had been worth it. I couldn't let my possible Nanette slip away. She was at a hotel near the airport for a reason, and she might be planning to catch a flight. If so, I needed to stop or delay her, or at least determine that she was defi-nitely not Nanette, and let her go.

I didn't have to wait long. At six-forty-five she came out of her room carrying a gigantic suitcase. She set it down, went back in, and came out with another. Just as big. Two giant suitcases? Wherever she was going, she clearly planned to stay for a while.

I watched her hoist one of them into the trunk of her car, then shove the other onto the back seat.

She went back in her room, then returned with a smaller green and blue flowered Victorian carpet bag. Her idea of a purse? If so, an unusual one.

She walked around the corner of the building, I assumed to go to the lobby to check out. Then came back and drove off, with me on her tail.

Just as I figured—crackerjack detective that I am—she was going to the airport. I still needed to get a good look at her face to confirm she was Nanette. Since she didn't know me, I hoped to be able to get a closer look at her there—and see where she planned to fly off to.

She pulled into the airport parking lot.

I parked a row behind her and watched her unload both suitcases. With one in each hand, she started lugging them toward the entrance.

I slipped out of my car and followed.

A skycap saw her struggling, hurried to meet her, and grabbed her bags.

I slowed my steps and watched him check them in. She handed him a tip and entered the airport.

I followed her in, keeping my distance.

She stepped up to the TWA counter, where an agent handed her what I assumed was a boarding pass. Okay, so she was flying on Trans World Airlines. But where to?

She headed toward the terminal gates. Unburdened by heavy suitcases, she picked up her pace. I still couldn't see her face. I still had no idea if she was Nanette.

If only she would turn around. No such luck.

She was moving at a surprisingly speedy clip, considering she was wearing high heels and a tight skirt. A matching dark blue blazer completed her outfit. She was so fashionably attired, she could have been a magazine model.

Gorgeous, glitzy, glamorous. Off to fly the skies.

I wouldn't know. I'd never flown in an airplane before.

I didn't let her out of my sight.

We entered a crowded hallway lined with TWA gates. Men, women, a few children. Everyone seemed to know where they were going and headed there as quickly as possible. Signs posted at each gate declared that flight's destination.

We passed flights going to Chicago, Miami, Seattle, New York, Boston...Cleveland.

It was a good thing I'd worn flat shoes. I was huffing and puffing to keep up with Miss Glamour Girl. Once she got to her gate, I'd go up to her, start a conversation. Keep it light, casual chitchat between fellow travelers.

And then what? What if she looked just like Nanette up-close? I had Nanette's photo in my purse. Maybe I'd confront her with it. Gage her reaction. Grab her arm if she still tried to get on the plane. Maybe even shout for the police if she resisted. Shout that this woman had been reported missing.

I didn't get a chance to do any of those things. She was too smart. And had timed it too well. Or maybe it just seemed that way.

She ran—literally doing a run-wobble—up to the Los Angeles gate. Clutching her carpet bag purse, she waved her boarding pass at the gate agent, who impatiently motioned for her to come through.

She disappeared.

I ran up, heart pounding, breathing hard to catch my breath.

"Plane's about to take off, lady." The gate agent stuck his hand out. "Got your pass?"

I shook my head. "I just wanted to say goodbye to a friend before she left."

He shrugged. "Looks like you missed her."

My heart dropped to the floor. I couldn't believe this was happening. "Please, could I board the plane, just for a minute, to say goodbye?" I gave him a pleading look. Did they let you do that? I had no idea, but it was worth a try.

He scoffed. With an impatient scowl on his face, he yanked a yellow tape across the boarding entrance area, looking at me like I was a not-too-bright child. "Like I said, lady, the plane is taking off. Right now. Your friend cut it mighty close. Just made it with not a minute to spare."

———

So, now what?

I'd been so close to victory. Now here I was, standing in the middle of a chaotic, crowded airport, no closer to finding my client's wife.

Indulging in self-pity was not going to help. But I was feeling pathetically sorry for myself.

I went over to the gate counter and asked if a woman by the name of Nanette Paulson had been one of the passengers to board the plane that had just departed.

As expected, the answer was no. Why would Nanette use her real name if in fact it had been her?

So, I muttered to myself again, now what?

I trudged back to my car, climbed in, and sat there contemplating my options. I could think of only one, and I wasn't keen on it. It was time to question Carolyn about her marriage. Without arousing her suspicions.

Did she have a clue that her hubby was cheating on her?

No matter who he was cheating on her with, I needed to know. I didn't believe she suspected he'd been fooling around with Nanette. I'd seen no sign that she believed that for a minute.

Still, did Alec have a history of philandering? And if so, was Carolyn aware of it?

I drove to the country club, hoping to find her there. I also wanted to talk to Steve. Maybe he'd dug up something useful about Alec and Nanette.

The receptionist at the front desk waved me in. She'd seen me there enough times with Carolyn that she apparently had me pegged as a regular. Such were the perks of having a rich friend. Her country club was now my country club.

How fun.

I also took it as a good sign that Carolyn would be there.

My instincts were right. She was playing golf with Steve and another couple—a short, stocky man with sandy blond hair, and a tall, willowy woman sporting a spiffy plaid golf outfit.

They were teeing off at hole number two.

Great.

I wasn't about to wait around for a few hours until the fine-looking foursome finished up at hole eighteen. I strolled toward Carolyn just as she was getting ready to tee off.

Her eyes were fixed on the ball.

Whack. She watched it sail through the air, then turned toward Steve with a proud grin. "Hey, I'm getting so much better, thanks to you. Landed it exactly where—"

She saw me standing there and looked more puzzled than pleased. "Story. Why...what are you doing here?"

"I was just about to ask the same question." Steve hurried up to me. "Do you have news about Nanette?"

"No. Yes. Well...not really...maybe?" I nodded at Carolyn. "I need to talk to you. It's important."

"Who are *you*?" Miss Best Dressed Golfer glared at me. I stared back. What a cute little plaid hat. Cute pale-green blouse, cute flared skirt—beige with a plaid trim that matched the hat. Why not have a golf skirt that matched one's hat? I suspected she was the envy of every woman on the course.

I ignored her question and hurried over to Carolyn. "I hate to interrupt, but I need to talk to you. Like I said, it's important."

She gave a pained frown. "*Do* you have news about Nanette? Because if not, I think I've told you everything I possibly can." She pounded her golf club onto the ground, clearly annoyed. "I don't know how much more I can say. And I'd just like to get back to living my life."

I nodded. "I understand, and I don't have anything I can share with you just yet, but—"

"But what? I've answered all your questions, I've introduced you to all her friends. I've even lent you my bodyguard, who you seem to have taken a shine to, and it's becoming very tiring."

So that was her problem. Now I was competition for Steve's attention? She'd been the one to come to me, offering to help me, and now she was beginning to regret it. If Alec truly had intended for her to fall in love with Steve, his plan was working.

"Carolyn," Steve said. "Come on, now. You're not being fair. You offered to help Story. You wanted me to help her. And she's just trying to do her job."

"I get it Steve, but I'm just trying to start living normally again." She gave him a half-flirty, half-serious pout. "Which at the moment means winning this round of golf, with you as my partner, so we can qualify for the club's upcoming tournament." She looked at me and lifted her chin. "I don't want to talk to you right now."

My face went hot. She was dismissing me. Acting like a self-centered brat.

This was new, and it almost felt as if she *knew*. Knew my investigation was uncovering secrets about her husband she'd rather not know.

Secrets that would destroy her perfect life.

But...how could she know?

It didn't matter. I would not let her dismiss me like that. "I only need a few minutes, Carolyn," I said through clenched teeth. "Only a few minutes."

Steve put his arm around her shoulder. "Come on, if you want, we can talk to Story together." He gave me a knowing look, like don't argue.

"Please, just get on with this, folks." The sandy haired man waved his club in the air. "People are coming up behind us and they're not going to be happy waiting around while you three have a leisurely chat. The woman says she only needs a few minutes. For God's sake, give them to her." He pointedly looked at his watch, then at me.

Carolyn's stiff stance softened. Steve's arm around her seemed to be doing the trick. She melted against him and put her head on his shoulder. "Okay. Fine."

"Over here." Steve motioned for me to follow him and Carolyn away from the others. "Quick, Story. What is it?"

I looked at him, then at Carolyn. I would rather have questioned her alone, but she gave me no choice. "It's about Alec. I hate to ask you this, Carolyn, but—as far as you know—has he ever been unfaithful to you?"

She widened her eyes. She stared at me as if I'd lost my marbles. Then she scrunched her eyes together and shook her head. "What?"

"Has Alec ever cheated on you, that you know of?"

Her jaw dropped. She didn't answer right away. Then she turned her shocked gaze to Steve, grabbed his arm, and clung to him, as if for emotional support. "I can't believe she's asking me this, Steve. She's interrupted our golf game for *this*?"

"Go ahead and answer her," Steve said.

"No!" The word came out as almost a scream. "No...Alec has never cheated on me," she snapped.

"Are you sure?" Steve asked softly.

Carolyn shook her head. "No. I know my husband. He would never cheat on me. Never."

I studied her face. "Are you absolutely, positively certain?"

She looked certain, and she looked like she wanted to kill me. "I. Am. Positive. And I'm insulted that you're even asking me this. Are we done?"

"I want to know why Story is asking the question," Steve said.

I shook my head at him. I wasn't ready to reveal to Carolyn what I knew or suspected. "I have my reasons," I told her.

"You think Alec is cheating on me?" She glared at me. "Don't be ridiculous. I believe you were hired to find Nanette, not investigate my marriage."

"True..." I let the word linger.

Her face flushed. "Just what are you saying?"

"Only that my search for Nanette has brought up some interesting questions about Alec. And that my job is to learn the truth, wherever it leads."

"Truth?" She spit out the word. She let go of Steve and leaned over and put her face in mine. "You want to know the sad *truth*, Story? I don't *care* if Alec is cheating on me. You know why? Because I could give a crap about him. All he does is work, work, work. The only thing he cares about is money, money, money. He can go to hell."

Steve put a hand on her shoulder. "Carolyn."

She turned and threw her arms around his neck, burying her face in his chest.

He stiffly put his hands on her waist and looked at me with an expression I couldn't read.

"Alec can go to hell because I have you, Steve," she murmured. "I thank God for you. You are the one good thing that has come from all this. From Nanette's disappearance..."

"He's your bodyguard, Carolyn. Your hired bodyguard!" I shouted before I could stop myself.

She stepped away from Steve and squinted at me. "So?"

I looked at Steve. He looked amused and curious, like he was just going to stand back and see where this went.

I was curious, too. But far from amused. "What happens when Steve is no longer your bodyguard?" I waved a hand at him. "What then?"

She shrugged. "I don't know...I don't like to think about that."

"Are you going to ask Alec to keep him around?" I was baiting her, but I couldn't help it.

"Alec can go to hell..." Carolyn looked like she might cry.

I felt ashamed of myself. I'd gone too far. I had wanted to see if she knew her husband was cheating on her. Now I knew she didn't believe he was. But that even if he was, she didn't care.

What a mess. It was time for me to get going.

Carolyn clearly thought so, too. She pointed to her golf buddies. "Come on, Steve. We're holding up play."

I glanced over. Golf Buddies were watching us. Of course, they were. They knew juicy gossip when they saw it.

"Come on, love." Carolyn grabbed Steve's hand.

Love? What was she doing? Purposely adding to the gossip?

She flashed me a smirk. Yes, she was.

Steve didn't pull away from Carolyn as they walked back to their game.

And, to my consternation, he was purposely avoiding my gaze.

Nineteen

I couldn't leave the Whispering Pines Country Club, not until I talked to Steve, alone.

How long did it take to play eighteen holes of golf? I had no idea, so I strolled over to the pool and settled myself down on a lounge chair to wait.

It was hot. But having dressed for the weather in a short-sleeve sun dress, I slipped off my skinny sandals, put my head back, closed my eyes, and fell asleep.

The next thing I knew, I was being jolted awake by Steve whispering in my ear. "Wake up, wake up, Sleeping Beauty. You're not going to find Nanette this way."

I blinked. He was leaning over me with a wide grin.

I sat up, shading my eyes from the sun. "Where's Carolyn?"

"Inside, at the bar."

"She let you off her leash?"

He dropped his grin. "Not nice."

"Sorry. Couldn't help it." I swung my legs around, smoothed out my dress, and slipped my feet into my sandals. "I've been waiting to talk to you privately. Looks like this is our chance."

"I've been wanting to talk to you, too—and I was hoping you'd hang around." Steve gave me a hand to help me up. "We can't stay here. Let's take a walk."

"Where?"

"I noticed a bench out by the tenth fairway, under some trees. Let's go there. It's on the other side of the course, where hopefully no one will notice us."

"What about Carolyn? Won't she come looking for you?"

He shrugged. "I hope not. And I don't really care at this point. Come on. I want to hear your latest. Based on that scene that took place between her and you, I have a feeling it's going to be juicy."

"Oh, it's juicy…"

I didn't say any more till we got to the bench.

I filled Steve in on what I'd observed when I tailed Alec, beginning with finding him at his business, then following him to that mysterious apartment building at lunchtime, then back to work. "You were right, he never went to Atlantic City," I said. "That was a complete lie."

"Not surprised. But what about that apartment building? What do you think he was doing in there?"

"I don't know, he wasn't in there more than thirty minutes, but based on what happened after he left work, I have my ideas. I think he's keeping a mistress there."

"A mistress…? Why? What happened after he left work?"

I described how I followed Alec to the French café. "Very romantic. Out in the boonies."

"And…"

"And he was dining with a woman. By candlelight. Pretty, dark hair…"

"My God. Nanette…?"

I sighed. "That's the problem, I don't know. For sure. I couldn't get a good look at her face."

Steve pressed his lips together. "Were you tempted to go over and confront them?"

"Not really, I wanted to wait to see if she really was Nanette."

"Okay, makes sense."

"And I didn't want Alec to see me, so I went back to my T-Bird and waited for them to leave. Then I had to make a choice about which one to follow since they left in separate cars. I followed her."

"Smart."

I described how I tailed her to a hotel in Philadelphia and then the next morning, when I followed her to the airport.

"But then I lost her." I shook my head. "I was so close. So close to getting a better look. And then she was gone. She'd timed it perfectly, as if she suspected someone might try to follow her. When she got to the Los Angles gate, she ran to make it, leaving me in the dust."

"She might have spotted you tailing her and hustled so you couldn't get on that plane."

"I wish I could have." I gave a loud, deep sigh. "Problem was, I didn't have the money to buy a ticket, even if I had time to buy one. Now, I don't even know if the woman was Nanette. It's so frustrating."

We sat there in silence for a few minutes, as if neither of us could think of a solution to my problem. Not that it was really Steve's problem, but I was grateful for any help he could give me.

He leaned toward me and gave me a warm, sympathetic smile, easing my frustration some. It was so charming, so caring. So genuine. No wonder women fell for him. "She might have just been a pretty woman having a fling with Alec and was then in a hurry to catch her flight home to California," he said. "Alec's a rich guy. Women like men with money. Whether this woman was Nanette or not, poor Carolyn."

"Carolyn says she doesn't care if he's playing around. Because now she's in love with you."

"Yeah," Steve sighed. "Yeah..."

I didn't know what Steve was going to do, but I knew what I was going to do.

"I need to fly to L.A. To find this woman," I said.

He stared at me. "What?"

"You heard me."

"But you just said you don't have the money."

"I'll find a way to get it."

"But you don't know what name she's using. Or where she's staying. Finding her will be impossible."

"I'll find a way."

Steve looked at me with admiration. Making me want to succeed just so I could feel I'd earned it. But despite the act I was putting on, I was feeling anything but confident.

"I'll go with you," he said.

"What? No."

"Why not?"

"You have a job. Here. Guarding Carolyn. Remember?"

He leaned toward me and whispered, "I could quit."

"No, no, please don't quit."

"Why not?"

"I need you to stay with Carolyn. Anyway, this is my case."

There went that sexy grin. "I know it's your case," he said, "and I'm not trying to steal your case. But I'm getting tired of this babysitting gig. It's not me. My skills could be put to better use in California, with you."

"Stealing my case..." I turned away from that grin. It would *not* work on me. "Please, no. I only confided in you because I trusted you. I guess I shouldn't have."

"I'm not taking your case. I only want to help."

I gave a deep sigh and looked back at him. He did look hurt. Like I'd misjudged him. "What's going on, Steve?" I asked. "There's something you're not telling me. About why you took this bodyguard assignment in the first place. I know it's not about the money. Why did you?"

He raised his shoulders, let them drop.

I waited.

He glanced at me, then away. "It's not something I like to talk about. I've never shared it with anyone."

"I'm flattered. I think."

"It has to do with a case I worked on a couple of months ago..."

"Tell me..."

"I had a client, who suspected his wife of adultery. He hired me to see if his suspicions were true, and it turned out they were..."

"That sounds like a fairly typical scenario."

"Yes. But my client was so outraged when he learned the truth that he shot and killed his wife and her lover. When they were together, in bed."

"Oh...how awful."

"I blame myself."

"Why?"

"Because I didn't see it coming."

"How could you?"

"I don't know, but I could have warned the wife he might try something. When he left my office, he was furious to the point of making me uneasy."

"But she wasn't your client. And that wasn't your responsibility. And you know it."

He looked at me, held my gaze. "I know. But I also knew that I needed a break. From the nasty, sordid side of being a P.I."

He looked away. "When Alec offered me the seemingly easy job of guarding his lovely wife, I took it. I told you that Carolyn and I had met at a party, and I thought how hard could it be? The money was nice, but you're right, that wasn't the real reason I took the job. I liked the idea of taking it easy for a while." He shot me a wry grin. "And look where that's taken me."

"She's fallen in love with you..."

"Right."

"You can't help it, Steve. That you're loveable. Women can't resist you."

He looked back at me with that sexy grin magnified. "What about you, Story?"

I felt my cheeks burn. "I'm the exception."

He laughed, didn't say anything. I didn't say anything.

A few golfers passed by and waved.

A breeze came through and cooled my cheeks.

I breathed in, breathed out. Coming out here with him was not a good idea. Because I was not the exception.

I was too attracted to him to hide it. And I had to hide it and I had to fight it. I finally found my voice to ask, "What are you going to do, about Carolyn's crush on you?"

He shrugged. "Don't know yet. I'm being used. And I hate that."

"I don't blame you."

He reached over and took my hand. "Let me go to California with you. Please?"

His touch burned my skin. I took my hand back. "No. If you really want to help me, stay here, with Carolyn. You can help me more from here than out in California."

It was true.

He held my gaze and sighed. "Okay."

"Thank you."

"The problem is, it will mean Carolyn and I will be spending even more time together," he said.

I slid him a sly smile. "Poor you."

He gave me an even slyer smile back. "Yes, poor me. I don't know how long I can hold her off." He took my hand again. "I can't help the effect I have on women, Story. So, hurry up and find Nanette, will you?"

———

Hurry up and find Nanette...hurry up and find Nanette...hurry up and find Nanette.

Hells bells. I'd nearly had her in my grasp at the airport, but she'd gotten away. Now I'd have to fly to California to find her.

On the way to my office, I stopped at the Exploring the World

Travel Agency to find out how much it would cost to fly to the City of Angels.

Having never stepped foot in a travel agency before, the exotic posters on the walls put me in an adventurous mood as soon as I walked in the door.

Paris. London. The Swiss Alps. Honolulu. Beautiful, faraway places I could only imagine jetting off to. Someday. After I made it big.

"Where would you like to go today?" A woman seated at the desk nearest the door greeted me with a smile. The kind of smile that said she'd like nothing more than to help me go somewhere dreamy.

I smiled back, feeling guilty that I was only there to ask the price of an airplane ticket. One that no matter how much it cost would be something I couldn't afford. "Well..." I cleared my throat. "I'm interested in finding out about flights to Los Angeles. I, uh...I'm not ready to go today, but I might need to fly there soon. And I was wondering..."

"From Philadelphia?" She grabbed her glasses, which were sitting on top of a pile of brochures and slipped them on. Then she reached for a large, thick book and pulled it toward her.

"Yes, that's right."

She nodded and opened the book. "Philadelphia to Los Angeles. Let's see...do you have an approximate idea of the date?"

"Not exactly."

Her smile slipped. "I'll need a date, dear. Let's pick one to check. Say, two days from now?"

I nodded. "Okay. Sure."

She flipped through pages of extremely fine print, which I assumed listed airline flights for all over the world. "Let's see, TWA has a flight that leaves at seven a.m. Nonstop, too. Very nice." She glanced back up at me, named a price that wasn't so nice, and picked up the phone. "I could call the airline and book you now."

I shook my head, swallowing hard to keep my pride intact. The seven o'clock flight was probably the one that my Nanette look-alike had taken, which at least I now knew was nonstop. Only it was nothing I could afford.

"I need to wait," I said. "I'm afraid I'm not quite ready yet. But thanks for the information."

"Certainly." She cocked her head. "Come back when you're ready. My name's Patricia." She handed me her business card, very fancy lettering, with the image of an airplane flying above a billowy white cloud. "By the way, where do you plan to stay when you get to L.A.? Will you need hotel reservations? I could help you with those as well."

I hadn't thought about that. "Yes, I suppose I would need a hotel."

"Will you be traveling alone?"

"Yes. Yes, I will."

She put down her glasses. "Is this for business?"

"Yes, but it's personal. I mean, for my personal business."

"I see." She looked at me like she didn't really see. "Would you need to rent a car, then? Los Angeles has no real public transportation. You will need a car to get anywhere."

Now I was really wasting her time, and mine. Things were looking bleak indeed if I had to pay for a hotel and rental car, too. I decided to play along and see how bleak. "Yes, certainly. I will also need a car."

She reached for another slimmer book, opened it, flipped through it, then quoted what it would cost for a rent-a-car for a week.

I did a pretty good job of not gasping.

"Thank you, thank you very much," I said, tucking her card it in my purse. "You've been very helpful." I turned and headed for the door before she could ask for my name and phone number, so she could start booking my trip.

I took a deep breath when I got back to my T-Bird.

Now, at least I knew. Knew what a trip to L.A. would cost, and that there was no way I was going.

Unless...

I drove to my office, thinking. I needed to go see Dr. Paulson again. Ask him if Nanette had any friends in California. If she did, I'd ask my parents for a loan. I didn't know how I'd ever be able to pay them back.

But I'd find a way.

TWENTY

It was four-thirty by the time I got to my office.

I'd stopped at home to change out of my sundress and into something fresher and make myself a tuna fish sandwich for a late-lunch-early dinner while I was at it.

I planned to type up my daily report and then head over to Dr. Paulson's office.

But Dora and Charlie Macy changed my plans.

I found them camped out in front of my locked office door, sitting on the floor, Charlie with his long legs spread out, taking up much of the hallway, Dora beside him, crossed legged.

"I told them I had no idea when and if you'd be in today," Wendy called out to me from her desk. "But they insisted on waiting."

I couldn't imagine what they wanted. Especially when they greeted me with matching scowls.

"It's about time you got here." Charlie bounded to his feet and came toward me. "We been waiting for hours."

"That's right." Dora scrambled up and faced me with a frightened child look in her eyes. "We weren't leaving, was we, Charlie?"

Still confused, I dug my key out of my purse, unlocked the door, and ushered them in.

I sat down behind my desk, then, leaning forward, folded my hands, acting as if their presence was perfectly normal. It wasn't, it felt weird. Still. "Have you heard from Nanette?" I asked. "Is that why you're here?"

"No." Charlie glared at me. "Have *you*? That's why we come here."

"No. No news yet." I narrowed my eyes at him. "How did you find my office?"

"You gave us your business card, lady. Remember?"

"Oh, yes, of course." I looked at Dora. "Where are your children?"

"Cut the crap," Charlie snapped. "As if you really care."

"They're with Charlie's sister," Dora said. "And Charlie, be nice. She was just being polite."

I was more confused than ever but decided to keep being polite. That old adage about catching more flies with honey and all. For some reason, he was riled up. I needed to stay cool. "How can I help you, folks? I wish I had some good news to give you about Nanette, but I'm afraid I have none. Not yet."

Charlie nodded at Dora. She squeezed her eyes closed, in a way that again reminded me of a child, this time one who was about to cry. Only, when she opened them, they were dry. "I'm really, really worried about my sister. So worried I can't sleep."

"I'm sorry to hear that. I'm trying my best to find her. And rest assured, when I do, I'll let you know."

"How come we ain't seen nothing about Nanette in the papers?"

Charlie came toward me. "That's why we come here, cause how else we going to know anything? Why ain't the world looking for her? A sweet innocent lady like her? A rich doctor's wife?"

His words didn't match his tone. His words conveyed concern. His tone was mocking.

It made me wary. "Martin Paulson wants to keep his wife's disappearance private. For the sake of his patients. But the police are looking for her, and so am I."

Charlie liked my answer, which made me even warier. A look of triumph spread over his face as he grinned at Dora, then flashed me an arrogant smile. "Just what I thought."

"Charlie..." Dora shook her head.

"Dora." He barked her name. "Tell her. Tell her, Dora."

Hesitant, Dora looked at me, then at Charlie. She swallowed and took a deep breath. "I'm so upset about my beloved sister being missing that I want it in the news."

Beloved sister? Nanette had abandoned her years ago. "I don't understand." I waved a hand. "You want what in the news?"

Charlie snorted. "Explain yourself, Dora. Get on with it, woman."

Dora shook her head, looking miserable. "You tell her, Charlie."

"Damn you!" He pounded his fist on my desk, making me jump. "Okay then, listen up Miss Detective Lady—my cousin's a newspaper reporter. And we're going to tell him all about Nanette. Tell him she's missing. And that nobody seems to care, especially her rich doctor husband. Who's keeping it quiet, so he doesn't upset his pregnant patients, because wouldn't that be a shame?"

He gave me a smirk that chilled my blood. "I think people will want to know about that, don't you? Sounds like a mighty good story to me. People might even wonder if he murdered her. Might even make the front page of those newspapers they sell next to the cash register at the grocery store."

"But that's not true." I looked at Dora, but she wouldn't meet my eye. "Dr. Paulson does care about Nanette. That's why he hired me."

"You're not doing a very good job." Charlie stomped his foot.

"Wait! I told you—"

"Shut up. You ain't found her—so why wouldn't you want the public's help?" Charlie wiggled his eyebrows in such an exaggerated, mocking way that I wondered what he really wanted.

If Nanette was hiding out in California, for whatever reason, she'd go more underground if she thought everybody in the country was looking for her. I couldn't tell him that, of course, and I couldn't let it happen. I sighed. "What do you want, Charlie?"

"Take us to meet Doc Paulson."

"Why?"

He folded his arms across his chest. "So, we can tell him to his face."

"Tell him what?"

Charlie chuckled. "That for the right price, me and Dora will keep our mouths shut. We won't go see my reporter cousin. We won't go to no newspapers. We won't go on the T.V. news."

"And then?"

"You go on looking for Nanette as long as you want, lady, and all will be swell."

———

Charlie was clever, I had to give him that.

He clearly hadn't kidnapped Nanette, but he was going to make Martin Paulson pay another way.

By blackmail.

By smearing the doctor's reputation unless he cooperated.

Charlie clearly didn't care if I ever found Nanette, although I suspected Dora did. She just lacked the courage to say so.

I picked up the phone and dialed Dr. Paulson's office and asked his receptionist if I could speak to him right away, that it was an emergency. Fortunately, he was between delivering babies and had a few minutes to give me.

When I explained that Nanette's sister and her husband were in my office, demanding to see him, he invited us to meet him at his home in an hour. He was no fool. He could tell by the tone of my voice that things were tense and in no way did he want us showing up at his practice.

He gave me his address and hung up.

Dora and Charlie followed me to the Main Line in their rusty Ford pickup truck, with an engine so loud it announced our arrival as we pulled into the long driveway of the Paulson mansion.

It was only a block away from the Lowell's place, and larger and grander than theirs, which was saying something. White brick with black shutters on its many windows. Two-story and sprawling, Roman-style pillars flanking the front door.

The spacious front yard was a rose garden, where red, yellow, and white flowers bloomed.

Dr. Paulson opened the door before I could knock, ushered us in, and locked it. "I was watching for you out the window." He gave Dora a tentative smile. "You must be..."

"Dora Macy, and this is her husband, Charlie," I said. "Thank you for agreeing to meet us on such short notice."

"Of course. Come in, come in." He waved a hand to follow him into his living room, dimly lit, cool, and subdued, with dark leather furniture, oriental carpets, and a marble fireplace.

Dora looked around, wide-eyed. Charlie's eyes held an ominous gleam.

Dr. Paulson, looking nervous and uncomfortable, waved a shaky hand. "Please, have a seat. He lowered himself down into one of two leather chairs angled before the fireplace.

I took the other as Dora and Charlie perched themselves on a sofa facing the hearth.

A painting above the mantle caught my eye. It was lovely. And it struck me as ironically sad. A woman, garbed in a flowing white gown, was strolling through a sunlit meadow, a rapturous smile on her face.

Nanette. Posing like the angel she wasn't.

Dr. Paulson was studying Dora's face. "You look like her, you know. I didn't believe Miss Smith when she told me Nanette had a sister. But now, I must admit the resemblance is unmistakable."

Dora's lips quivered in a tentative smile. "Really, do you think so?"

"Yeah, Dora, he thinks so." Charlie's tone was snide. His eyes cut to the doctor's startled frown. "But we ain't here to talk about family resemblances."

"What are you here for...exactly?" Dr. Paulson stood and jammed his hands in the pockets of his gray trousers. "I could tell by the little that Detective Smith told me on the phone that it was important. And I was anxious to meet Dora, anyway, so that's why I invited you to my home. I was shocked to learn Nanette had a sister, and I apologize for not inviting you sooner, but I've been going through an extremely difficult time."

He turned and looked at the painting above the mantle, then back to Dora. "I'm not myself, so forgive me, I'm a nervous wreck. I also can't imagine why Nanette never told me about you."

He sat back down, fished a handkerchief out of the pocket of his starched white dress shirt, and dabbed his eyes with it.

"She never told you about me because she wanted to start a brand-new life when she left the orphanage," Dora said, no longer trying to hide her bitterness. "And I wasn't permitted to be part of it."

Martin Paulson shook his head. "I'm sorry. I had no idea."

"Apparently, Nanette did a pretty good job of leaving her past behind," Charlie said, his tone smooth and sarcastic. Tense and glowering, he looked like a copra ready to spring. "My wife accepted that Nanette had created a new identity for herself, so she stayed away. But now that her sister is missing, Dora is beside herself with grief. Ain't that right, Dora?"

Dora nibbled at a finger. "That's right."

Dr. Paulson glanced anxiously at Charlie. "I'm pleased that you folks came to see me. I wish we could have met under better circumstances. But I assure you that when Nanette is found she and I will have you here often. You will be part of our lives from now on."

I wished it could have been left at that. Wished we could have parted on a friendly basis. Wished that Martin Paulson's apologies would have been enough.

But Charlie wasn't interested in playing nice.

"Where is Nanette, doctor?" He sprang to his feet. "Where is she?"

Startled, the doctor met his angry gaze. "I don't know. That's the problem, good sir."

"Don't 'good sir' me...I want to know why more isn't being done to find my sister-in-law."

The doctor stood and faced him. "The police and Miss Smith are desperately searching for her. What more do you want?"

"Funny you should ask." Charlie waved his arms in the air. "How about putting posters up all over town? Missing-lady posters, with Nanette's picture on them? How about going to the newspapers? How about going on TV? Or...if you won't, maybe Dora and I should."

Dr. Paulson looked at me, clearly confused at Charlie's emotional outburst about a woman he'd never met.

"This is why the Macys wanted to meet with you." I gave him an apologetic grimace. "I'm sorry, but there was nothing I could do. If I didn't bring them here, they would have caused a scene in your office in front of your patients."

He blinked and blinked again. "I don't understand. What do you want, Mr. Macy? Miss Smith is aware that I want this to remain out of the public eye. I assume she explained that to you."

"Money," I whispered, then said it louder, "he wants money."

"Yep." Charlie chuckled. "That's right. Dora and I will keep quiet and not tell the whole world how upset we are about her dear sister being missing—for the right price."

Realization dawned in the doctor's eyes. He shook his head. "Are you blackmailing me?"

Charlie shrugged. "Call it what you want."

"How much do you want?"

Charlie grinned. "A thousand bucks. For now. And then another thousand a week from now and then every week until Nanette is found."

I gasped. His demands were outrageous. And this was partially my fault. By tracking down the Macys, I'd inadvertently awakened a sleeping giant, adding to my client's already unbearable situation.

To my surprise, Dr. Paulson didn't flinch. He looked at Dora, sadly out of place amid such opulence in her faded brown dress and scuffed work shoes. Then at Charlie, in his dirt-streaked farmer's overalls, cool and defiant.

Clearly angry but resigned, the doctor mumbled, "I'll get my wallet."

He disappeared into an adjacent room, then came back. Slowly counting out the money, he handed the bills to Dora. "I'm sorry we had to meet this way," he told her softly, with a degree of compassion that neither she nor her husband deserved. "I'm also sorry that you must need money so badly that you would do this to me."

Dora stared at the bills in her hand. Then she glanced at Charlie, gave a loud sob, and ran to the front door.

We heard it slam shut.

Charlie raced after her. We heard it slam shut again.

Martin Paulson went back to his chair and sank down into it. He leaned his head back and closed his eyes. He grew so quiet and so still, I wondered if he'd forgotten I was there.

Or, if he expected me to show myself out.

Or, if he was working up the energy to fire me, then personally show me out.

I stood up to go.

He opened his eyes and met my anxious gaze. "Money means

nothing to me when the woman I love more than anyone in the world is gone, detective."

"I'm sorry, doctor. I never imagined this would happen."

"Of course not." There was sorrow in his eyes, but I also saw something else. Hope. "I'm not blaming you, but then again, I don't expect to be giving them any more money, Miss Smith. Do you know why?"

"Yes." I knew why. "Because I'll find Nanette before the week is up."

"That's right." He sat up and squinted at me. "And you know why I believe that?"

I hesitated. "Because I'm a good detective?"

He gave a pained smile. "That remains to be seen. But I do I believe you've discovered some things about Nanette that you've been holding back from me. Which I want you to tell me. Right now."

———

"Nanette might be in California." The words just flew out of my mouth, and what a relief.

I was done sparing this man's feelings. He wanted to know everything. I was happy to tell him everything—the good, the bad, and the really bad.

What was good? That it looked like Nanette was alive. Bad? That she'd lied to him about many things. Really bad? That she'd been cheating on him with his best friend.

He listened. The color drained from his face as I summed up what I'd learned and what I'd witnessed. "No, no, no, no, no..." he said when I stopped and eyed him with sympathy. "No...this can't be."

"But you're not totally surprised, doctor, are you?" I asked softly. "That's why no posters around town, no stories in the papers, no heartfelt pleas to the public. It wasn't just to spare your patients, preserve your practice. Deep down, you knew."

He went over to the mantel, and with his hands clasped behind his back, stared up at the angelic portrait of his wife. For a long time.

Then he came around and met my gaze. "But why would she go to California? Why would Nanette—assuming this woman you saw was Nanette—why would she go there?"

"I was hoping you could tell me. Does she know anyone in Los Angeles?"

He shook his head. "I don't think so."

"What about her friends from nursing school? Did she keep in touch with any of her classmates?"

"No...wait." He held up a finger. "There was one. Only one, because Nanette left nursing behind when she married me. But she and this woman had grown really close in school, so they stayed in touch, writing letters mostly, an occasional phone call." He pressed the palm of his hand to his forehead. "What was her name?"

"Did you ever meet her?"

"No, I don't think so. As I recall, she took a job out West immediately after graduation." His eyes lit up. "I think maybe California. Could it be?"

My heart started racing. Maybe, maybe, maybe. "Think, doctor, think. Can you remember her name?"

He shook his head slowly back and forth, then he pointed to a massive desk on the other side of the room. "Like I said, they wrote to each other. I think Nanette kept her stamps and stationery in there."

He walked over, yanked open a side drawer, rummaged around,

then held up a pale blue envelope. There was a card inside, which he pulled out and read. "Faith Young," he said, his voice tight. "That's her." He tapped on the envelope. "There's no return address, but it's postmarked Los Angeles, mailed last month."

"Bingo." I couldn't keep the excitement out of my voice. I held out my hand. "Can I see the card?"

It contained nothing special, a watercolor image of bluebirds on the front, and inside a scrawled message that Faith hadn't heard from Nanette for a while and hoped all was well.

Dr. Paulson took the card back from me. "So, what does this mean? What do we do now?"

I held his anxious gaze. "I need to go to California. And you need to help me get there."

"What? How?"

"I went to a travel agency to see how much it would cost to fly to Los Angeles. And it costs a lot, doctor. More than I can afford. Much more."

He groaned. "I should have known."

Alarmed, I asked, "*What* should you have known?"

"I hired a rookie in the business. Someone just getting started who's operating on a barebones budget. And this is what I get."

Alarm turned to anger, which ballooned in my chest. "Just what are you insinuating?"

"I've just shelled out a thousand dollars in blackmail money that I should not have had to pay." He waved a hand. "And now you expect me to shell out at least that much or more to send you to California and back—to look for a woman who might not even be my wife."

"There's a good chance she is your wife," I said through clenched teeth.

"And if she's not? What happens if you get there and find out she's not? What then, Miss Smith?"

"It's a chance we will have to take, doctor."

"No." His eyes snapped fury and frustration. "It's a chance you'll have to take. Because I will pay for your trip, for your airfare, for your hotel, for a rent-a-car, but only on one condition. That if you come back without my wife, you will pay me back. Every penny."

Twenty-One

It was risky. But what choice did I have? To find Nanette, I had to go to California.

Before I went, I needed to get the stitches out of my hand. And let Steve know my plans.

The next morning, I went to the hospital emergency room, got the stitches removed, then drove to Carolyn's country club, where I found him. Or, rather, them. Steve and Carolyn were on the tennis courts this time. Playing doubles with another couple, which, by the look of things, was an intensely competitive match.

I walked over to the court and sat down on a bench to watch and wait. Carolyn spotted me and missed the ball. She stopped the game.

"Story! Again? Really? What do you want now? Tell me you've found Nanette or…" She jerked her thumb in the direction of the exit. "Go and leave me alone."

I stood up. "I'm here to talk to Steve. I just need a minute."

She pointed her tennis racket in his direction. "Well, Steve's busy, as you can see. So…"

Steve calmly went and picked up the ball and came over to me. His face and arms and legs were covered with a fine sheen of sweat, and in his tennis whites, he looked more handsome than ever. I tried not to notice.

"I've got a minute, Story," he said. "Is this something we need to discuss in private?"

Carolyn looked like she might explode if I said yes.

"No." I flashed her a sweet smile, then waved a hand in apology to the other couple for interrupting their game. I looked back at Steve. "I just wanted to let you know that I'm planning to fly to California tomorrow. I'll be in touch when I get back."

"Nanette's in California?" Carolyn looked at me like I'd lost a few screws.

"Story must have a good reason for going." Steve gave me a concerned frown. "Are you going alone?"

"Yes, and I'm not sure how long I'll be gone, but it's for the reason we discussed." I pressed my lips together and tried to signal with my eyes that I dare not say more.

He tossed Carolyn the ball, put his hand on my arm, and steered me away. "Story and I do need to talk," he called over his shoulder. "I'll be right back."

"No!" Carolyn screamed and stamped her foot.

We turned to look at her.

Everyone on all the courts stopped playing and turned to look at her.

Waving her tennis racket like a wild woman, Carolyn threw it down, like a petulant child, and stomped over to Steve and me.

"What's this secret you have to discuss with my bodyguard?" she hissed, thrusting her face inches from mine. "I think you're creating drama just so you can have an excuse to be around Steve. What a pathetic detective! You have no idea what you're doing! Get out of my life and get out of Steve's life and stay out!"

Too shocked to defend myself, I just stared at her.

She grabbed Steve's arm and yanked him away from me.

Clearly furious, Steve shook himself free. "What are you doing, Carolyn? Calm down!"

She shook her head. "I'm sorry Steve," she whined. "I'm sorry that I ever got you involved in Martin Paulson's problem."

Martin Paulson's problem? Anger surged through me. "We're talking about your best friend, Carolyn. I'm searching for your best friend!"

"Then go find her already." She sniffed. Waved her arms. "Go to California—if that's where you think she is. What a joke...you're a joke."

Steve met my gaze. I could tell he was trying to keep his anger in check, but he looked ready to explode. "Story's doing a fantastic job. She's making amazing progress. She just came here to let me know where she's headed next. What's wrong with that?"

"Plenty!" Carolyn screamed. "There's plenty wrong with that. You're supposed to be guarding me, not traipsing off with *her*." Carolyn gave me a shove.

I stumbled back but didn't fall.

Carolyn ran over and threw her arms around Steve.

Steve's anger vanished, morphing instead into disgust. I could see it in his eyes as he met my gaze. He was disgusted with Carolyn. And disgusted with himself.

"Let go of me, Carolyn," he said. "Let go, now."

"No…"

"Let go—because I quit…"

"No, no, no…"

"I'm done being your bodyguard, your plaything, your toy!"

She backed away with a sob. "No. You can't quit. You can't leave me…"

"Steve, what are you doing?" I hiss-whispered.

"I'm going to California with you. I won't let you go alone."

"No." I shook my head. "You're not going. This is my case."

Carolyn was staring at us aghast, tears streaming down her face. "You can't quit, Steve," she wailed. "I need you."

"No, you don't." Steve took my arm. "Come on, we need to find a place where we can talk privately."

I pulled away. "No. This isn't right. You need to talk to Carolyn. You owe her that."

He shook his head and grabbed my hand. "She and I can talk later. Let's go."

He hurried me along. I looked back at Carolyn. She looked like her world had just ended.

I felt guilty, and alarmed. "What are you doing, Steve?" I pulled him to a stop. "This isn't right. I know you're fed up with your job, but this isn't a good way to quit."

He whispered in my ear, "I want to see what Alec will do."

"What? What do you mean?"

"I want to see what he will he do now. Things are becoming mighty uncomfortable between me and Carolyn, dangerously so. I can't let this go on. I just can't."

I looked back at the tennis courts. Carolyn seemed frozen in place.

The other couple was trying to console her, the woman had her arm around her shoulder.

"What do you think Alec will do?" I asked as we moved toward the pool.

"That's what I want to find out. It should be interesting. In the meantime, this will free me up to go to L.A. with you."

He still had a firm grip on my hand, and I pulled us both to a stop again. I gave him an I'm-serious look. "I do not want you to come with me. This is my case and I have things under control. It turns out Nanette has a friend who lives out there. I have an address and everything I need."

He let go of my hand and narrowed his eyes. "What do you mean? How are you paying for this?"

"Martin Paulson. I brought him up to date. It was time, and he was ready." I bit down on my lip. I wouldn't mention Dora and Charlie. Steve didn't have to know about their shameful scheme.

He shook his head. "My God, Story—did you tell him about Alec?"

"Yes."

"And...?"

"And he's resigned to learning the truth. And more desperate than ever for me to find Nanette. Which is why he's paying for my flight, hotel expenses and to rent a car."

Steve studied my face, like he was trying to read my mind. He knew there was more. "And what if you don't find Nanette out there? What then?"

I shrugged. "I'll have to cross that bridge—"

"Don't give me that. He only gave you another week. What if you run out of time and come up empty?"

He knew. I might as well tell him. "I'll be fired." I shrugged again. "And...I'll have to pay him back."

"That's outrageous. And no way to do business."

I sighed. "You're right. But I'm going to do this. Because I'm sure the woman I saw get on that plane was Nanette."

A slow smile formed on Steve's face. "You're a gutsy woman, Story."

"Thanks." I returned his smile.

"But a stubborn one, too."

"If that's what it takes to be gutsy."

"And you're really not going to let me go with you, are you?"

"Nope."

He sighed.

"But I do want to come with *you*, Steve."

"What? Where?"

"When you and Carolyn go back to her house—which you'll have to do to collect your things. And to tell Alec you're quitting. I want to be there."

He nodded, holding my gaze. "Why?"

"I think you know."

He gave me that slow smile again. "Oh...so you can see Alec's reaction when I tell him I'm quitting?"

I gave him my best gutsy grin. "Yep. Great detectives think alike."

———

I'd hoped to remain a fly on the wall during the Lowell drama I was certain would unfold.

That didn't happen. I felt more like a fly dodging a fly swatter.

Alec eagerly cast me in the role of villainess, which I should have seen coming. Although in my defense, I hadn't expected him to be waiting for us the minute we walked through his door.

"What's *she* doing here?" He looked at Carolyn and Steve, then waved his hand wildly in my direction as we entered the living room. "Get out Miss Smith, now, before I throw you out."

I suspected, by the thunderously annoyed expression on his face, Carolyn must have called him from the club and told him to get home immediately. And to brace for trouble. He was dressed in an impressively tailored black suit with a pin-striped tie, and she'd probably pulled him out of a very important meeting.

My being there didn't help.

I'd followed her and Steve from the club. Steve drove Carolyn's Lincoln Continental. Of course. He was her chauffer as well as her babysitter. I didn't even know what kind of car he drove.

Not that it mattered.

And anyway, he wouldn't have to be her chauffer anymore. That thought made me smile as I took a seat in front of the fireplace, ignoring Alec's order to leave.

Carolyn and Steve stood side by side, facing Alec. Steve didn't waste any time, announcing that he was quitting. "I assume Carolyn called you and told you, and yes, it is true. I don't believe Carolyn needs protection any longer, if she ever did, and therefore, I quit. Effective today."

Alec glared at Steve, then shook his fist at me. "Why are you still here? I said get out. You get out."

"No." Steve turned to Carolyn. "Let Story stay. This has nothing to do with her."

Carolyn pouted. "I think a lot of this has to do with her."

Alec stomped over to me and our eyes locked. I gave him my best unruffled smile. He narrowed his gaze. For a second I thought he was going to grab me and haul me to the door, which would have been interesting.

Because I would not have gone quietly.

He was too much of a gentleman, though. Too well bred. Too afraid of what it would look like to start a fight with a woman.

I'd come to witness Alec's reaction to Steve's resignation. Here it was. He was clearly outraged that he'd lost control. Of Steve, and of me.

Enjoying myself, I didn't move. I gave Alec a stone-faced, raised-eyebrow stare and waited to see what he'd do. Knowing what I did about him gave me a feeling of power. Which I could tell confused him, because he didn't know that I knew what I knew.

Finally, after several moments, he gave up on me and turned to his bigger problem.

Steve.

"I don't understand why you are abandoning us now." Alec waved a hand at him. "Explain that to me, please."

"I'm not abandoning you." Steve glanced at Carolyn. "It's just that I don't believe your wife is in any danger, and I have other things I want to do with my life right now."

"Story's going to California," Carolyn sang out. "I bet—"

"I'm not going with her," Steve said. "If that's what you're thinking."

"Did you say Story is going to California?" Alec eyed me with suspicion. "Why? Aren't you supposed to be looking for Nanette Paulson? Did Martin fire you?"

I felt my face flush. Damn it. I didn't want Alec to know I was going to California. "Oh...well...I'm not going there immediately." I gave him a tight smile. "It's just that I'm planning to go there on vacation. After I find Nanette. You know, to celebrate."

Alec snickered. "And just how close are you to finding her?"

Another thing I didn't want him to know. "I'm getting there."

"That's not a reassuring answer."

"It's all I can tell you at the moment."

Alec grunted, then turned back to Steve. "In the meantime, while Miss Lady Detective is getting there, as she so cutely puts it, Carolyn might still be in danger because you are going to leave her unprotected. I can't believe you would do that."

Steve shrugged. "There are plenty of bodyguards in this town. I'll find you a good one."

Carolyn grabbed his arm. "I don't want anybody else, Steve, I want you."

Pleading. Frantic. The look she gave him was wretched. She was desperately in love with him, and she didn't care who knew it.

Any man who loved his wife and valued his marriage would have reacted with alarm.

Not Alec. He chuckled with glee. "See, how can you resist that pretty face, Steve? She only feels safe with you. Come on, stay. I'll double your pay."

"I can't be bought," Steve said. "So, no."

"Please!"

We all looked over at the staircase. Freddie stood at the top, clutching the banister, looking panicked.

We all turned to watch him race down the stairs. "Please, please, please don't quit, Steve." He was close to tears. "I need you. My mom needs you. Don't leave us now."

I'd forgotten all about Freddie. Apparently, the others had, too. He was distraught, which surprised and saddened me. I hadn't thought about what Steve's plan would do to him, or that it would upset him. The cocky teenager had been replaced by a little boy.

I glanced at Steve, who looked as rattled as I felt. "I'm sorry, Freddie," he said. "I'll miss you, but I need to get on with my life, get back to being a P.I. You understand."

Freddie shook his head. "No."

"Don't worry, I'll come back and visit sometimes. We'll keep making music together. Maybe I'll even help you start a band."

Freddie shook his head harder. "No. You're my friend. I don't want you to go."

"I must."

"Why must you?" Freddie demanded. He jabbed his finger at me. "It's because of her, isn't it? You're sweet on her."

———

Me? Why did the conversation keep coming back to me? I stood up. Time to go.

"I don't know what you're talking about, Freddie." Steve put up a hand to stop me. "My leaving has nothing to do with Story."

"So, what's she doing here, then? Why is she always hanging around?"

"What are you talking about?" Alec's head swiveled back and forth between me and his son.

"She's come to the house when you're at work, Dad. And she's always at the club. It's ridiculous and annoying."

"Is that true, Carolyn?" Alec snapped.

"She only came here once." Carolyn's lower lip trembled. "And she has been to the club many times, but only to look for clues about Nanette. Although lately it has gotten ridiculous."

"Out." Alec jerked his thumb at me. "Get out now. Before I call the police."

He didn't have to ask me again. I'd seen and heard all I needed to, and more.

TWENTY-TWO

My dad agreed to drive me to the airport the next morning to catch my ten o'clock flight to L.A. He wasn't thrilled about me going but wanted to make sure his little girl got off safely.

My bags sat by the door, and I had my ticket securely tucked in my purse before the sun came up. I'd been too nervous to sleep. I was scared to fly. Afraid I'd miss my plane. And wracked with worry about whether I was doing the right thing.

When someone knocked on my door at six-thirty, I about jumped out of my skin. Dad wasn't due to arrive for another two hours.

I opened the door a crack and sucked in a breath. "Steve."

How did he even know my address...? Stupid question. He was a detective. But...?

Peering at him in the dim early morning light, I could see he was upset. Uncharacteristically disheveled. Wrinkled khaki pants. Wrinkled T-shirt. His hair sticking up in places, as if he hadn't bothered to comb it.

"Can I come in?"

I didn't like the look in his eyes either. "Of course, of course." I ushered him into my tiny living room, confused. "I told you my dad's taking me to the airport. You didn't have to—"

"No. I'm not here about that. I wanted to catch you before you left. It's about Carolyn."

"Carolyn?"

"She's been rushed to the hospital. Emergency."

"Oh my God." He wasn't making sense. "What...why?"

"I'm not sure. Freddie found her unconscious, pounded on my bedroom door, woke me up. There was an empty bottle of sleeping pills next to her bed. She was barely breathing. I called for an ambulance."

He still wasn't making sense. "But where was Alec?"

"Gone."

"Gone? What do you mean—gone? And why were you even there? I thought you'd quit."

He took a deep, shaky breath. "After you left, Alec and I got into a big argument. He said he had an important meeting later in Atlantic City, and that it would go late, and that he had no idea when he'd be home."

"Atlantic City, that's a crock. He likes to use that place as a cover for whatever shady stuff he's really doing."

"I don't know. No telling. He ended up pleading with me to at least stay the night, pack in the morning. I agreed. Didn't see the harm. And I wanted to spend some time with Freddie, anyway, calm him down, convince him I wasn't abandoning him, that I'd still be his friend."

"So, Alec ended up not coming home?"

"Seems like it. Freddy said he slept poorly, off and on, because he was waiting to hear his dad come home. Finally, around five, he decided to peek into his parent's room because he'd never heard him. The poor boy. That's when he found his mother alone. He tried to wake her up, but he couldn't. It's a good thing I was there."

"How was Freddie the night before?"

"We talked for a while and then turned in around nine."

"And Carolyn?"

"She wasn't speaking to me. And I have no idea when she went to bed." Steve raked his fingers through his hair. "I can't stop blaming myself for this."

"For what? This is not your fault."

"I should never have taken this job. Or at least I should have gotten out sooner, when I started suspecting I was being used."

"You stayed to help me." Now, I felt guilty. "Do you think Carolyn tried to commit suicide?"

He backed over to my sofa and collapsed onto it. "I don't know. I swear to God, I had no idea she took sleeping pills. Never saw any signs of it. She never mentioned to me that she did. I never got the impression she needed them."

"And the prescription?"

"In her name." He met my gaze with narrowed eyes that held grief and anger. "Except I don't believe she'd do this to herself. This is not Carolyn. She wouldn't. And she wouldn't do this to Freddie."

"People do crazy things when they're in love, Steve." I went and sat down on the other end of the sofa and turned to face him. "When you told Carolyn you were leaving her, maybe she just couldn't take it."

He closed his eyes, nodded his head, then opened them and looked at me. "She did feel abandoned by Alec. But having me in her life made it okay." His tone held bitterness and guilt. "She was clearly hoping that I was in love with her, and then when I said I was leaving..." He shook his head. "She couldn't have...wouldn't have...but maybe that's what Alec wants everyone to believe."

"What?"

"Maybe he wants people to think she tried to kill herself. But maybe he did come home last night. Maybe he poisoned her."

"*Attempted murder*?"

Steve slapped his knee. "Maybe when Alec saw his little scheme wasn't going to work, that Carolyn and I weren't going to run off into the sunset together, that she wasn't going to initiate a divorce, maybe he resorted to plan B."

"Murder," I whispered.

"It's possible."

I stared at him. "What are you going to do now?"

"Go to the hospital. See how she is. God help her, she's got to live."

"What about Alec?"

"It's too early to contact anyone at his office. He left no clue as to what hotel he might be staying at in Atlantic City, if that's where he really is."

"And Freddie? Where's he?"

"He's home, alone. I told him to stay put and stay calm and that I would go be with his mom and that everything would be okay." He slid me a sideways glance. "But here I am with you."

I felt my face flush. Freddy's words the night before haunted me. But this was no time to think about the undeniable something that was going on between Steve and me. The something that part of me didn't want and the rest of me very much did.

"Thanks...thanks for stopping by," I said. I put a hand to my forehead. "This is awful and upsetting and I wish there was something I could do, but it can't change my plans. I've got to go to California."

He stood up. "I know. But I want you to keep in touch."

I stood and faced him. "Yes, of course. I'm worried about Carolyn, and this could have something to do with Nanette."

"When you get to your hotel, call my office and leave Alice the phone number."

I nodded. We stared at each other in awkward silence. I didn't want to say goodbye, and I suspected he didn't either.

"Don't worry about any long-distance charges you run up by calling me from out there. I'll pay for them." Steve gave me that slow, eye-crinkling smile of his that always made my heart rate skyrocket.

Long-distance phone call charges had been the last thing on my mind. My blood went hot.

"That's nice of you," I finally managed to say. "I'll call Alice as soon as I get there."

Twenty-Three

"Don't worry, you'll be fine," my dad told me as we hugged goodbye at the American Airlines gate, destination Los Angeles, with a planned stopover in Chicago. "It'll be a long flight, you know, so just take a nap," he said. "And if things get bumpy—and there's a good chance they will—keep that airsickness bag they give you ready, just in case."

Airsickness bag? Great. I was already a mass of quivering nerves before he gave me that helpful advice.

Fortunately, my flight was amazingly smooth. So smooth that I relaxed and enjoyed the stunning view out the window, the meandering rivers, the vast squares of green and golden farmland.

Not only did my breakfast stay down, but so did the full course lunch of grilled chicken, green beans, and baked potato that a cheerful stewardess served me on porcelain china after we left Chicago.

Miraculously, I caught up on my sleep. After the plane touched down in sunny California ten hours after we left Philadelphia, I felt refreshed and energized.

Ready to track down my prey.

Nanette's nursing school friend, Faith Young, lived in Los Angeles, according to the postmark on her card. I just needed to find her address. I also had to assume she might be working as a nurse, probably in a hospital. And if so, I needed to learn which one.

Martin Paulson had agreed to pay the expense of a Hertz Rent a Car for three days. Since he'd footed the bill in advance, a shiny, brand-new blue and white Chevrolet Bel Air convertible awaited me when I got off the plane.

I had to smile. Why not drive a convertible in California, too? Might as well enjoy the balmy weather, blue skies, and palm trees on my make-or-break-my-career adventure.

He'd also given me enough money for three nights in a hotel. I needed to find one that was safe, clean, and conveniently located. Stopping at a gas station just outside the airport, I bought a map, found Hollywood on it, then headed there. Why not? Because in this huge, sprawling region, I'd at least heard of Hollywood.

The land of movie stars, glitz, and glamor.

I had to pinch myself, I couldn't believe I was driving its streets. Wide-eyed and excited, I hoped to spot someone famous. No such luck. I didn't see any movie stars among the beautiful men and women walking up and down the sidewalks. But I did pass some iconic landmarks, including a few movie studios. I couldn't believe I was cruising through this land of dreams, a place I'd heard of all my life.

Then I gripped the wheel and reminded myself I needed to find a place to stay.

I passed several hotels and finally pulled into the parking lot of The Sunset Strip Hotel, where a flashing neon sign proclaimed they had vacancies. It also had a swimming pool out front, and more importantly, a phone booth between the office and the pool, which I was going to need to call Steve's office as well as area hospitals.

The clerk behind the office counter could have been a movie star. Strikingly handsome, like a young Cary Grant, I was mesmerized by his dazzling smile as he quoted me a nightly rate within my budget, collected my money, and handed me a room key.

Lugging my heavy suitcase to my room on the first floor, I felt pretty good about all I'd accomplished so far. I was exhausted, but I'd survived flying on an airplane, I'd navigated the busy highways of Los Angeles during rush hour without wrecking my fancy rental car, and now, I had a safe place to stay.

My room was standard hotel décor, one bed, a bureau, and a clean bathroom. What more did I need?

A phonebook. I needed a phonebook and couldn't find one in the room.

Tossing my suitcase onto the bed, I headed back to the office.

"You'll need dimes for the phone booth for local calls," Young Cary Grant told me, flashing that polished smile again as he pushed the fattest phonebook I'd ever seen across the counter.

I couldn't resist. "You know, you ought to be in pictures. Has anyone ever told you that?"

He laughed. "All the time—and thank you very much. I'm an actor. This is just a part-time job, until I make it big."

"I hope you do make it big." I picked up the phonebook and nodded to a table on the other side of the room. "Do you mind if I go sit over there?"

He lifted a shoulder. "Go right ahead."

I nodded thanks and sat down, quickly flipping to the white pages to search for Faith Young.

There were many Youngs, but no Faith.

A pang of disappointment burst my bubble. Did I really think it was going to be that easy?

I turned to the Yellow Pages and searched for hospitals, then pressed my lips together. More than I'd expected. I pulled a notebook out of my purse, jotted down a bunch of names and numbers, then returned the phonebook as I cashed in a few dollars for a bunch of dimes.

Armed and ready, I headed to the phonebooth.

I wanted to call Alice first, but hesitated, thinking about what time was it was back East. It had to be getting late. Still, I decided to at least try to put a call through to her.

I closed the glass door and dialed the operator. "Long distance please." When she came on, I gave her Steve's number, and told her that his office would be accepting the charges.

"Hello, Story." Alice's cheery voice came across loud and clear. "I've been waiting to hear from you all day. I was afraid to leave until I did. Are you in California?"

"Yes, yes, yes." It was so good to hear her voice. "I'm sorry to have kept you waiting. And I only have three minutes, or you'll get billed extra, so are you ready to take down the name and number of my hotel? I'm in Hollywood."

"Hollywood? How exciting. Of course, dear, go ahead."

I rattled off the name and hotel phone number and then gave her the number marked on the phone in the phone booth, just in case.

"Wonderful," she said. "I will pass this along to Steve. He's still at the hospital. Been there all day."

Carolyn. The poisoning. Alec, where was Alec? The problems in Philadelphia suddenly seemed so far away. And I was running out of minutes.

"Do you have any news about Carolyn?" I held my breath.

"Not yet, dear. But Steve said for you to call anytime, and not to worry about the expense."

"Thank you," I said, touched, and grateful. "I'll call tomorrow when I have news on my end."

I hung up. Fished more dimes out of my wallet. Time to call the hospitals.

I dialed the first one on my list. They'd never heard of Faith Young. I shrugged and dug out another dime.

One hour and many dimes later, I still hadn't found her.

She wasn't working at any of the hospitals on my list. I wondered if she'd changed her name—gotten married—in which case she might not even be working anymore. It was also possible that she'd hated nursing and was now a secretary or a salesclerk or a teacher.

Then what?

Forcing back panic, I went back into the office to ask the clerk if he had any other phonebooks for other areas around L.A.

"Pasadena," he said, handing me a much smaller book. "What exactly are you looking for? Maybe I can help you."

"I'm looking for a woman named Faith Young, who's a nurse. I think she might be working at a hospital around here." I quickly flipped to the Y's and ran my finger down the list of Youngs. No one named Faith. I sighed.

"Why are you looking for her?"

"I'm a private detective." I flipped to the Yellow Pages and searched for hospitals.

"Private detective? Cool."

I glanced up at him and grinned. "Thanks. I think it's cool, for a woman, which is probably what you're thinking."

"I was thinking you should be in pictures. You're pretty enough."

Flattered, I widened my smile. "Thanks, I bet you say that to all the girls."

"Not really. If you want, I can give you the name of my agent."

"Hey, if this detective business doesn't work out, I might take you up on it."

Since my detective business was seriously at stake, I put my eyes back on the Yellow Pages. Only two hospitals were listed: St. Luke, and Huntington.

I jotted down the phone numbers and told the clerk to wish me luck.

"Maybe you will get lucky," he said.

"I hope so, I'm running out of dimes."

This time, though, luck was on my side.

Faith Young worked at St. Luke Hospital.

I almost fell out of the phonebooth. Shoving the door open, I danced my way back to the office.

"She works at St. Luke," I announced. "Now tell me, how far away is Pasadena?"

He beamed. "Not far, eleven or twelve miles. It's an easy drive. Take the Pasadena Freeway. Straight shot."

"Thanks," I said. "I'll head there first thing tomorrow."

It was growing dark. Time to call it a night. And since I was feeling proud of what I'd accomplished, I expected to sleep well.

All I had to do was find St Luke Hospital, learn which shift Faith Young worked, then follow her home.

If my luck held out, Nanette Paulson was staying with her. It was a long shot, but it was the only one I had.

Twenty-Four

The Pasadena Freeway was anything but a straight shot. It was a curvy highway, running between hills along the Arroyo Seco River.

Not a bad drive, once I got onto it without getting killed.

To merge onto the freeway, I had to floor the Chevy, going from a dead stop at the bottom of the ramp to sixty miles an hour in a matter of seconds. All while gritting my teeth and muttering "go, go, go."

It was Sunday morning. Where was everyone was going, and why were they in such a hurry to get there? I didn't have a solid plan for the day because it all depended on whether Faith Young was working.

But it had occurred to me before I left the hotel that I would need an excuse for knocking on her door—and a plausible reason to be invited inside—once I followed her home from the hospital.

I decided I would pretend to be a door-to-door vacuum cleaner saleswoman, which I figured would do the trick. All I needed was a vacuum. Which I borrowed from the hotel, from the middle-aged woman who'd replaced Young Cary Grant on the morning shift. She told me I could borrow the one the maid used, since she didn't work on the Sabbath.

Thirty minutes after leaving Hollywood, I took the off ramp to Pasadena, with an Electrolux in my trunk, and hope in my heart.

Fortunately, St. Luke Hospital was not hard to find. Situated at the edge of a canyon, northeast of downtown, it was an off-white-stucco multi-story structure, with a chapel on one corner and several wings branching off the main building.

In the front lobby, stationed behind a desk, sat a volunteer in a pink uniform wearing a name tag that said "Zelda."

I asked Zelda which floor nurse Faith Young worked on.

She frowned. "Why, I have no idea." She gave me a curious look. "I only have a list of patients. Are you here to visit someone?"

"No. I'm trying to find Miss Young."

"I see." She shrugged. "I'm sorry, but I'm afraid I can't help you."

I couldn't give up. I pressed a finger to my lip. "I'm an old friend of hers, and I've just pulled into town. And I heard she works here. And I was hoping to surprise her. Can you at least tell me if she's working today?"

Awkward. Really awkward. I was fishing. But...

Zelda looked at me with a mix of compassion and uncertainty in her eyes. Which told me she wanted to help but wasn't sure how. "I don't know," she said. "I don't know which nurses work which shifts on which days. It changes all the time, anyway..."

"Any chance you could go ask?"

"Well...I'm not supposed to leave my post." Her eyes brightened at the sight of someone coming down a set of stairs to her left. "Wait, here's Dr. Jadestone now. He's head of medical surgical, perhaps he can help."

Dr. Jadestone was clearly in a rush. "Faith Young? She's working now, seven to three, second floor." He kept going down a hall, disappearing through a set of double doors.

Zelda raised her eyebrows at me. She smiled. "So, there you go, you're in luck. Your friend will be available to meet you later today. Isn't that nice?"

It was great. Only, I didn't know what Faith looked like. "Do you think I could just run up to the second floor really quick, and give her a wave?" I asked, pointing to the set of stairs the doctor had just come down.

Zelda shrugged. "I suppose that would be okay."

"Thanks, you're a peach."

I took the stairs slowly, formulating in my mind what I was going to do next.

I couldn't just go up and introduce myself to nurse after nurse until I found Faith Young. I didn't want her to see me, because later that day I was going to knock on her door and try to sell her a vacuum cleaner.

Pushing open the door to the second-floor wing, an unsettling, empty silence greeted me.

The hallway was lined with half open doors to patient rooms. Suddenly, I remembered how much I hated hospitals. As a teenager, I'd visited my grandmother in one just hours before she died. Now, that old feeling of hopelessness came flooding back.

A nurse came out of one of the rooms and walked toward me. I froze, then relaxed when I saw the name tag pinned to her starched white uniform. Not Faith Young.

"Can I help you?" she asked.

"Uh..." I mumbled. "I think I might be lost."

"Are you looking for a patient?"

Patient? I blurted out the first name that came to my mind. "Wendy Castillo. But I think I might be on the wrong floor..."

"I don't know of any patient by that name. I'm sorry."

"Thanks," Hugging my purse to my side, I gave her a sheepish look. "I think my mother might be looking for Wendy on this floor, too, so I'll just..." I waved my hand. "Keep looking for my mother."

I kept walking, slowly, waiting for her to stop me. But she was clearly too busy to care about confused little old me. When I turned around to look, she was entering another patient's room.

I breathed a sigh of relief and kept going, keeping my head down, trying to look as unobtrusive as possible. I caught a glimpse of patients in rooms that I passed. But didn't see any more nurses until one suddenly skirted out of a room in front of me.

She had dark hair pulled up under her nurse's cap, a sweet face, and big eyes behind wire rim eyeglasses. My breath hitched.

I turned my head, avoiding eye contact, and she kept going down the hall.

Which was a good thing. Because her name tag said Faith Young.

Faith Young walked home from work. Which took me by surprise.

After driving into downtown Pasadena to grab lunch, I'd parked at the back of the hospital lot, waiting for her to come out at three o'clock and get in her car.

Instead, she kept walking, making it difficult for me to follow her in my colorful convertible. I was forced to drive at a slow crawl, keeping her in sight as she made a left turn, then a right, then a bunch more turns before entering an attractive neighborhood of cute, cozy bungalows.

Her house was as cute as the others, if not cuter. Tidy, two-story, with a flower garden, and pots of red and yellow flowers on every step leading up to the front porch.

I watched her climb those steps and disappear inside. So far, I was impressed with Faith Young. She'd carved out a nice life for herself with a rewarding job, at a nice hospital, in a pretty city. Living the California dream.

What were the chances her old school chum Nanette had interrupted that dream?

I was determined to find out.

I waited at the end of Faith's block for about fifteen minutes, then pulled up to her house and parked. I pulled the Electrolux out of my trunk, lugged it up her to her porch, and knocked.

She opened the door, looked at me, then down at the vacuum, then back at me. "Can I help you?" She sounded annoyed. She'd changed out of her uniform and was dressed in a sleeveless blouse and pedal pushers. Ready for a relaxing afternoon, until I showed up.

"I don't need a new vacuum cleaner," she said as she started to close the door. "Thank you anyway and have a good day."

"Please," I said, "just give me a minute."

She hesitated. "Why should I? I don't need what you're selling."

"Oh, but you do, you do." I flashed her an earnest, trust-me smile. "You might think your house is clean but let me show you how much cleaner it could be with this wonderful machine."

There must have been something to my pathetic attempt at a

phony sales pitch, because she opened the door all the way and stared at me, then at the vacuum I was clutching. "Looks kind of old." She wrinkled her nose. "Is this your latest model?"

I nodded eagerly. "Yes, this is it. And if it looks a little beat up, that's because it's my demonstration model. I've whisked this baby across many a carpet in Pasadena, and if you'll let me, I can show you how clean it can get yours."

I peered inside her living room, as if assessing the type of carpet she had on her floor, while really looking for any signs that she had company. The room was neat and cheerfully furnished. If Nanette was staying with her, she was being careful to stay out of sight.

Faith tilted her head. "I think my house is clean enough." She narrowed her eyes at me. "But you look familiar. Do I know you from somewhere?"

Uh, oh. Was she remembering me from the hospital? I hoped not, although stupidly I had on the same outfit, a navy-blue blouse and black pants.

When I'd dressed that morning, I had thought those clothes resembled something a door-to-door saleswoman might wear. I hadn't thought about wearing something different to the hospital. I was learning. A good private eye needs a variety of disguises.

"I don't think I know you," I said, giving her an innocent smile. "But come on, what do you say, how about letting me in for a few minutes? I promise, this won't take long."

My voice sounded whinier than I'd intended. My sales pitch sounded sad, even to me. Which, to my amazement, ended up being to my advantage. Another valuable P.I. lesson learned: stay alert and stay flexible.

"You look tired," Faith said. "I think you have a real hard job, but

I'm sorry, I can't help you. I would be wasting your time to let you in because I have absolutely no interest in buying what you're selling."

I gave a loud sigh. "You're right, I am tired." I hung my head. "And yes, my job is so, so hard. But I need to pay my bills, and I need to keep going." I wiped imaginary sweat off my forehead and gave her an apologetic grimace. "Could I at least trouble you for a glass of water? I would be so grateful."

The woman was a nurse. Of course, she'd get an exhausted, thirsty woman a glass of water. It was the least she could do.

She nodded. "Yes, certainly. You wait right here. I'll be right back."

Success. Just as I'd hoped. She left the door open and left me alone long enough to take a quick step inside.

Which was all I needed.

Because that's when I saw it. The green and blue flowered Victorian carpet bag. On the floor. Beside the sofa.

My heart jumped into my throat. I swallowed hard. Stopped breathing.

I'd seen that bag before. In the hands of the woman who looked like Nanette. As she hurried to catch her plane.

Twenty-Five

"Steve, I think I've found Nanette." I pressed the phone tight against my ear as I watched a bunch of kids playing in the hotel pool. "I'm pretty sure she's staying at the home of her friend, Faith Young. Her friend from nursing school."

"What do you mean by pretty sure?" Steve's voice sounded so close it made my heart swell in my chest. He was in his Philadelphia office, three thousand miles away, because he'd been hoping I'd call, waiting for me to call.

Suddenly feeling warm inside that phonebooth, I cracked the door open, fanning my face with my free hand.

I told him how I'd followed Faith Young home, how I'd managed a sneak peek into her living room, and what I'd seen there. "The carpet bag has a unique blue and green flowered pattern. I'm sure it was the one I saw at the airport. It belongs to the woman who boarded that plane. Since I have proof from my client that Faith and Nanette recently corresponded, it's got to mean the woman is Nanette."

"Slow, slow down. Take your time, don't worry about the minutes." I could hear the smile in Steve's voice. I could picture it on his face. "We need to talk this through, decide what you should do next."

"How's Carolyn?" I felt guilty for not asking about her first, before blurting out my news.

"Still the same. Still in a coma," he said, his voice grim.

"I'm so, so sorry to hear that. We still don't know how or why she overdosed?"

"No. But believe it or not, Alec is blaming me."

"What?"

"He says that if I hadn't told Carolyn that I was quitting, she wouldn't have tried to kill herself."

I gasped. "That's ridiculous."

"Says she was that attached to me."

"Do you think there could be any truth to that?"

"No, I believe she was poisoned. By him. It was his plan B. To get out of his marriage. But that scares me because I have no proof. And she's still alive. So who knows what he might try to do next? I'm afraid to leave the hospital because now she really does need a bodyguard. I slipped out to wait for a call from you, but I need to go back."

"Where's Alec?"

"He visits off and on. When he's in her room, I make sure I am, too. Which infuriates him. He tells me to leave. Says I have no right to be there, because I quit. Then I tell him I changed my mind, and we get into heated arguments in front of the nurses. It gets ugly. I would've been fired by now if it wasn't for Freddie. Even a man with a heart as black as Alec's doesn't have the heart to fire me in front of his sobbing son."

"I'm sorry, Steve," I said in a hoarse whisper. "I'm glad you're there for her."

"Which means I can't be there for you. And I want to be."

"No...don't worry about me. I'm doing fine on my own. I can do this."

He didn't say anything, like he was thinking that over. "Okay, champ. Tell me what your next move will be."

I took a deep breath, let it out, took another deep breath, let it out.

"You still there, Story?"

"Yes."

"Well?"

"I need to go back to Faith Young's house and stake it out."

"Yep. But how?"

"It's not going to be easy because I can't tip Nanette off that anyone is looking for her." I sighed. "I'll need to use my camera. My brother gave me a Brownie as a going away present before I left. Said I might need it."

"Good for him. That's great. But you'll need to get damn close to get decent shots. Do you know how to use it? Do you have film?"

"He showed me how to use it, and I'll get film."

"You've got a lot to learn. A camera and a gun are prerequisites for being a P.I."

"I know, I know. I don't have a gun yet." I was annoyed that he kept bringing that up. "But I'll be okay for now."

Steve groaned.

"At least with the camera, I'll be able to prove to Martin Paulson that I've found his wife," I said eagerly. "I'll have pictures. Even if she refuses to listen to me, and refuses to go back to him, at least he'll know where she is."

"You're going to confront her?" Steve asked. "I don't like the sounds of this. I wish I could be there with you."

Part of me suddenly wished he could, too, but I stifled those silly, weak feelings.

"Thanks, but no thanks," I said, flashing a steely smile that I hoped he could hear from three thousand miles away. "I can do this. Stay tuned."

Twenty-Six

The best way to do surveillance on Faith's house was on foot. So, the next morning I parked at the hospital and hoofed it to her neighborhood.

I had my hair in a ponytail and wore over-sized sunglasses to hide half my face. With my comfy Keds sneakers on my feet and my trusty Brownie on a strap around my neck, I was ready.

I prayed that I looked nothing like the vacuum cleaner saleswoman I'd been the day before.

But in any case, the first thing I needed to do was check out Faith's garage.

Like all the homes in her neighborhood, she had a one-car garage beside her house. It occurred to me that maybe she was walking to work so Nanette could use it.

Unfortunately, from the sidewalk, I couldn't see into the garage because the door was closed. Its only window, on the side, faced the house, and I didn't want to risk going up there to peek in, as I might be seen.

Casually strolling past the bungalow, I noticed that the blinds on all the windows were partially closed, making it impossible to see into the house, either.

I went around the block to view her backyard. I could see part of it between houses. It seemed to be occupied by a well-maintained vegetable garden.

Interesting.

Only I didn't see Nanette—weeding, watering, picking peas, or doing anything else.

Too bad.

So…what next?

I went back to the front of the house, scouting the area across the street for a bush to hide behind. A property cattycorner from Faith's had several promising prospects. I picked the tallest bush closest to the sidewalk and settled myself down behind it.

Yuck. On grass, damp with dew. Within minutes the bottom of my pants were soaked through. Oh, well. Drawing my knees to my chest, I watched and waited for something to happen, cradling my heavy, black camera in my hands.

I watched and waited for Nanette to come or go from the house.

I watched and waited for Faith to come or go from the house.

I watched and waited for *anyone* to come or go from the house.

Nobody. Nothing. House and neighborhood, quiet as a mouse.

An hour went by, and my legs started cramping in places I didn't know could cramp. My back began to ache. Wincing, I shifted position.

More time went by. Some kids ran past me on the sidewalk. I held my breath. Thank God, they didn't notice me.

More time went by. A big black dog bounded up to me. I tensed up. Thank God, all he did was sniff my hair and leave.

Lucky me. I hadn't been spotted or mauled.

But not lucky me. Because in all that time, no one had come or gone from Faith's house. And I wondered if anyone ever would.

I was beginning to think I should call it a day when the front door opened, and a woman stepped out onto the porch.

My heart leapt into my throat. I froze.

She was young and slim and not Faith Young.

I couldn't see the color of her hair because she wore a scarf over it. In mid-summer... why wear a scarf in mid-summer—unless you didn't want to be recognized?

I watched her walk down the steps. She had the scarf half pulled over her face, covering her forehead and much of her eyes.

No matter, I needed to take pictures, anyway.

I gripped my camera and stood up. Click.

She turned toward the garage.

I advanced the shutter.

Click.

She reached into her purse and pulled out car keys.

I advanced the shutter again, click.

She opened the garage door—click—and seconds later, was backing out in a shiny black Ford.

Click, click, click.

She drove off.

I got in one last click. Of a shiny black Ford motoring down the street with my mystery woman inside.

My heart pounded, sweat ran down my face, but I was grinning from ear to ear.

She was Nanette. I was sure she was Nanette.

———

Now all I had to do was prove to my client that I'd found his wife.

Steve had seemed apprehensive about me confronting her and asking her to just go back to her husband. And I knew he was right.

When I took the case, I had no idea what I would be dealing with, or how it would end.

Would I find a kidnapped woman or a dead woman or a woman with amnesia? Or a runaway? In any case, I'd always imagined returning Nanette to her husband in some form or fashion, even if it was in a coffin.

I'd also assumed that if she had run away, I'd simply convince her how much her husband loved her, and she would gratefully run back into his arms.

Now, I knew. I was learning. The P.I. business wasn't that simple. It was messy. And I'd have to fight my way through the mess.

I needed to get my film developed. That was my next step. Then get the photographs to Martin Paulson, pronto. In my heart I knew they might not be good enough to satisfy him that I had, without a doubt, found his wife. But right now, they were all I had. And until I saw the developed prints, I didn't know what I had.

I drove to a drugstore in downtown Pasadena and learned that if I dropped my film off there, it would take a week to get my pictures back. Not good enough. I needed them now.

I drove back to the Sunset Strip Hotel and found my handsome clerk behind the counter.

"Hello, gorgeous." His eyes sparkled at the sight of me.

Really? He was being kind, or maybe he was just a good actor. Because I felt anything but gorgeous. More like damp, dirty, and disheveled after the long day I'd spent behind that bush.

He cocked his head. "How's the detective biz going?"

"Fantastic. I'm making progress." I grinned. "But I need something, and I'm hoping you can help."

"Anything for you, doll."

"Do you know anyone who has a darkroom?"

He gave me his wide, pearly-white smile. "Of course. I know lots of photographers in this town. Actors need photographers and photographers need actors and serious photographers have their own darkrooms. Why do you need a darkroom?"

I set my camera down on the counter. "There are important pictures in here that I need to see right away. This is a Kodak Brownie, so they're not professional level shots, but they're evidence in the case I'm working. And I can't wait a week for the film to be developed through a drug store."

He rubbed his hands together. "How exciting. This reminds me of a movie I was in as an extra a few years ago. The detective, who was a guy, had this real cool camera, and the pictures that the dude took were life and death important. And..."

I put my hand up to stop him. "Cary Grant, just give me the name of a photographer who can develop *my* pictures."

"Cary Grant?"

I smiled. "You look like a young version of him, okay. What's your real name, by the way?"

He flushed, clearly flattered. "Randy Dawson."

"Okay, Randy, which of your many photographer acquaintances do you recommend?"

He gazed up at the ceiling, then looked at the phone, snatched it up, and started dialing. "John Smiley, I know his number by heart."

"Smiley. Great name for a photographer."

"He thinks so." Randy held up a finger to signal he was waiting to be connected, then, "Hello John…" he lowered his voice to a mellower actor's tone. "I have a favor to ask you. We have a young lady here at the hotel who's a private eye—yeah, a real one—and she needs a darkroom."

A few minutes later, he hung up the phone, and I had what I needed. If I headed over to John Smiley's studio right now, he could develop my film.

"He also said he'd be glad to take some pictures of you. You know, in case you get tired of what you're doing, want to go into acting." Randy scribbled down the address on a piece of paper, then handed it to me and winked. "Think about it, doll. You got the look."

That was flattering. It truly was. But I was feeling good about what I was doing now.

"Thanks, Randy." I picked up my camera and put it around my neck. "But I'm enjoying my real-life career. Why would I want to play a detective in a movie when I'm living the real thing?"

———

John Smiley was a big, burly guy, who obviously thought of himself as a beatnik.

His beanie was slanted, just so, over too-long, uncombed hair. He sported a dark, pointy beard. And he was dressed in nothing but black, all the way down to his jet-black boots.

He also had an impressive studio a few blocks from MGM Studios, including a fully equipped darkroom, which he proudly showed off when I arrived. It was filled with complicated looking equipment and smelled of awful chemicals.

I did my best to look suitably impressed. And handed him my Brownie.

"A Brownie Hawkeye?" He sniffed. "This is an amateur's toy."

"I know, most people get their Brownie Kodak memories developed by dropping their film off at a drug store," I said. "But I need these pictures right away."

He palmed my amateur camera in his huge hand, bouncing it up and down as he fixed his gaze on me. "Randy told me you're a detective. Impressive, girl. And, okay, I got your jive, got you covered. You want to watch me work?"

I shook my head. "Not necessary. Is there someplace I can wait?"

"Sure, my waiting room, follow me."

His waiting room, at the front of his studio, included a comfortable sofa. He disappeared with my camera, and I went over to the sofa, put my head back, and fell asleep.

I wasn't sure how long I was out, but when he woke me up, my photos were in his hand.

"Long day?' He sat down beside me and spread the pictures out on a coffee table in front of us.

I rubbed my eyes. "A challenging one. Took me hours to get these pictures."

"Not bad for a Brownie," he said grudgingly. "Take a look."

I leaned over and studied the black and white prints. They were clear and sharp, although obviously taken from a distance. Pictures of a woman in a baggy, gray dress. With a scarf over her head.

Who could have been just about anybody.

I sighed. I'd done my best. I just hadn't been able to get any closer to her. I told myself that one day I'd be able to afford a better camera, and a long lens.

I picked one of the photos up and studied it. I could see her eyes, but barely, as she walked down the front steps of Faith Young's home. Her eyes looked dark, and furtive, like a cat.

I pulled the picture of Nanette that Dr. Paulson had given me out of my purse. I held it up next to the one I'd taken, then handed both photos to John Smiley. "Do you think these could be the same woman?"

He studied them, carefully. "Hard to say..."

I waited.

He squinted at one, then the other, then shook his head. "Could be...but then again..."

"Then again, what?"

"*Are* they the same woman?"

"I want them to be."

He grunted. "Too bad you couldn't have gotten any closer."

I met his gaze. "I know. But if she was your wife, do you think you would recognize her behind that scarf?"

He looked back at the pictures. "You know...I think it depends."

"On what?"

He looked back at me with sympathy in his eyes. "I think it would depend on what you wanted to see."

TWENTY-SEVEN

I had a message from Steve when I got back to my hotel.

"He says it's urgent, to call his office right away." Randy handed me a piece of paper. "He said you know his number, but I jotted it down just in case."

"Thanks," I said, then cashed in a dollar for more dimes.

With my heart racing, I headed back outside to my trusty phone booth.

I'd been planning to call Martin Paulson, and on my drive back from the darkroom, had been rehearsing in my mind what I would say to him.

But now, I needed to call Steve first. He answered the phone himself on the first ring. "Story, what is going on? Did you stake out that nurse's house? Get any pictures?" He sounded breathless.

"Yes, and yes."

"Who'd you get pictures of?"

"A woman, but she had a scarf over her head, and most of her face."

"That's promising. You're in Fat City."

"What?"

"You got the goods, Story."

"I suppose…I did the best I could with the camera I had. Got the pictures developed already, and I'm about to call Martin Paulson, so he can tell me what he wants me to do next. Should I stake her out again? Then follow her to wherever she's going? Then what? Confront her while I get some closeups?"

"That wouldn't be a bad idea, under ordinary circumstances."

Something in his tone made me uneasy. "What's wrong?"

"Things just got more complicated, that's what's wrong. Alec is apparently on his way to California."

My heart slammed against my chest. "Oh my God, he's coming here?"

"According to Freddie, he's flying out today or tomorrow. Supposedly for a business meeting. Only, I doubt that—and I thought I should warn you."

"Do you think he's coming for Nanette?"

"Who else?"

"But what about Carolyn? How is she?"

"She's opened her eyes a few times. But she hasn't spoken, and the doctors don't know…" His voice broke. He cleared his throat.

I waited. Was he swallowing back tears? Was it possible that he was a little in love with Carolyn after all? He clearly cared for her, and Alec had hired him because he'd noticed that his wife and Steve had a bond.

An irrational jab of jealousy pierced my gut. "What is it that the doctors don't know, Steve? What are they saying?"

He coughed, cleared his throat again. "They don't know if she will be able to make a full recovery. They are hopeful at this point, which gives me hope. She's the only one who can tell us what really happened. Maybe Alec put the pills in her orange juice, or in her coffee, or cereal, or something. But if she doesn't...come around...if she dies...he'll be free to be with Nanette."

"And that's what Nanette is waiting for? Hoping for?"

"Seems to me."

"Me, too." I let out a loud sigh. "Poor Freddie."

"I'm worried about you, too, Story."

"Me? Why me?"

"A man who we both believe tried to kill his wife is headed your way. And when he discovers that you are in *his* way, who knows what he's capable of?"

"He doesn't know I'm out here, does he?"

"I think he might. It might be one reason he's flying out there. He's afraid you're going to blow things wide open."

"Which means I need to blow things wide open." I gripped the phone. "I'm going to call Martin Paulson. Right now. Tell him I have pictures. Tell him I'm going to get more pictures. Tell him I have proof that his wife is here. That she left him voluntarily."

I took a deep breath. "Then, that's it. I said I'd find her, and I found her. Case closed."

Steve didn't say anything. I was afraid we'd been disconnected. "Steve?"

"I'm going to fly out there, too. And this time I'm not going to let you tell me no."

I sucked in a breath. "Why?"

"Because Alec is on his way there." Steve's tone was don't-argue-with-me determined. "And I have a bad feeling about that."

———

The minute I hung up with Steve, I plinked another dime in the slot to call to my client. Worried that I might run out of change before I was ready to end the conversation, I told the long-distance operator that Dr. Paulson's office would accept the charges, hoping it was true.

Fortunately, he must have alerted his staff that I might do that, because I was put through, and a minute later, had the doctor himself on the line.

I got right to the point. "I think I've found Nanette. I don't have absolute proof, but I have pictures. And I'm almost certain it's her."

That shocked him. I could hear him breathing. Heavily. Labored. As if he was trying to process the news. "What do you mean?" His tone was accusatory. "What do you mean? Is she alive? Is she okay?"

"She's alive. She looks well. That's the good news." I took a deep, shaky breath. "The unfortunate news is that it looks like she doesn't want to be found."

"What? Have you talked to her? Where is she?" He was whispering, and I realized that some of his staff might be listening.

"I have not talked to her because I didn't want to spook her, tip her off that—"

"What do you mean spook?" He shouted the last word. Clearly now not caring who was listening.

I didn't know how else to say it. "I think she left you, doctor. I think she ran away. I'm sorry, but—"

"That's nonsense. What you're telling me is complete nonsense. You must be mistaken."

"I don't think I am. I tracked her down to her friend's house. Faith Young, her nursing school friend. Nanette seems to be staying there, but in hiding."

"Hiding? Why do you think she's hiding?"

"Because when I watched her leave the house, she was wearing a scarf over her head and most of her face. I took pictures from across the street, and I don't think she saw me, but—"

"So, you didn't really see her at all? Is that what you're telling me, Miss Smith? That the woman you saw might have been Nanette, or maybe not. That maybe she was somebody else?"

He was practically screaming now. I had to calm him down. He was going off the rails. Acting like a complete lunatic.

"That's right," I said, pitching my voice low and steady. "That's what I'm trying to tell you. Except, I'm pretty sure—"

"Go back! Go back to that house! Get more pictures! Or knock on the door and speak to that woman, face to face. Ask if her name is Nanette Paulson. And if she says yes, ask her what she's doing there. Tell her that her husband loves her. That he wants her back. No questions asked."

He started sobbing. His cries grew louder and louder.

I didn't know what to do.

A woman was with him. I couldn't hear what she was saying. Because her voice was muffled. But she was trying to comfort him.

Thank God.

"Okay, doctor. I will do as you ask," I said. "I just wanted to make sure that's what you want me to do. Because I need to warn you—that she might run when she realizes she's been found. Then there's no telling where she'll go next."

I didn't mention Alec Lowell. That he was on his way to California. I didn't know what that man was planning. Until I did, why add more drama to the drama?

"Don't let her run," he wailed. "Just don't let her run. Bring her back to me. I insist that if this mystery woman you've found is my wife, that you bring her back to me."

Insist? How could he insist such a thing?

"That's impossible, doctor." I let that sink in. "If she doesn't want to go back to you, I can't make her."

"Give me the address, then!"

Alarm bells jangled in my head. "What?"

"I said give me Faith Young's address."

"Why?"

"Because I'm going to fly out there, myself. I'll make her come back to me."

"No. What about your patients? Your patients need you. And I have things under control here. You don't need—"

"Give me the address, Miss Smith. Now. I've paid you handsomely. Which means what you have found belongs to me. Give it to me *now*."

I didn't see that I had a choice. I gave him the address. Then I implored him not to get on a plane until he heard from me again. That, for all I knew, the woman I had found was not his wife.

"If she's not," he snapped, "you will have wasted my time, a lot of my money, and a fortune of your own money on a cute little California vacation."

Twenty-Eight

Okay, so now three men were threatening to come to Los Angeles to mess with my case.

Alec Lowell, Martin Paulson, and Steve Evans.

What was I supposed to do?

I had to get ahead of all of them.

Early the next morning, I took a fast shower, threw on some pedal pushers. a short-sleeved shirt, and my sneaks, and headed out the door to my rental car.

One way or another—and I wasn't sure how—I had to confirm that the person staying at Faith Young's house was Nanette.

Even if it meant pounding on her door so loud it brought the police. Maybe it was time to get them involved, anyway. What was the worst that could happen? They'd arrest me for disturbing the peace?

"Story!"

I froze in my tracks. A long white Chevy pulled into the hotel parking lot. With Steve behind the wheel.

I thought I was dreaming. How did he get here so fast?

My feet wouldn't move. I just stood there, utterly shocked. Clutching my car keys, my mouth hanging open.

"Steve?"

"Surprise!" He grinned as he got out of the car and sauntered over to me. "Told you I was getting on a plane."

"But when? When did you get on a plane?"

"Late yesterday. Caught the night flight out of Philly—and what a night I just had. Hard to sleep with all that turbulence, but I did manage to get some shut eye. Off and on. Mostly off." He yawned, then widened his grin as he met my shocked gaze. "It was worth it, though, to be here with you."

I blinked. "Thanks. I think. But I didn't ask you to come, remember? In fact, I have things firmly under control."

That, of course, was a lie. And damn, if he didn't look good for a man who'd spent the night curled up in the seat of an airplane bumping its way across the continent.

The part of me that was flattered he would do this for me was secretly swooning inside. But I wasn't going to let it show. I didn't want to be swooning. The last thing I needed was to be swooning.

Focus. I needed to focus, focus, focus.

I tore my eyes away from Steve's and pointed to his car. "Where did you get that?"

"Where do you think? From the airport. Rented it."

"This trip must be costing you a fortune."

He lifted a shoulder. "I can afford it."

I shook my head to clear it. "How...how did you know where to find me?"

He put his hands on his hips. "Really? You told me the name of your hotel, remember? Wasn't hard."

"Right..."

He pointed to the keys in my hand. "Where are you going? To breakfast?"

"Breakfast?" I was indignant, though also hungry. "No. I was heading to Faith Young's house. Hoping to beat the crowd there."

"Crowd?" He frowned.

"Yes. You. Alec. Martin Paulson."

"Paulson? He's coming here?"

"Yes. Possibly. Probably." I sighed. "I tried to talk him out of it. But he demanded that I give him Faith's address when I told him that our mystery woman didn't want to be found. He didn't like that. He blew up."

Steve dangled his car keys. "Let's go, then. I'll drive."

I hesitated, held back.

His face darkened. "Come on. We're not really going to argue about this, are we? I know it's your case, and you want to feel like you're in the driver's seat with it. And you are. But let me do this for you. I'll drive to the nurse's house, and you give me directions."

I pressed my lips together. Hard. To bite back the smile that threatened to slip out. "You came all this way..." My smile escaped, despite my best efforts. "So, okay."

———

Steve talked me into stopping at a diner for breakfast, where we made it quick by sitting at the counter for some eggs and bacon before gulping down our coffee and heading back out.

"My number one rule as a private eye is to always fortify yourself for what might be a long day ahead," he said as he opened the door for me to get in the car. "It's something I learned the hard way, because you never know."

Traffic was slow on the Pasadena Freeway. And I was glad Steve was driving because smog was starting to blanket the area, making it more and more difficult to see. Choking, dirty yellowish-white stuff. Disgusting.

I realized I'd been lucky so far to have clear, sunny days, but it seemed my luck had run out. I hoped the gloom wasn't a portent of what was to come.

"You're really worried about Alec, aren't you?" I angled myself to face Steve.

He was keeping a sharp eye on the road and nodded. "Yep."

"That's why you're here."

"Yep."

"What do you think he's going to do?"

"No telling. That's the problem." He shot a quick glance at me. "What do you think he's going to do?"

"Pick up Nanette and run."

"Where?"

"I don't know, and that's the crazy part." I gave an exasperated sigh. "He has a wife, and she has a husband. They can't just ignore that."

"He's hoping his wife will die soon," Steve said bitterly.

"True. Horribly true. But what about Nanette?"

He grunted. "She obviously doesn't care what her husband thinks, or how he feels. She pulled a disappearing act on her sister, and it appears she's planning to do the same thing to her husband."

"You mean like, 'Bye-bye, honey, it's been nice knowing you. Now get out of my life and stay out'?"

Steve grunted. "Something like that."

"How cruel."

"It is cruel. Some women are like that. And some men."

"You've seen it all in this business, haven't you, Steve?"

"Yes, and so will you, Story. Get used to it."

Sadness descended on me like the smog on the freeway.

Martin Paulson was an emotional man. But he seemed like a nice enough person. Who didn't deserve what was happening to him.

Carolyn didn't deserve being poisoned, either. She had to live. She had to pull through. So good could prevail over evil. And for her son's sake.

I kept my musings to myself. I didn't want to talk about Carolyn right now. Steve needed to concentrate on the insane traffic, which eased up as we took the exit for downtown Pasadena. As did the smog. The sun was trying to make an appearance as we entered the city, and I was rooting for it. For light to banish darkness.

I directed Steve to Faith's house, and he parked out front. We got out of the car and Steve went around to his trunk, pulled out a black camera case, then removed a big camera from the case along with a few flashbulbs.

He stuck the flashbulbs in his pocket, slung the camera around his neck, then reached back into the trunk and pulled out a gun. A revolver. He tucked it into his pants and covered it with the bottom of his shirt.

My eyes went big. "What are you doing?"

"Getting prepared, for anything." He gave me a knowing wink. "Watch and learn, Story. Watch and learn."

TWENTY-NINE

Steve and I climbed the steps to the porch, then I went ahead of him, knocked on the door, and held my breath.

No one answered.

Steve whispered, "Try again."

Rap, rap, rap.

Same result. I looked at him and shrugged. "Faith is probably at work already. And I don't think Nanette is going to come to the door."

He went up and knocked. Nothing. Again, harder. Then again, so hard I worried he'd slice his knuckles open.

"The garage..." I pointed to it. "I wonder if the car's there?" I scurried down the steps and over to the small window and peered in.

"It's there," I told Steve as I came back to him.

I took over the knocking, loud and obnoxious enough to be annoying. And impossible to ignore.

I had my hand up to rap again when the door jerked open, knocking me into Steve, who grabbed me before I toppled over.

A woman stood there, glaring at us like we'd lost our ever-loving minds.

She was stunningly pretty. Sleek, shiny, dark hair. Sensuous, rose-pink lips. Deep tan that flattered her shapely body, clad in a tight white dress that looked amazing against her tawny skin.

But her eyes were her best feature. And what gave her away. Big and brown, like those of a doe. Like those in the picture. My heart soared. I'd know those eyes anywhere.

"Nanette Paulson?" I gave her an I-can't-believe-I-found-you grin. "Are you Nanette Paulson?"

She squinted at me, clearly annoyed, and not a little alarmed. "Who wants to know?"

"My name is Story Smith..." My hand shook as I reached into my purse, pulled out a business card, and handed it to her. "I'm a private detective, hired by your husband—"

"No...go away!" She tried to close the door, but Steve grabbed it before she could.

She gave him a how-dare-you stare. "Who the hell are you?"

He kept a firm grip on the door. "*Are* you Nanette Paulson? Answer the question."

Her eyes went to the huge camera around his neck. "What's that for?"

"Answer the question," Steve snapped.

She hesitated. Then something in her melted, surrendered. Like she was tired of running. Tired of hiding. Or maybe she just didn't see the point of lying. Her shoulders slumped and she whispered, "Yes. That's me."

Relief rushed through me. I flashed Steve a triumphant smile. Finally, finally, finally! The person I had to find—knew I would find—was right in front of me.

"I've been searching for you everywhere." Without thinking, I reached out to touch her arm, to be sure she was real. But the frigid scowl she shot me made me draw my hand back. "I'm sorry," I said. "But your husband is beside himself with grief. That's why he hired me. I must talk to you. Can we come in?"

She shook her head. "No. I don't want to talk to you."

"Please? It's important."

Her scowl went icier. "My friend is asleep upstairs. She owns this house...she's a nurse...she worked the overnight shift last night. I'm surprised you didn't already wake her up with your ridiculous pounding."

I winced. "I'm sorry, but you and I really need to talk and I'm not going to leave until we do. Can we come in? Unless you'd rather come out here on the porch..."

She huffed and threw the door open. "Okay, come in, if you insist. But keep it quiet and make it quick. I don't have much to say. Just tell Martin that I want a divorce. I should have told him that myself."

"Would have been quicker and easier," Steve muttered as we moved into the house.

The living room was as neat as before. Nanette closed the door behind us but didn't ask us to sit down. She faced us with her arms folded across her chest, her stance defiant.

I figured I might as well lead off with the first obvious question. "Why did you run away?"

She wrinkled her cute little button nose. "I was bored."

"I mean, why did you run away instead of just asking for a divorce?"

She sighed. "I assume you've met Martin?"

"Yes, of course."

"He's an extremely emotional man, wouldn't you say?"

"That's one way of putting it..."

"He would have blubbered and cried and screamed if I'd asked for a divorce. He would have begged me to stay. I didn't need that. So, I just left." She gave a petulant shrug.

I couldn't believe this woman. What a spoiled, selfish hussy. "You left your best friend, Carolyn, behind on the Ocean City boardwalk when you sneaked out the back of that candy store," I said. "Leaving her wondering what happened to you. That was your plan?"

She lifted her chin and gave a haughty sniff. "It worked."

"You scared her to death."

She shrugged. "I'm not proud of that."

I was outraged. "Carolyn has been beside herself and so has your husband and all your friends. Don't you care?"

She gave a loud sigh. "What do you want me to say? That I'm sorry? Okay, I'm sorry. Now are you done with me? Just go tell Martin that I want a divorce."

I couldn't believe this was it. That she was going to dismiss me so easily, just send me on my way.

I glanced at Steve. He was fiddling with his camera. Attaching a flashbulb.

Nanette noticed. "Wait." She waved a hand at him. "What are you doing?"

He aimed the camera at her. "Smile pretty."

Click.

The flashbulb went off. *Poof.*

Nanette blinked and blinked again. "Hey—why did you just take my picture?"

Steve grinned. "Your husband hired Story to find you, so now she has proof that she did."

Nanette narrowed her eyes and studied his face. "And who are you, again? This chick here calls herself a private eye. But...who...the...hell...are you?"

He grinned. "I'm her chauffeur."

My chauffeur? I bit back a snicker.

Nanette cocked her head. "What's your name?

"Steve Evans."

Recognition sparked in her eyes. "Wait a minute, I've heard of you."

"Really?" Steve gave her a knowing look. "Maybe it was because I was hired to be Carolyn's bodyguard after you disappeared. By her husband, Alec. You know Alec of course."

She stiffened, then shrugged. "That explains it."

"You've been in touch with Alec, then?" I raised my eyebrows.

She stared at me. I had her.

I smiled. "Alec is your lover. He's the real reason you ran away —isn't he?"

She shook her head. "No.... Where did you hear that? That's crazy."

"You stole your best friend's husband."

"No. I did not."

"And do you know what else?" She was squirming, and I was enjoying watching her squirm. "Alec poisoned Carolyn. He fed her an overdose of sleeping pills so he could be with you. Did you know that?"

It was impossible to tell if she knew. Or even cared. She just stared at me with those big eyes, shaking her head back and forth, back and forth.

Something thumped on the porch.

Startled, we all turned toward the door.

Somebody was there. Alarm shot through my veins.

The door burst open. It was Alec.

Of course, it was Alec.

He'd arrived.

And he had a gun.

THIRTY

"Put the gun down." Steve waved his pistol at Alec. "Now!"

Alec sauntered toward him. "I will...if you will..."

"Okay...then—now!" Steve dropped his weapon.

Alec let his drop to the floor. It hit the carpet with a thud.

Thank God. I swallowed hard. Remembered to start breathing again. "Alec, fancy meeting you here," I said with strangled sarcasm. "We were just talking about you."

Nanette ran to him. He caught her in his arms, and they embraced. She stepped away and met my gaze with a cheerful smirk. Her cheeks pink, her eyes dewy, she was obviously done denying that Alec was her lover.

"She found me, Alec." Nanette jerked a finger at me. "Can you believe this female dick traced me all the way to California?"

Alec grunted. "Story Smith..." He spit my name out with disdain. "I knew you were trouble from the get-go. Unfortunately, I was right."

Nanette grabbed his arm. "But it doesn't matter now. She doesn't matter. I told her to just tell Martin that I want a divorce. Now you and I can be together at last."

Steve shot me an I-can't-believe-this look. "But what about Carolyn?" His tone was snide. "Have you forgotten that Alec is married?"

Alec's eyes cut to Steve. "You fool, Evans. You could have had Carolyn. You should have taken her. She was yours for the taking. Instead, she lies in a coma in a hospital bed, and it's all your fault."

"Like hell!" Steve stepped toward him. "You tried to kill her, Lowell. And don't think you're going to get away with it. The minute Carolyn wakes up, we'll all know the truth."

"Coma?" Nanette grabbed Alec's shoulders and shook him. "Wait —Carolyn's in a coma?"

He nodded grimly.

She looked at him wide-eyed. "You mean she's not *dead*? Why isn't she dead?"

My jaw dropped. Icy chills slithered down my spine. Nanette was truly evil.

"Nanette, what's going on here?"

We turned. A woman was making her way down the stairs in fat, fuzzy slippers, her hair askew. Faith Young. We'd obviously woken her from a sound sleep.

Looking confused, she rubbed her eyes and clutched her robe. "I don't understand, Nanette, you have company?"

Nanette nodded. "I'm sorry they woke you up, Faith. I begged them to keep it down."

"But I thought..." Faith put a hand to her forehead. "Oh, no...did Martin find you?"

Her eyes darted back and forth between Steve and Alec. As if she was trying to figure out which one was Martin. The horrified look on her face told me what I'd suspected. That Nanette had lied to her friend about her husband to gain her sympathy and support. She'd probably fed her wild lies about him being cruel and abusive.

"Martin's not here, but I'm the private investigator he hired to find Nanette." I went over to Faith as she came all the way down the stairs. I held out my business card.

She didn't take it, looked at me with suspicion. "You tried to sell me a vacuum cleaner yesterday, lady."

"Yes, I did, but I was just trying to get a peek inside your home...to see if Nanette was staying here."

Faith's eyes went to the guns on the floor. "Guns?" she screeched. "Whose guns are those?"

Nanette just stared at her. Alec just stared at her. Steve and I looked at each other.

"Look, I don't know what's going on here, Nanette," Faith said, "but I let you stay with me so you could hide from Martin. You said that you were scared to death of him. That if you asked him for a divorce, you had no idea what he might do. Now I'm scared. I'm going to call the police."

"Don't." Nanette put a hand up. "I can explain."

"Don't listen to her, she's a liar," I said. "Martin never abused her. He loves her. She ran away because she's having an affair." I pointed to Alec. "With him."

"An affair?" Faith shook her head. "I don't...I don't understand."

"Meet Alec Lowell, Nanette's secret lover and the husband of her best friend," I said. "I suspect Nanette ran away to buy time until Alec did what she wanted—ask his wife for a divorce. Only Alec didn't want the messiness of that, especially the expense. So, he stalled, dragged his feet. Am I right, Nanette?"

Nanette scoffed. "You don't know what you're talking about, you bitch. Faith, don't listen to her, she's—"

"Alec hoped his wife, Carolyn, would fall in love with me," Steve said. "He hired me to be her bodyguard, forcing us together day and night. When that scheme didn't work, he poisoned her."

"I did not," Alec growled. "How many times do I have to—"

"Doesn't matter," I said smugly. "As soon as Carolyn comes out of her coma, and tells the police what you did, they'll arrest you, Alec." I enjoyed taunting him. And Faith needed to know the truth.

Bad idea, though.

Alec reached down and grabbed his gun. He kicked Steve's under the sofa.

He waved his gun at me, then Steve. "We're leaving, Nanette...but first we have to take care of these two—they need to go bye-bye."

Alec glanced at Faith, who was pale, trembling, and looked about to faint. "Faith, my dear," he growled, "I know it's awkward meeting like this, but do you have any rope?"

She whispered, "Rope?"

He pointed the gun straight at my head. "That's what I said."

"In the basement," she said, her voice shaky.

"Go get it. Nanette, go with her."

Alec motioned for Steve to come stand next to me, then waved his gun back and forth between us. Steve stayed unbelievably calm. I tried to, but inside I was quaking.

Faith and Nanette came back with a long, coiled rope. Nanette handed it to Alec.

"What are you going to do?" I asked.

"You'll see," Alec said. "Nanette, go get two chairs from the kitchen."

"What are you doing?" Faith wailed.

"Shut up," Alec snapped at her, "or I'll shut you up."

Nanette dragged two chairs into the room and Alec motioned with the gun for Steve and me to sit.

"Nanette, stop him, stop him!" Faith whimpered. "What is he going to do?"

"I told you to shut up," Alec said. "Nanette, go get another chair—looks like we'll need to take care of your friend, too. And grab a sharp knife while you're at it. We'll need to cut the rope into pieces. Tie them all up, make it look like a robbery."

"No," Faith cried. "No...no...no..."

I felt sorry for Faith. She'd just been trying to help a friend. Who she now knew was a monster.

No time for self-pity, though. I glanced at Steve. He gave me a reassuring flicker of a smile, as if to say all would be okay. Or so I hoped because his eyes gave nothing away.

When Nanette came back with the third chair, Alec pushed Faith into it. Then, while holding the gun on Steve and me, barked at Nanette to tie up her friend first.

"What are we going to do, Alec?" Nanette sawed off a long piece of rope.

"We are going to fly to Paris today. It's what you've always wanted—for us to get married there, right?" Alec said.

"Yeah...but..." Nanette jerked Faith's hands behind her and started winding the rope around them.

"We got to speed up our plan. I need to get out of the country before Carolyn wakes up."

Nanette stopped winding. "And why *is* she going to wake up?" Her tone had shifted from lovey-dovey to flippant and furious. "You obviously screwed up, Alec. You fed her enough sleeping pills to knock her out but not kill her? Now look at the mess we're in."

"How was I to know what dose would do the job?" Alec's face grew redder by the minute. "I don't know anything about sleeping pills—that was your brilliant idea, Nanette."

"You could have just asked her for a divorce, like I wanted," Nanette said. "It would have been so much easier."

"That's what I keep saying," Steve whispered to me under this breath.

"Carolyn would have taken me to the cleaners if I'd asked for a divorce." Alec frowned. "She would have hired the best lawyer in Philadelphia, who would've made sure she not only got the house, but also the cars, Freddie, half my estate, and a lifetime of alimony to boot. I wasn't going to let that happen. You should have been more patient."

Tears slid down Faith's cheeks. "Please, Nanette, please...don't do this to me." She sobbed. "I can't believe you are doing this..."

"I ran out of patience, okay, Alec." Nanette secured the rope around Faith's wrists. "I waited and waited until I realized you were never going to ask Carolyn for a divorce. You were playing me for a fool—and I couldn't stand one more minute with my stupid, suffocating husband."

Nanette shoved Faith's ankles together and started wrapping rope around them. "Every time Martin touched me, I wanted to scream. But no, I had to pretend I was Miss Perfect Wife. And Carolyn's best friend...I couldn't do that forever, Alec. I was too in love with you."

Alec tightened his grip on his gun, keeping it pointed at me and

Steve. "If you'd loved me so much, you would have trusted me and waited. Instead, you pulled your stupid disappearing act. Which just brought more trouble."

"I couldn't stand seeing you and Carolyn together. Picturing you and her together in bed. Pretending to everyone at the club that I was her friend. I just couldn't..." Nanette was whining now.

Faith rocked back and forth in her chair. She arched her body in a futile attempt to get free.

"Tie her waist to the chair," Alec growled. "And hurry up. We still have to take care of Miss Sherlock Holmes here..." He jerked his gun at my face, then swung it toward Steve. "And her boy assistant..."

Nanette glanced over. "Some plan you had, Alec. Expecting Carolyn to fall for her bodyguard. Really?"

"It would have worked," Alec snapped. "If the fair Miss Smith hadn't come along and distracted him."

"Yes, and too bad Story figured you out." Steve said, staring down the muzzle of Alec's gun. "Story caught on to what you were up to before I did. I couldn't believe it at first, but it all made sense. You saw that Carolyn and I had hit it off—and instead of being jealous—you tried to use it to your advantage."

"Shut up," Alec barked.

"Then I quit, to see what you would do. Only it never occurred to me that your backup plan was murder."

"Like I said, Evans, Carolyn's unfortunate condition is all you fault."

Nanette had a new piece of rope ready. She turned to me.

If I was going to stop her, it had to be now.

I knew Nanette and Alec weren't just going to tie us up and leave us there. Before jetting off to France. No, they were going to shoot us in the head and leave us for dead.

I tried to think...looked around the room.

Steve's gun. Under the sofa.

Maybe I could somehow grab it...

I bent over and pretended to gag, like I was sick. About to throw up. With my head almost to the floor, I glanced under the sofa. I could see it.

I sat up, coughing. Steve glanced at me, and I signaled to him with my eyes.

He gave a quick nod.

Nanette came over to me, twirling the section of rope meant for my hands. "What's the matter, dear, are you feeling ill—"

I shot a foot out, kicked her in the abdomen. Hard. She flew back.

I launched myself toward the sofa, landed on my stomach, reached for Steve's pistol, and shoved it toward him.

He scooped it up and aimed it at Nanette. She scrambled to stand.

Alec growled and tackled Steve, knocking the pistol out of his hand as he went down.

I snatched Steve's gun off the floor.

Steve grabbed Alec's ankle. His gun went flying as his feet cut out from under him.

I beat Nanette to it. Pointed both guns at her, one in each hand. Hoped I didn't have to fire either weapon. Just squeeze the trigger?

I faked a cocky grin, like I knew what I was doing, and Steve jumped to his feet.

I handed him his gun, keeping Alec's.

Steve pointed his pistol at Alec, then motioned for Nanette to get down on the floor with him. "Call the police, Story!" he shouted. "Then untie Faith. Hurry."

I ran toward the phone.

Halfway there, a shot rang out. A bullet whizzed past my head.

I froze. Turned.

It was Martin Paulson. At the door with a gun.

Damn it. Why couldn't he have stayed home and let me do my job?

"Put the gun down!" Steve shouted, keeping his pointed at Alec and Nanette.

"No!" Martin's eyes blazed fury. "I'm going to shoot the son of a bitch who stole my wife." He advanced toward Alec, then stopped when he saw Nanette. She was crouched on her knees, cowering behind her lover.

"Don't shoot, Martin," she whimpered. "Please..."

"You left me for him..."

"Please!"

"Why did you leave me for him?"

"Please, don't shoot him, don't shoot him!"

"Do you love him?" Martin was a volcano ready to explode. Red-faced, fiery eyes.

"No!" Nanette wailed.

"Liar!"

"Yes...yes..." Her voice broke. "Yes, I'm sorry, I'm sorry..."

"Put the gun down, Dr. Paulson," Steve said. "This is not the way to settle things."

Martin kept his gun trained on Alec. "I want to know how long this affair has been going on, Nanette."

"It doesn't matter." She gave a strangled sob. "It's over, okay. Just don't shoot him, don't shoot…"

"Tell me how long."

"Uh…ahh…two years, three years…I don't know…I'm sorry, I'm sorry…"

"Three years! You've been making a fool of me for three years!?"

"I'm sorry!"

"No, you're not."

Nanette's eyes bulged with terror. "I'm telling you the truth, Martin. You must believe me."

"Everything was a lie."

"No, no, no. Not everything…"

I didn't like the look in the doctor's eyes. Wild. Broken. Unhinged. "All those Monday nights…you never volunteered to feed the poor. Did you?"

"No." Nanette shook her head. "I'm sorry…"

"You were with *him*, we're you?"

"No."

"You're lying now!"

"Yes, yes, I was. Okay, I was, but now we're done. I'll come back to you, Martin, I will. I swear. Please…"

"I met your sister. The one you left behind at the orphanage. The one you forgot to tell me about."

"Dora?" Nanette rasped her name.

"Yes, Dora. You abandoned her. Left her behind and never looked back. Were you planning to do that to me?"

"No!"

"Liar…"

"Yes."

"Why?"

Nanette shook her head.

"For him?" Martin stepped closer to Alec, pointing the gun at the spot between his eyes.

"No...yes..."

Martin pulled the trigger.

BAM.

Alec ducked.

The bullet hit Nanette. Square in the chest. She flew up, then back, landing face up.

Faith screamed.

I think I did, too.

Blood was spurting out of a gaping hole in Nanette's pretty dress. Crimson pooling on white.

My heart was pounding, and my ears were ringing from the blast, and I was shaking so bad I couldn't move. I looked at Nanette's eyes. They were open, but unseeing.

She was dead.

Alec threw himself on top of her. "No...no...no...my love...my love..."

Martin dropped his gun, collapsed to his knees.

I ran over and picked up his gun. Once again, I was holding a gun in each hand.

"Call the police, Story," Steve shouted as he kept his aimed at Alec. "Then untie Faith. Hurry."

I turned back to the phone.

Martin was making noises that sounded more animal than human. Keening. Mewing. Wailing.

I put his gun down on the table, put Alec's down on the table, then picked up the receiver and dialed O for the operator.

But Alec was too quick for me. And for Steve.

He jumped up, launched himself in my direction, snatched his gun off the table.

And shot himself in the head.

————

I don't remember how long it took for the police to arrive. It could have been five minutes, or thirty, or an hour.

Because everything for me, while we waited for them, felt like a hazy dream. Like I was trapped in a nightmare.

I remember untying Faith. I remember her standing up, looking down at Nanette in horror. I remember her seeing what remained of Alec, his crumpled body, his head blown-to-bits.

Then screaming and screaming and screaming.

I also remember that I wanted to run to Steve. Have him hold me. Comfort me. Tell me everything would be okay. Which would have been a bad idea. Not to mention unprofessional.

Because I needed to be strong.

And everything would not—could not—be okay.

The reality was that two people were dead. Including the woman who I'd been hired to find. Shot by my client.

This was not how my case was supposed to end.

Standing there, numb, and in shock, I couldn't stop wondering how much of it was my fault.

"It's okay, Story," Steve said. "None of this is your fault. We're alive. That's what matters."

When police finally came, they arrested Martin Paulson and led him away.

Then they told me and Steve and Faith that we needed to go down to Pasadena police headquarters for questioning.

———

"Buck up," Steve told me when we walked outside. "This is going to be an interesting ride."

When I saw the crowd gathered in Faith's yard, I realized he didn't mean the ride to police headquarters. Gawkers were spilling onto the sidewalk and into the street.

Screaming and gunshots in a normally peaceful neighborhood will attract curious onlookers, so I shouldn't have been surprised.

I was eager to tell my story to the authorities. Close my case. Put it behind me. Go home. Find more business, hopefully. And learn from my mistakes, just as soon as I could figure out what, if anything, I could have done any differently.

But now my first case was about to become national news. Because the jumble of onlookers included newspaper reporters waving notebooks and photographers snapping pictures.

I didn't think this was what my brother Rob had in mind when he predicted this, my first case, would do wonders for my reputation as a female P.I.

A police officer ushered Steve into the backseat of a patrol car, then told me to get in next to him, then Faith.

"Will this making-the-news be good, or bad, for my P.I. business?" I asked Steve as the car took off. "Just wondering."

Wedged between him and Faith, I was no longer feeling cold and numb. Acutely aware of Steve's body pressed against mine, I was getting warm.

He took my hand and patted it. Warmer still.

"I'm not sure if this is good or bad," he said. "But look on the bright side, Story Smith. After today, I think a lot of people are going to know your name."

THIRTY-ONE

More reporters and photographers waited outside the police station, an adobe brick, two-story building with a front entrance framed by willowy palm trees.

Television cameras were there, too.

We were hustled inside, then ushered through a large room where uniformed officers swarmed about amid ringing telephones and clicking typewriters.

Metal doors along one wall led to what looked like meeting rooms. Faith and one of the officers disappeared into one of them. Steve and another officer went into the next. And a third officer took me into room number three.

He closed the door with a firm click.

The room was small, claustrophobic. Gray walls. No windows. One table. Two chairs.

God, I hoped I wouldn't have to be there long.

I sat down behind the table, and the plain clothed officer sat across from me.

He looked close to retirement age. Steel-gray hair, with a lined face wearing a jaded expression that told me he'd seen it all, and had lost patience for any of it a long time ago.

"Detective Sergeant Tom Kent." He slapped a notebook on the table and fished a pencil out of his shirt pocket. "And you are?"

"Story Smith. Private investigator."

His weary face brightened. Then he grinned. "Really?"

I tilted my head. "Really what? My name?" I spelled it out.

"No. That you're really a private investigator...a dame?"

I nodded, trying not to look insulted. "From Philadelphia. And proud of it."

"Proud to be from Philadelphia, or proud to be a female P.I.?"

"Both," I said, just then realizing the truth of it. Los Angeles was glamorous, and Philly was gritty, and I looked forward to going back to gritty. And my one-woman business.

He asked me what I was doing in Faith Young's living room.

I told him my story, which took about an hour. He didn't interrupt. Took lots of notes.

"So...this was your first case?" Now he looked impressed.

"Yes. It was daunting but do-able. I found her, which is what I was hired to do. Sadly..." I let my words trail off.

"Your client was quite a firecracker."

"That's one way of putting it."

"Why do you think he hired you?"

"You mean why did he hire a dame?" I smiled. "I think he thought a woman might have a better chance of finding a woman."

"Interesting theory."

"I'm glad that he took a chance on me, at least. I could tell from the beginning that he was emotionally on edge. But I wasn't prepared for the end. Tragic."

The detective sighed. "Your client will get one call from jail, and I assume it will be to his office."

"I hope so. He had an extremely successful practice as an obstetrician, which I assume he won't be going back to any time soon?" I winced at the thought of all his pregnant patients, who would be devastated to learn the news.

"I don't think he'll be able to get out on bail. But he will get a fair trial. After that? Who can say?"

"The press is on this story already." I met his gaze.

He nodded. "From what you've told me, it has all the elements that sizzle. Money. Sex. Murder. Only, I hope I don't have to caution you not to talk to any reporters. It might compromise Dr. Paulson's case."

"I understand." I leaned forward. "Wait a minute. What about Nanette's sister, Dora? Who is going to tell her that her sister is dead? I don't want her learning it through the news."

"We'll contact police in her area. Send someone to her home."

"Thank you." It was the right thing to do, but I doubted that Dora would grieve. She'd been doing that for years. She'd lost the sister she knew, and loved, a long time ago. Her husband, Charlie, on the other hand, could go to hell as far as I was concerned.

I stood up. "Alec Lowell's wife, Carolyn, will need to be contacted. I think my colleague, Steve Evans, will want to do that—call the hospital, see how she is. And Carolyn has a son. He's only fifteen."

Detective Kent nodded and stood. "We're done here," he said. "I'll take you to Mr. Evans now."

———

To my surprise, Steve was waiting for me behind the wheel of his rental car, parked at the back of the police headquarters lot.

When he saw me, he got out and opened the passenger door. I hopped in before any reporters could spot me.

"They didn't want us to have to fend off the press back at Faith's house, so I gave them my keys, and an officer drove this baby here while we were being questioned," Steve said.

He closed my door, got back behind the wheel, then turned to me with a smile. "And I have great news."

"Carolyn?"

"Yes. She's awake. Hasn't said much yet, but a doctor I just spoke with on the phone said he thinks she'll recover completely."

I returned his smile, truly relieved. "Finally, some good news. The best we could hope for."

"Yep. Sure is." Steve put the keys in the ignition, then hesitated. "Uhm, where we going? Back to your hotel?"

The question took me by surprise. After all I'd been through, after all *we'd* been through, everything felt weird. My case was closed. Nanette was dead. Alec was dead. Dr. Paulson was in jail.

I'd been on an emotional rollercoaster for so long that getting back to normal felt strange. What was normal, anyway? I pressed my lips together. "My hotel? I guess... I mean, where else should we go?"

"Your hotel it is, then." Steve started the car and headed out of the lot. He glanced at me. "When were you planning to fly home?"

"Tomorrow. I have an open ticket for a flight back to Philadelphia, which Martin Paulson paid for in advance. Fortunately. All I need to do is find a travel agent to finalize the reservation."

"Okay," Steve said. "I'll go with you."

I looked at him. "What? Where?"

The corners of his mouth turned up in a teasing grin. "To the travel agent. Might as well get on the same plane as you. We can sit together."

I felt my face flush. "Oh, okay, that makes sense. Cool."

Cool. And hot, hot, hot. How was I going to survive hours on a plane sitting next to Steve? My heart started racing just thinking about it. We'd have hours to talk. We didn't really know each other...and I wanted to get to know him better...but it made me nervous. And I didn't want him to know it made me nervous.

"Glad you approve us flying together," Steve said as he deftly weaved through traffic. "Because I also need a place to stay tonight." He winked at me, then put his eyes back on the road.

At least, I think he winked. Maybe it was just my imagination. Maybe he didn't really wink.

I swallowed hard. Didn't know what to say. Was he hoping that I'd invite to let him stay in my hotel room? Plenty of women would have jumped at that chance. But not me. My reputation and pride were at stake. Not to mention my business.

Back in Philly we'd be competitors. And friends? Maybe...?

Could I be friends with a guy like Steve? Ahhhh...only if I lied to myself about not feeling attracted to him.

He laughed. "Why so quiet all the sudden, Story?"

Now I was really blushing. "I have no idea where you can stay tonight, Steve. Maybe you can ask the travel agent."

"I was thinking about your hotel."

"Were you?"

"Thinking that maybe I can stay there..."

Oh, God.

He laughed harder. "Oh, I get it. You think I'm trying to wrangle an invite to stay in *your* room? I hope that's not what you're thinking. Because I'm too much of a gentleman for that."

Now it was my turn to laugh. Although it sounded forced. "Your reputation proceeds you, sir." I poked him in the arm.

He gave a fake pout. "But I'm reformed."

"Since when?"

"Since I met you."

My breath hitched. My eyes went big. Should I believe him? Or was this a line he used with all the girls?

My brain told me it was a line he used with all the girls. My heart told me...I don't know what my heart was telling me because it was beating so fast, I couldn't think.

"You don't believe me?" He glanced at me out of the corner of his eye.

"I'mmmm not sure. I honestly don't know what to think. Like I said, your reputation..."

"Is exaggerated," he said, now annoyed. "No matter what your brother says."

My brother, yes, my dear brother, Rob. Who'd been my protector all my life. Whose advice had never failed me. Except once. With Dean. He'd assured me that Dean would get over me. After I broke up with him. That he would find someone new. And go on with his life.

He didn't. He'd ended it instead.

"You're being quiet again, Story. Are you okay?" Steve tightened his grip on the wheel. Traffic, which had been crazy, had slowed to a bumper-to-bumper crawl.

"I'm okay," I said, my voice cracking. "It's just that, I can't stop seeing Nanette and Alec. All that blood."

Steve glanced over at me. "It was a shock. A lot to deal with. But I thought you handled it well. For a rookie in the P.I. biz. Do you want to talk about it?"

"My fiancé died the same way..." The words rushed out of my mouth before I could stop them. "The same way as Alec..."

I squeezed my eyes closed. I couldn't believe it. What had I just done? Why had I just told Steve that?

"Oh, God...oh, God. I'm sorry, Story." Steve slammed on the brakes. Just in time to avoid hitting the car in front of us. Traffic had come to a complete stop.

I covered my face with my hands. "I'm sorry. I don't know why I told you that."

"I'm glad you did." Steve's voice was soft.

"His name was Dean...he shot himself. After I ended our engagement. Our secret engagement. Rob was the only person who knew I planned to break up with Dean. But even he didn't know Dean and I were engaged."

I turned to face Steve. "You're the first person I've ever told."

"Wow." Steve's voice was even softer. "I'm flattered. Flattered that you trusted me enough to tell me this. It's not good to keep something like this bottled up. You don't blame yourself, do you?"

"Unfortunately, I do."

"*Don't*. You were just being honest. If he was too fragile to handle it, it's not your fault."

"I wasn't in love with him. I wanted to be. I thought I should be. But I wasn't."

"We can't control our emotions, Story. Sometimes we think we can. We try. But we can't."

"I know." Tears clogged my throat and I swallowed hard to clear it. "I know…"

Neither of us said anything more as traffic picked up again, and Steve concentrated on keeping up with it.

Then he took the next exit, pulled into a parking lot, turned off the engine, and turned to face me. "This explains something that I've been wondering about you, Story. I'm glad you told me."

I wiped a tear off my cheek. Damn it. I didn't want to cry.

"Ever since I met you, I've sensed there was something wounded in you," he said. "Deep down. In your soul. Subtle, but guarded."

I nodded. Sniffed. "You're very perceptive. And you're right. You might know me better than I know myself."

"I don't really know you at all," he whispered. "But I'd like to. Because you're fascinating."

I froze. Stopped breathing. I'd been believing that I didn't deserve love. Now Steve was telling me that I was fascinating.

Fascinating sounded fun. I could handle being fascinating.

"I kind of like being fascinating." I gave a trembling smile. "Whatever that means to you."

"It means you're a mystery that I'm enjoying trying to solve," he said with a grin.

He started the car back up. "Anyway, I do need a place to stay tonight. And I was only suggesting that I get a room in your hotel. Since we're both flying to Philadelphia tomorrow. Hopefully on the same plane."

Now I felt like a fool for thinking he'd been trying to get me into bed.

After all Steve had done for me, I was judging him based on what someone else had told me about his past. Was that fair? No, it was not. The man I had come to know in the past couple of weeks was kind, smart, and brave. "Of course, it makes sense for you to get a room in my hotel," I said.

"It's settled, then." He grinned. "Let's go find a travel agent. And then head to the Sunset Strip."

Thirty-Two

Our flight left L.A. at ten o'clock the next morning, with a planned stopover in St. Louis, and then on to the City of Brotherly Love.

The plane was only half full, so Steve and I were able to sit together. I took the window seat. Which was good, because unlike my previous flight, this one got bumpy almost out of the gate.

"Are you okay?" Steve asked when I grabbed the arm rest between us, squeezing it so tight my fingers went white.

"I will be," I said through clenched teeth. "As long as I can see the ground."

"Feel free to hold my hand, if you're scared," he whispered.

"Thanks," I said jokingly, "I just might do that."

I wondered what would happen if I did hold his hand? I wanted to, more than anything. So badly that I found myself gripping the armrest harder to keep myself from doing that. Because if I did, what kind of message would it send?

Because once we got back to Philly, he and I would be competitors. Even if he did find me fascinating. There was no getting around that. Steve would get the big and important cases. And if I was lucky, I'd get enough to eat and pay my rent while building my business.

Which would be ruined if I succumbed to my silly schoolgirl infatuation with him. Oh, we might date for a while. And who knows where that might lead? Because I would fall madly in love. Then, undoubtably, lose my virginity. And then what? Would he throw me over, like he had the others Rob had told me about?

I didn't really know Steve.

And the thought was unbearable.

I turned to look out the window, to send California a silent goodbye. We were leaving the City of Angels, and I wondered if I would ever see it again. Then the smog cleared, and a vast expanse of desert opened below, arid land, all yellow sand, with no trees and no water and no vegetation as far as the eye could see.

Beautiful in its emptiness.

For some reason that made me think of Nanette Paulson. She was beautiful. But empty. All show. No heart. She'd had everything to live for, a life most women would envy, but it wasn't enough.

Had she deserved to die the way she did? No. Had she brought it on herself? Yes. But I still couldn't help thinking it was partly my fault.

"It wasn't your fault, you know," Steve said, as if he was reading my mind. "Nanette, Alec, Martin Paulson. None of what happened to them was your fault. You did a fantastic job as a P.I. and I just want you to know that."

I turned to look at him. He'd never looked so handsome, and he was giving me that grin that made me go all gooey inside. "Thanks," I said. "I needed to hear that. And it means a lot coming from you."

"I mean it. Although I sense that you do blame yourself."

I sighed. "I do. I can't help it. I keep asking myself—if I had done anything differently, could there have been a happier ending?"

"You mean like Nanette going back to her husband and pleading for his forgiveness?"

"Yes."

"She wasn't that kind of woman. So that was never going to happen, no matter what you did. It was out of your control."

"If only he could have forgiven her," I said. "Let her go."

"Martin Paulson wasn't that kind of man, Story. And that wasn't your fault, either. You can't blame yourself for what other people choose to do, how they behave. I finally get that. It was an important lesson I needed to learn, and I did, thanks to this case."

"It's sad." I met Steve's gaze. "Because he was blind to who his wife really was. He never really saw the real Nanette, only the Nanette he wanted to see."

Steve smiled. "I have a philosophy, which I try to live by, and you might want to try it, too. Look for the good, see the good, be the good. But keep your eyes open, and don't be blinded by the bad."

"He was blinded by the bad."

"Unfortunately, and he wasn't the only one who got hurt."

"Poor Carolyn." I tore my eyes away from Steve's and looked back out the window.

"And Freddie. But the good part is that she's going to live. And she and Freddie will go on."

I looked back at him. "You really cared for her," I whispered.

"Yes, I did. And I still do. I'm going to go see her in the hospital tomorrow. Do you want to come with me?"

"I don't think that would be a good idea. She's in love with you, and I think you two have a lot to talk about."

"Maybe."

"She is in love with you, Steve. Do you think Alec's plan might have worked? If I hadn't come along?"

"You mean, would we have fallen so head over heels for each other that she would have told Alec she wanted a divorce?"

"That was Alec's plan."

Steve reached over and touched the tip of my nose. "I don't think so, Story. I'm not a homewrecker. I'm not that kind of guy." He grinned. "I might have a reputation as a love 'em and leave 'em kind of guy, but I'm not a homewrecker. Like I told you, I don't go for married women. I go for single ones."

"Alec's plan wouldn't have worked on you, then. That's good to know. But it also means when he figured it out, murder would have been his next step, no matter what."

"True. Sad but—"

The plane hit a weird pocket of air. We pitched sideways, then dropped.

I grabbed Steve's hand. And held on. Tight.

The plane climbed, then righted. My heart pounded and my stomach roiled as it smoothed out and then kept flying smooth.

I didn't let go of Steve's hand. It was too warm and too comforting. And life was too short.

"We'll be okay, Story," he said softly. "Just a little turbulence, happens all the time."

"Feel free to change seats if I end up needing to use the airsickness bag," I said. "I won't be insulted."

"Are you kidding?" He laughed. "We've been through far worse, you and I. Change seats? I wouldn't abandon you now."

Oh boy. I swallowed back tears that threatened to escape and roll down my cheeks. "Thanks," I said. "Thanks for everything. You've been such a good friend."

"I would like to be more than your friend."

I whispered, "I had a feeling…"

"And…?"

"And I need to think about that Steve. I really do."

"You're afraid of my reputation?"

"Yes, and I need to think about my business."

He put my hand to his lips and kissed it. "I understand. No pressure. But I do want to see you again. This can't be goodbye."

My hand where he kissed it burned. "It won't be goodbye, I promise." I slid him a shy smile and before I could stop myself, blurted out, "There's a little restaurant near Lancaster called The Old Barn Inn, where I'd planned to go to celebrate after finding Nanette. Maybe you can join me?"

He beamed. "I'd love it."

Flustered, I took my hand back and rubbed my eyes, pretending to be sleepy. But I was really trying to compose myself. I needed to think. I had a lot to think about. "I'm going to take a nap now," I lied.

"Okay." His voice was husky. "Maybe I'll try to get a little shut-eye, too."

I leaned my head back and closed my eyes, and I had no idea how long I tried, but I didn't go to sleep. I was too aware of Steve next to me. Every nerve in my body was buzzing.

Then I heard him singing. Softly. Lightly. Like he was composing a song. Right there on the plane as we headed home.

"If you were mine...we'd fly into a rainbow. You and I...across the sky." He sang it again and again, as if he was trying it out, listening to how it sounded. But I knew the real reason.

I opened an eye and looked at him. "I'm awake," I said.

He grinned. "I know."

Acknowledgments

Writing fiction is an exciting journey, and I am blessed to be traveling it with the assistance of many people in my life, including family, friends, fans, writing instructors, and fellow writers, including members of my Jacksonville, Florida-based writers group, First Coast Romance Writers.

Thank you, all.

I also want to give a huge shout-out to my wonderful editor, Caren Burmeister, who is not only a good friend but also a fantastic writing teacher. She has helped me grow as a writer in ways that continue to astound, encourage, and humble me. And I'm forever grateful.

Thank you as well to my cover designer, Robin Johnson, of RL Design, who continues to amaze me with her talent.

And thank you, thank you, thank you to all my readers who leave me reviews. I write to bring you joy!

Maggie FitzRoy is the author of three historical romance and romantic suspense novels, *Mercy's Way, Beacon Beach*, and *His Haven*.

She first fell in love with reading in third grade, when she discovered Nany Drew mystery books. Since that time, she has always enjoyed reading mystery and romance, which inspired her to write *Never on Monday*, the first novel in her Story Smith Mystery Series.

Maggie is a former journalist and magazine and newspaper editor who holds a bachelor's degree in history from Ursinus College and a master's degree in education from the University of Virginia.

She lives with her husband, dog, and two cats in Ponte Vedra Beach, Florida. When she's not writing, she enjoys reading, travel, swimming, choral singing, pickleball, yoga, and Pilates.

For information about Maggie's previous novels, or to sign up for her newsletter and receive updates about her next Story Smith book, visit her website www.maggiefitzroy.com.

facebook.com/maggiefitzroyauthor
instagram.com/maggiefitzroy
twitter.com/maggiefitzroy

facebook.com/maggiefitzroyauthor
twitter.com/maggiefitzroy
instagram.com/maggiefitzroy

www.ingramcontent.com/pod-product-compliance
Lightning Source LLC
Chambersburg PA
CBHW051130190726
48290CB00006B/1783